A Fa[...]

A fearless governess comes to the aid of five young girls in need of a home—and catches the eye of one rugged Montana businessman with a wounded heart. Their desire is strictly off-limits, but it only takes a spark to unleash the heat of forbidden love!

"Western readers longing for authentic settings and sweet romance will find it all. . . . Rich in colorful, historical details. A memorable love story."   —*RT Book Reviews*

"*A Family for Maddie* has vividly described adventures and heartwarming romantic moments."   —*Single Titles*

Hearts Afire

In the wake of a shattering betrayal, a dazzling actress flees New York. Arriving in Colorado Springs, she is swept into a tumult of striking gold miners— and rescued by a mine owner who knows when he's found something precious.

"Love and excitement fill every page of Luck's story. *Hearts Afire* is the kind of romance you can't put down."
    —*Fresh Fiction*

"*Hearts Afire* will capture your senses. This book will show readers true love is worth risking your heart for, and maybe much more."   —*The Bibliophilic Book Blog*

Hearts Unbound

A captivating Basque beauty sparks the desire of a hard-living Boise physician—but her father has chosen a man for her, also a Basque. Will the challenges of the lonely Idaho range force tradition to cross a daring boundary?

"Not your typical Eastern-lady-meets-frontier-doctor Western . . . If you're looking to be transported some-where unusual, and if you enjoy family/cultural conflict, I recommend *Hearts Unbound*. . . . A solid read."

—*All About Romance*

Rimfire Bride

A pretty and courageous schoolteacher comes to Bismarck and turns heads as a dress model in a shopwindow! And in the arms of the handsome single father who owns Rimfire Ranch, she discovers what home feels like.

"Luck's devotion to historical accuracy shines again . . . *Rimfire Bride* warms the heart." —*RT Book Reviews*

"Exciting . . . A must-read . . . You feel as if you are there in 1882." —*My Book Addiction Reviews*

Tallie's Hero

A *Publishers Weekly* Top 10 Romance for Fall 2012

The dangerous American West is no place for a genteel British novelist fleeing a scandal . . . but one plucky lady embraces the spirit of Wyoming— and captures the heart of her new hero, a daring rancher with big dreams of his own.

"The Wild West retains its appeal in *Tallie's Hero*."
—*Publishers Weekly*

"Steamy Western romance."   —*Fresh Fiction*

Claiming the Heart

As the Texas and Pacific Railroad expands
across the wild frontier, a spirited young woman
experiences the triumphs and tumult of building a
part of history . . . and loving a track man
bound to a politically powerful family.

"Terrific . . . An enjoyable nineteenth-century Americana
tale."   —*Genre Go Round*

"Fast-paced, engaging."   —*Romantic Times*

Susanna's Choice

Sara Luck's "promising debut"! (*Romance Reviews Today*)

In a dusty Nevada mining town, an aspiring news-
paperwoman crosses paths with a wealthy entrepreneur from San Francisco, and everything
changes—including her own uncertain destiny.

"Heart-warming . . . Sensual . . . This one's a keeper!"
—*Night Owl Reviews* (5 stars, A Night Owl Top Pick)

ALSO BY SARA LUCK

Susanna's Choice

Claiming the Heart

Tallie's Hero

Rimfire Bride

Marci's Desire

Hearts Unbound

Hearts Afire

A Family for Maddie

Available from Pocket Books

UNDER THE DESERT SKY

SARA LUCK

Pocket Books

New York   London   Toronto   Sydney   New Delhi

Pocket Books
An Imprint of Simon & Schuster, Inc.
1230 Avenue of the Americas
New York, NY 10020

This book is a work of fiction. Any references to historical events, real people, or real places are used fictitiously. Other names, characters, places, and events are products of the author's imagination, and any resemblance to actual events or places or persons, living or dead, is entirely coincidental.

First Pocket Books paperback edition April 2016

POCKET and colophon are registered trademarks of Simon & Schuster, Inc.

For information about special discounts for bulk purchases, please contact Simon & Schuster Special Sales at 1-866-506-1949 or business@simonandschuster.com.

The Simon & Schuster Speakers Bureau can bring authors to your live event. For more information or to book an event, contact the Simon & Schuster Speakers Bureau at 1-866-248-3049 or visit our website at www.simonspeakers.com.

Manufactured in the United States of America

10 9 8 7 6 5 4 3 2 1

ISBN 978-1-5011-0355-1
ISBN 978-1-5011-0357-5 (ebook)

Preface

I hope you enjoy *Under the Desert Sky*. People often ask writers where they get their ideas. Every family has stories that are told over and over, and through the years they get a little embellished. This is one such story. My grandmother often told us how her father, who had been a wealthy banker, lost the family fortune by investing in ostrich farming in Arizona. I wondered if this might be the genesis for a story, so I began my research, and what I found was fascinating.

Ostriches were indeed raised in the Salt River Valley, Arizona Territory, the first one being hatched in 1891. From then until the beginning of World War I, ostrich feathers were in worldwide demand in haute couture. In 1900, the United States imported $300,000 worth of feathers, and by 1910, South Africa was exporting ostrich plumes to the tune of $15 million, $5 million of which came to the American market. When I read these figures, I could understand why my great grandfather decided to sink his money into an ostrich farm. I just wish he'd been better at market timing!

UNDER THE
DESERT SKY

Prologue

Mount Olive, Illinois
1894

"**D**aughter, I think it's time you and I had a talk." Malachi Pence disappeared into his bedroom and returned with two envelopes. "I want you to read this." He handed Phoebe an envelope.

Phoebe withdrew a piece of paper and began to read:

> *Young woman with good moral*
> *upbringing wishes a position as cook or*
> *general housekeeper, city or country: latter*
> *preferred. Box 27, Mount Olive, Illinois.*

"Papa, what is this? That's our address."

"Yes, it is." Malachi lowered his head. "You can't stay here. Everybody knows what your mother did, and they aren't going to let you live it down. I want you to marry a nice boy and have a family and be happy, but you saw what Virgil Hemann's ma did when she found out your mother ran off with the preacher."

"It's all right, Papa. I didn't want to marry Virgil anyway."

"But don't you see? There'll be other Virgils who'll think because your mother divorced me, you'll do the same. You need to leave Mount Olive."

"I can't do that. I can't leave you all alone."

Malachi smiled. "You don't have to worry about me. We both know Mrs. Droste has her cap set for me."

Phoebe's eyes began to cloud as she focused on the paper in her hand.

"That's a classified I ran in a half dozen newspapers. I figured you'd enjoy the West."

"Nobody's going to answer an ad like that." Phoebe held back tears.

"They already have. How does Phoenix, Arizona Territory, sound to you?" He handed her the second envelope.

1

Cape Town, South Africa
1900

Christian De Wet paced back and forth in the library of the house of Mrs. Marie Van Koopmans, the woman who'd raised him. Nineteen years ago he'd been living on the docks, surviving by his wits and the occasional handouts of strangers. Called Jacktar by the sailors, that was the only name he had ever known. When he was injured by a horse, Cecil Rhodes, a British businessman who had just stepped off a ship returning from England, took the injured boy first to the doctor, then to his good friend Mrs. Van Koopmans.

Rhodes and Mrs. Van Koopmans had named him, Rhodes calling him Christian, and Mrs. Van Koopmans giving him the surname De Wet, which had been her maiden name. She had assigned him the age of ten, by which reckoning he was now twenty-nine.

Mrs. Van Koopmans became his surrogate mother and Rhodes his mentor, providing an education for him at the Oriel College in Oxford. After graduation, Rhodes employed him in the offices of the Chartered Company in London for eight years.

Over the last few years Christian had been caught up in the Boer War, which pit the Dutch against the British. What made the war particularly painful for him was that he was a child of both cultures. Mrs. Van Koopmans was Dutch, Rhodes was British, and Christian spoke both languages with equal facility. Because he knew nothing about his birth, he had no idea whether he was Dutch or English.

Today, a troubled Christian had come to see Mrs. Van Koopmans, saying, "During the siege, when we were trapped in Kimberley, I was sure the Boers were the aggressors. I saw how they dropped shells into the civilian population, hoping to do as much damage as possible.

"But when the siege was broken, I left Kimberley to be attached to the British columns—and what did I see? The British are burning houses to the ground and putting the displaced people into concentration camps where they don't give them enough to eat. In Kimberley we were rationed because we were running out of food, but the British are doing this deliberately. They are starving their prisoners, who are mainly women and children."

"I think you need to leave South Africa for a while," Mrs. Van Koopmans said. "Does Rhodes have someplace else for you to go?"

"No, he's hiding out in Rhodesia. After 126 days in Kimberley together, he and Colonel Keke-wich are no longer on speaking terms."

Mrs. Van Koopmans laughed. "And that's bad? I think I have more respect for the British officer just hearing that."

"I have to say, I thought when I was Jacktar and living on the docks, I had a hard life. But this war is much worse."

"What do you plan to do?"

"I've written my letter of resignation and I intend to deliver it to Groot Schuur myself. I'm sure Gordon Le Sueur will be happy to accept it. He's never liked me—I never quite had the right pedigree."

"If you do this, you know you can't stay in South Africa. Rhodes doesn't like people whom he considers to be disloyal."

"I know. There's a steamer that should be leaving for New Zealand in a few days."

"Tell me, do you really care where you go?"

"I don't. New Zealand, Australia, India—it doesn't matter."

"What about America?"

"America? I hadn't thought of that. I'm a British citizen, and I only considered the colonies."

"It wouldn't have to be permanent, but I do have something that might interest you. What do you know about ostriches?"

"Ostriches? I know during the early part of the siege some men brought in some eggs that made a fine breakfast."

"You won't be eating eggs, my boy. You'll be escorting two pair of ostriches to my old friend Yhomas Prinsen. He bought an ostrich farm in Phoenix, Arizona Territory, and he wants to introduce some new stock into his flock. He asked me to arrange getting them out of the country."

"Why?"

"The exporting of ostrich feathers to the United States is a big business for the Cape Colony. Now Yhomas thinks he can take some of that business for himself. He's found the Salt River Valley in Arizona to be a perfect place to raise ostriches. The only problem he's encountered is that the colonial authorities only allow birds to be exported for exhibits in zoological gardens."

Christian smiled. "And so you are facilitating getting an exhibit out of Cape Town. Is that right?"

Mrs. Van Koopmans nodded. "I just hadn't found someone I could trust to get them to Yhomas. Will you do it?"

"Shouldn't I know something about these birds?"

"Would you do it if July went with you?"

"July? Is he still working for you?"

"Of course. He's worked for me for twenty years. Why wouldn't he still be here?"

Maricopa County, Arizona Territory
1900

Phoebe Sloan took off her brown felt hat and wiped her brow with the back of her sleeve as she rested on her rake. It'd been a long time since the last rain, yet a cloud was gathering in the west. She looked over to see that Trinidad was still mowing the alfalfa, so she began waving her hat to get his attention.

"Don't you want me to finish the mowin', Miss Phoebe?" her hired man asked.

"No, I want you to help Cornello get what's cut into haycocks."

"It's not dry yet. Shouldn't we leave it in the swath?"

"Yes, but if it rains, it's ruined. So stop and help Cornello."

"Yes, ma'am."

Trinidad lifted the sickle bar and moved toward Cornello, who was at the other end of the field. Soon the two men, who were both in their sixties, were pitching the hay into mounds.

Phoebe had been out in the sun for most of the day. She'd made a pallet for Will in the shade of a mesquite tree, and the two of them had eaten lunch together before her son had fallen asleep. She walked over to see if he was awake.

There was Will, her beautiful four-year-old, resting innocently on the patchwork quilt. She smiled when she saw where he'd built a house out of sticks, and fences out of seed pods. All his carved ostriches were separated into pairs.

Phoebe shook her head, wondering how many children would find enjoyment by playing with carved ostriches. She looked toward the sky. The cloud was getting darker, but she was reluctant to wake the sleeping child. Instead, she walked to the other side of the tree and knelt down beside her husband's grave, where she began rearranging the rocks that outlined the site.

"I need to talk to you, Edwin." She said the words conversationally as if her husband were sitting beside her. "I went to see Mr. Forbes this week to renegotiate the loan. He said he'd drop the interest rate to four percent if I could pay five percent by the end of the summer." Her voice began to shake. "I don't know if I can do it. Buck tells me Mr. Prinsen wants to buy every ostrich in the valley, but if I sell our birds now, I won't have any way to make a living."

"You're a fool, Phoebe."

Phoebe jumped when she recognized her brother-in-law's voice. "Frank, what're you doing here?"

"I came to talk to you. Charles Forbes told me you'd been in to see him."

"That's none of your business."

"Oh, yes it is. That's my nephew over there, and I won't let you kill him like you did my brother."

Phoebe took a deep breath, but didn't speak. They'd had this conversation before.

"You know what he did was because of you and your big ideas. What fool thinks there's money to be made in ostrich feathers?"

"Mr. Prinsen thinks there's money in it."

"He grew up in South Africa—he knows something about ostriches, and there's one thing he has that you don't: money. Haven't you learned that it takes a lot of money to keep this place going?"

"Our first birds are mature now—all it takes to keep them is alfalfa."

"That's a lie. You keep those two old men around. What do you pay them?"

Again Phoebe didn't answer.

"Whatever it is, it's too much. You should sell out and move into town."

"I won't do that. Not as long as there's a breath in my body." Phoebe gritted her teeth.

"It won't be long until you'll be lying right there beside Edwin. Have you looked at yourself lately? You look like a dried prune. Your hair is always a mess, your clothes are in tatters. What money you do have, you pour back into this worthless piece of sand."

By now, tears were streaming down Phoebe's face.

"I've told you before, I'll take care of you." Frank's voice softened. "You don't have to be here."

"Yes, you have told me before, and you've told

me what I have to do to earn it. But no matter how desperate I might get for money, I'll never warm your bed, Frank Sloan."

Frank stepped up to Phoebe. He wiped the tears from her cheeks. "Never say never, my dear Phoebe. You might find my bed much more to your liking than you ever found my brother's."

Phoebe slapped Frank hard.

A sardonic smile crossed his face. "A spit-fire—that's what I like about you. If only it had been me that came to your bed that night, Will would've been my son."

Just then, in the distance, thunder rumbled.

Phoebe left Frank standing by his brother's grave as she gathered Will in her arms and ran to the house.

New York

Christian stood on the deck of the RMS *Campania* as tugs moved it into position at the Cunard pier. The ship had made the crossing in just six days, much faster than was the first leg of his voyage from Cape Town to Southampton.

He had no idea how difficult it'd be to take four ostriches out of South Africa. First of all, he had had to pay a $500-a-bird tariff just to get them out of the country; then the steamer, from New Zealand, had a flock of at least fifty sheep bound for England. The sheep upset the skittish birds, but the hardest part of the trip was traveling with July. Not even a first-class ticket would've enabled July to travel anywhere but in strictly segregated steerage.

Once they'd docked in New York, customs personnel came aboard to process the first-class passengers. This was little more than a cursory inspection, though when the inspector saw Christian's rifle, which had been a gift from Mrs. Van Koopmans, he commented. "I'm not sure I can let the rifle through."

"It was cleared in Cape Town."

"Cape Town? What is your nationality?"

"I have a British passport." Christian held his passport out.

"You don't need that for entry into the US. Do you have paperwork on the rifle?"

"I do. Here are the authorization papers from both the American and British embassies."

The official looked at the papers for a moment, nodded, then issued a letter of clearance.

At that moment, Christian saw July, along with several other passengers, being loaded onto a ferry. "Where are they going?"

"Ellis Island, but that's not for you, sir. You've been cleared. You may go wherever you want."

"But that's my employee and I need to be with him." Christian pointed to July. "We have live cargo that must be cared for."

"Very well, sir, if you'll get in the line to the far right"—the officer handed Christian a pass—"you'll be on the next ferry."

• • •

Stepping onto Ellis Island, Christian located the ostriches and arranged for them to be put in the required quarantine for incoming animals. Then he went in search of July and found him being interrogated by a self-important, overweight official.

"July? This isn't July, it's August, and I didn't ask you for the date. Now, let's try again. Tell me your name."

"July."

"No. I need your name." The overbearing man was becoming more agitated.

"*Laat my dit hanteer,*" Christian said, speaking in Afrikaans, telling July to let him handle it. "I'll tell him you aren't that proficient in the language."

"*Ja, meneer,*" July replied.

"What was all that?"

"This man works for me," Christian said. "But he doesn't speak English all that well. If I may, I'll answer your question."

Christian wasn't telling the truth; July had lived and worked in Cape Town for more than thirty years and he was conversational in English, Afrikaans, Malay, Hindi, and several Bantu dialects, as well as his own Zulu language. But Christian recognized that he might be better able to deal with this pompous ass than July.

"I require a full name," the official said.

In all the years they'd known each other, Christian had never heard July called anything other than that. If Mrs. Van Koopmans had given Christian the surname De Wet, he thought he could just as easily give July a name.

"His name is Julius Van Koopmans."

July smiled broadly.

"You say he works for you? In what capacity?"

"He's a certified keeper of rare birds, specifically ostriches. We're transporting two pair to Phoenix.

"You have the proper paperwork for this, I suppose?"

"Yes, these birds are going to the Arizona Ostrich Farm, in care of Mr. A. Y. Prinsen, and here is the paperwork showing we've paid the tariffs on each bird."

"This says you paid two thousand dollars. How many birds did you say you're bringing?"

"Four."

"Mister, they have to be mighty special birds to have a tariff like that; but no matter how special they are, they still have to stay in quarantine for seven days. Your man here might want to stay close to them if they're that valuable."

"We appreciate that. Is there a bunk room where July—Julius can stay?"

"Sir, this is not a hotel. There's a bench down there where he can bed down if he wants, but that's about it. Oh, there's a place where he can get a bite to eat and a washroom nearby, but that's all I can offer."

"Thank you."

• • •

"If we're going to be stuck here for seven days, I think we should trade off every other night. That way it won't be too hard on either of us," Christian said. "If you'll take the first night, I'll find us a hotel."

July shook his head. "Do you see all these signs around here—COLORED drinking fountain, COLORED waiting room, WHITES ONLY. What makes you think the hotel you find for you would work for me?"

Christian had no answer. Blacks had been emancipated in South Africa since the last apprentices were freed in 1840.

"I'll stay with the birds," July said. "You wouldn't know what to do with them anyway."

Phoenix, Arizona Territory
September 1900

The first thing Christian noticed when he stepped down from the train in Phoenix was how hot it was. The oppressive heat seemed to bear down on him like a great weight. He looked around for July, as he'd not been able to ride in the same car. July was easy to find, not only because he was the only black person on the depot platform, but also because, at six feet nine inches, he was head and shoulders taller than anyone around him.

"July, over here," Christian called.

With a broad smile, July picked his way through

the crowd to join him. "What do we do now, Christian? Where do we take the birds?"

"I'll be honest with you, July, I don't have the slightest idea. My directions ended with—" Christian pointed. "I think that's where we start."

The sign read CHRISTIAN DE WET. A tall, slender young man, dressed in Levi Strauss waist overalls and a short-sleeved denim shirt, held it. His high-crowned, wide-brimmed hat seemed to be part of a universal uniform for all males in this part of America. Christian and July walked toward him.

"I'm De Wet." Christian extended his hand.

"I'm Andy Patterson. Mr. Prinsen sent me here to meet you and the birds."

"We were wondering what we were going to do with our stock. This is my friend and partner, July—that is, Julius Van Koopmans."

Andy looked at July, lifting his eyes as he took the measure of his size. "Damn if I don't think you're about the biggest man I've ever met. Whoowee, I sure don't ever plan to get on your bad side."

"My bad side?" July asked, confused.

"I don't ever want to get you mad at me," Andy explained.

Christian chuckled. "July's a good man, and it takes a lot to make him mad. But you're right, when he gets angry, you don't want to be on the opposite side of him."

"I can tell you right now, we're going to be great friends." Andy reached out to shake July's hand.

"I assume you have some sort of conveyance for the birds," Christian said.

"Yes, sir, I sure do. Let's get them settled. It's not much of a ride out to the ranch. I expect you men are hungry. Mrs. Prinsen said we shouldn't tarry—she'll be holdin' supper for you. Besides, I'm one cowboy who's never late for a meal."

"So you're a cowboy," Christian said. "I've read about cowboys and I'm glad to finally meet one."

"Yeah, well, right now, workin' for Mr. Prinsen like I do, I guess you can't rightly call me a cowboy. But I'll be damned if I'll ever let myself be called a bird boy."

Christian and July were warmly greeted by Yhomas and Katie Prinsen, and Yhomas's farm manager, Rueben Bucknell, and his wife, Gwen. The supper was a huge piece of beef that had been cooked over an open fire, and a pot of beans.

"We thought we'd initiate you to the Western way of eating," Katie said as she ushered them to a long table in the shade of a cotton tree. For July's sake, Christian was glad to see a couple of black faces were included. "Have you ever eaten barbecue?"

Christian laughed. "Yes, ma'am, I know what it's like to eat meat cooked over an open fire."

"Young man, until you've eaten Memphis barbecue, you've not eaten. Lorenzo grew up there, and the first time I ate his cooking, he lost his job rounding up ostriches. From then on, he became the bunkhouse cook, isn't that right, men?"

Several of the men responded, and one of the black men was slapped on his back good-naturedly.

"Well, real Memphis barbecue is pork. But I do my best," Lorenzo said.

When the meal was over, July excused himself to make certain the new ostriches were settling into their environment. Lorenzo accompanied him while a couple of the others set about cleaning up after the meal.

"Christian, bring your things in and let's get you situated," Yhomas said. "Lorenzo will see that July gets settled. I would never have thought that Marie would let him out of her sight. How long has he been working for her?"

"Close to twenty years. For her to let him leave just shows how much Mrs. Van Koopmans values your friendship."

"The feeling is mutual. Do you think she'll be safe in Cape Town? Everybody knows where her sympathies lie."

"That may be her salvation. She's an Afrikaner and she's never denied that." Christian picked up his belongings and followed the Prinsens into the house.

After Christian was settled, Yhomas invited him into the library. "Have a seat." Yhomas indicated a leather sofa. "I think you'll find that quite comfortable."

Christian sat down. "Yes, it is."

"Marie sure thinks a lot of you."

"She thinks I'm her son."

"Oh, I know the story well, my boy, how she took in an urchin and turned him into, in her words, 'one of the smartest and finest gentlemen in all of Christendom.' You've made quite an impression on her."

"She's a wonderful lady. I can't imagine caring for a flesh-and-blood mother any more than I do for Mrs. Van Koopmans."

"And yet, you continue to call her 'Mrs. Van Koopmans.'"

"I called her that when I first came to live with her, and now it just seems awkward to change."

"Well, she adores you, whatever you call her. How do you like your martini?"

"I don't know. Mrs. Van Koopmans insisted that I take it, but obviously I haven't had the opportunity to try it out yet."

"What're you talking about?"

"My rifle. Isn't that what you asked me?"

"Your rifle?"

"Yes, my Martini."

Prinsen laughed. "Oh, yes, the Martini-Henry. I'd forgotten about that. Actually when I say *martini*, I'm talking about a drink that's popular here. It's really quite good."

"I've not had the pleasure."

"Well, then I must make one for you." Prinsen opened the liquor cabinet and began mixing the drink. "I'll have to take you and your Martini over to the Tonto Range sometime soon. That's where people around here hunt elk."

"Yes, I think I'd like that."

"I can't thank you enough for bringing these new birds. You know, almost all the ostriches in America are the progeny of the same two birds, and I think it's time to introduce a new bloodline."

"That seems strange. How did that happen?"

"Some well-meaning, uninformed handler covered the first shipment with a canvas and smothered all but two. That's why Marie was so careful about who she got to deliver them."

Christian laughed. "I didn't have much to do with getting them here. It was July who took care of them. I just rode on the same ship with them."

"Well, they're fascinating creatures, and I must say they're proving to be quite profitable. And having lived in both the Cape Colony and here, I believe I can say with no little authority that the Salt River Valley could be the best area in the world for raising ostriches. And as long as the ladies want their fashionable hats, there can be no end to the amount of money I can make."

"Is there a chance the market will fade away?"

"When a New York lady will pay as much as sixty dollars for a prime starched feather, do you think she'll grow tired of her hat? I don't think so."

"For your business, I hope that is true."

"The biggest problem we have now is this drought. If we don't get good rains this fall, we'll really be in a pickle."

"How long have you been in a drought?"

"This'll be the third year." Prinsen handed the

drink to Christian. "Try this, my boy, and tell me what you think."

Christian took a sip. "Well, it's got gin, and I developed a taste for gin when I was in England."

"I thought you might've. Tell me, is the war really as bad as the American papers say? I can't tell if it's the Dutch or the British who are favored to win."

"I don't think anyone knows."

"But you have experienced the war, haven't you? I mean, firsthand?"

"Yes." Christian began telling about the siege of Kimberley.

Christian was surprised at how closely Yhomas had followed the war. He wanted to know what Christian knew of Bloemfontein, of Johannesburg, of Pretoria—all cities that had fallen to the British—and now he'd read that President Kruger had withdrawn to Lydenburg. "The Boer cause is lost, isn't it?"

"You can't say that yet. The word when I left was that President Kruger has escaped to Mozambique, and he intends to sail for France. Perhaps he can garner some support there."

"Uncle Paul is no longer relevant," Yhomas said, referring to the president of the Transvaal. "If the Afrikaners have a chance, it'll be up to the man for whom you are named."

Christian laughed. "I don't think Mrs. Van Koopmans was aware of General De Wet when I was named."

"It doesn't matter. You should be proud to bear

the general's name, no matter how you came by it. I'm glad you're here. Not many people in Phoenix are interested in what happens so far away. They only care if there's a cloud in the sky that may bring a drop of rain. Oh, and they care if McKinley gets elected again."

The mantel clock struck two.

The long train trip, and perhaps even the alcohol, made Christian's eyelids droop.

Yhomas set his drink down and stood. "My goodness, what kind of host am I? You look tired. Come with me, and I'll show you to your room."

When Christian climbed into bed, he thought he'd fall asleep immediately from exhaustion, but he missed the rocking of the train that had brought him to Phoenix. And the talk this evening had been unsettling. Yhomas was obviously an expatriate and an entrepreneur who was trying to make his home and his fortune in Phoenix. Yet, from the conversation tonight, South Africa was never far from his thoughts.

Christian closed his eyes. He envisioned Table Mountain in half-light, its foursquare rock guarding the bay as it rose over Cape Town. He saw the red glow on a winter morning as the sun searched for the veiled rocks beyond. Perhaps he shouldn't have been so anxious to leave his homeland.

But then he thought of Kimberley and what he'd endured at the hands of the Boers. But they were not the only agents for hardship. Lord Kitchener, who had been the British commander during the siege, had imposed the dreaded martial law that had created so much unnecessary mayhem for the people. As Christian recalled his time at Kimberley, his thoughts returned to a young woman he'd met there.

"Ina Claire. I need to tell you where I am," he said aloud, even though he was alone.

Christian jumped out of bed and lit the lamp that sat on a table by his bed. Across the room was a writing desk. Opening the drawer, he found some ink, a pen, and some stationery. He smiled when he saw the woodcut head of an ostrich in the corner, its wide eyes staring at him. Miss Woodson would be amused when she received his note.

> *Dear Ina Claire,*
>
> *I'll bet you are quite surprised to hear from me. I am in the United States, in a place called Arizona. I came here to deliver some ostriches for Mrs. Van Koopmans to a man named Yhomas Prinsen. I have thought often of the siege of Kimberley, and although the recollections of the investment of the city aren't pleasant, the memories of you are. I hope your thoughts of me are just as agreeable, and I hope there is an opportunity for us to see each other while I am in the US.*
>
> *Yours truly,*
> *Christian De Wet*

Christian reread the letter. It seemed to have just the proper amount of familiarity, one that could be taken as a friendly reminder of the time they had spent together, yet one that held open the suggestion of renewing their friendship. He folded it, put it in an envelope, and addressed it. He had no idea how to post it, but he'd ask Yhomas tomorrow.

2

"**B**e careful, Will," Phoebe called as her son put his ear down on an ostrich egg. "We'll help the little babies out when it's time."

"I hear him, Mama. I hear him scratching." Will picked up the seven-inch egg. "He wants to come out."

"Not yet. He needs a few more days."

"Here you are." Gwen Bucknell entered the incubator house. "I should've known you'd be here. Are your eggs about to hatch?"

"Will would say so." Phoebe chuckled. "But I think we have at least another week." She lowered the top on the incubator box. "Why don't you come up to the house and join us for a cup of root beer?"

"Root beer!" Will shouted. "Miss Gwen, please come. I want some root beer." The little boy ran out of the building, and as he did, the flock of chicks in the adjoining pen began to scurry.

"Will, slow down. You're scaring the little birds," Phoebe called.

"He's grown into such a little helper. What would you do without him?"

"He wears me out, but he's a great joy. Now tell me, what brings you over this afternoon?"

"First of all, I haven't seen you for a while. But more importantly, Buck said you weren't at the Dorris Theater yesterday."

"You mean for the water meeting?"

"Yes. Most of the farmers in the valley were there."

"What difference does it make? They're never going to get anything accomplished. The day Edwin bought this farm, he was told a reservoir was going to be put in the Tonto Basin, and now, five years later, there's still nothing."

"Yes, but this time it's different. We can't survive another year of drought like we've had for the last two years. Everyone agrees something has to be done—they just can't agree on how to do it."

"And we're right back where we were with the Hudson Company. Like I said, nothing's going to be done," Phoebe said.

Just then Will opened the door to the kitchen. "I got the cups." He held them up.

"Good for you. I'm so thirsty," Gwen said.

Phoebe went into the main house and got the root beer from the icebox. She grabbed a loaf of bread and sliced off three pieces, then slathered on some of her freshly canned pear preserves. She wished she had some butter, but with the drought many of the dairy cows had stopped giving much milk, and the price for butter was more than she was willing to pay.

Will was showing Gwen some of his toys. "She likes my ostriches. Mr. Lopez made them for me."

"Which reminds me, I didn't see either Cornello or Trinidad. Where are they?"

"Just guess. Sunday is September sixteenth." Phoebe smiled.

"Oh, yes. Mexican Independence Day. But it's only Wednesday. Has the fiesta started already?"

"No, but the community was a little late getting organized, so Trinidad's putting a volunteer band together. He says they have to practice."

"Hah. They won't be back next week either. You should get someone else to work for you beside those two old men."

Phoebe looked down.

"Oh, Phoebe, I'm sorry. It's just that there's so much work to be done, and you can't do it all by yourself. How many birds do you have now?"

"I have six pairs of full-grown birds and about forty feather birds. And this'll be my third hatching this year, so if all my eggs survive, including the ones that are in the nests, I should have close to eighty young chicks."

"I had no idea you had that many. Mr. Prinsen's going to want to buy some of those chicks."

"What do you think he's paying?"

"I think he'll pay twenty-five dollars per bird. But you can ask him yourself. That's why I'm here. Mr. Prinsen is having a water meeting tomorrow evening and he wants you to come."

"I can't do that, Gwen. What would I do with Will?"

"Bring him along. Hannah and Adeline love to play with him. They think he's a doll."

"I'm not a doll; I'm a boy."

"Of course you're a boy, Will, but you remember Hannah and Adeline. They're big girls now, and I'll bet they'll have some root beer," Gwen said. "They may even want to bake some cookies if they had somebody to help them."

"I know how. Mama lets me help her. I can do it."

Phoebe rolled her eyes. "You've left me no choice, Gwen. What time does this meeting start?"

"Be there at seven."

Phoebe laughed. "That's late. I'll try to keep my eyes open."

"Phoebe Sloan, you're twenty-four years old. You need to get away from this place more often. Other people have fun, have you forgotten?"

"Maybe it's because I spend so much time with Trinidad and Cornello. They go to bed as soon as the blackbirds take over the nests."

"You don't really mean they go to bed at five o'clock!"

"Well, maybe that is a bit of an exaggeration, but we don't see much of them after I serve supper."

"You just wait, my friend. I'm going to see that all of that is changed. I have a big surprise for you."

"No, no, no—no matchmaking."

"Well, I have to admit Baron Goldwater wasn't right for you, but I'll find someone you'll like. I promise."

"Gwen, please don't do that. I don't have time. I have too much to do."

"We'll see." Gwen untied her horse. "Don't forget, Will, my girls need you to help with the cookies tomorrow night. You make your mama come, all right?"

"I will." The little boy went back to his toys.

"What time will your people be arriving?" Christian asked as he helped Yhomas move extra chairs into the parlor.

"I've said seven, but out here, everyone is on their own time."

"When they start arriving, I'll go out and see how July is getting along."

"No, no. I'd like you to stay. With all the experience you've had in the shadow of the Colossus, you might be able to offer a suggestion or two."

"The Colossus—I haven't heard Rhodes called that in a long time."

"You call Marie 'Mrs. Van Koopmans', but it's just 'Rhodes' for your employer."

"Former employer. Rhodes and I aren't exactly on the best of terms right now. That's one of the reasons I came to America."

"Well, then, there's no reason you have to hurry back to Cape Town, now, is there?"

When Phoebe and Will arrived at the Prinsen home that evening, they were met by Andy Patterson, who was supervising those parking the visitors' vehicles. One part of Prinsen's side yard had been turned into a parking lot, and it was filled with conveyances of all kinds.

"Good evenin', Miz Sloan," Andy said as Phoebe arrived in her buggy.

"Hello, Mr. Patterson." Phoebe passed over the reins as she stepped to the ground. She reached back to help Will.

"I can get down myself, Mama." Will jumped down. "Do you think my friends are here yet? We're going to make cookies!" Will started to run toward the house.

"Will, wait!" Phoebe called. "You can't go into someone's house unless they tell you we can come in."

"I don't reckon he's much of a problem, seein' as how folks are comin' and goin' this whole evenin' long," Andy said.

"Nevertheless, Will has to learn some manners." Phoebe then said to Will, "You wait right there, young man."

Will stopped and waited until his mother caught up with him. Reluctantly, he let her take his hand.

"Phoebe," Katie Prinsen said as she opened the door. "I'm so glad you could join us."

"Where are Hannah and Adeline?" Will asked. "We're going to make cookies."

"Oh, yes, I've heard about that. Do you think you'll have enough to share? If this meeting lasts a long time, I'll bet these men will like a cookie later on."

"Oh, dear," Phoebe said. "Are there no other women?"

"I expect a couple more ladies, but you're the only woman landowner, I believe. The meeting is convening in the parlor, so why don't you go on in while I take Will to the girls."

When Phoebe stepped into the parlor, she saw at least two dozen others. She recognized most of the farmers and ranchers and several of the businessmen in town. The Salt River Valley had four ostrich farmers, but Prinsen and Phoebe were the only two now present.

"Mrs. Sloan, it's so good of you to come," Yhomas Prinsen said as he came to greet her. "I believe you know most of the people here." He took in the room with a sweep of his arm.

"Yes, I think I know every . . ." Phoebe stopped as she saw a man whom she clearly didn't recognize. Slightly taller than most, he had ash-brown hair and blue eyes and was wearing brown jodhpurs tucked into high boots, a silk shirt with a string tie, but no vest. He was one of the most handsome men she'd ever seen.

No, *handsome* wasn't the right word. She equated *handsome* with some drawing-room dandy with slicked-down hair and well-defined features. This man was much more masculine than that. He had broad shoulders and a narrow waist, and she wondered what he'd look like without his shirt.

What was she thinking? Phoebe felt her cheeks inflame, and she hoped she wasn't visibly blushing.

"Oh, of course, you haven't met my houseguest." Prinsen called, "Christian."

The man looked toward Prinsen when summoned, then, with the suggestion of a smile, walked over.

"Mrs. Sloan, may I present Christian De Wet, a fellow countryman of mine."

"Mrs. Sloan." Christian took her hand. "I'm pleased to meet you." His accent was not harsh but rather pleasing.

"My pleasure, Mr. De Wet."

"Christian, you'll be interested in this: Mrs. Sloan is also raising ostriches," Prinsen said. Then to Phoebe: "Christian brought two new pair of ostriches that should improve our bloodlines. We'll exchange chicks at some time in the future."

"Oh, Trinidad told me you were expecting some new birds."

"Christian brought them over from Cape Town."

"Well, I'm glad to see you didn't smother them." Phoebe laughed nervously. "It must've been quite an adventure, bringing these skittish birds all the way from Africa."

"I'm afraid I was little more than a passenger. It was my friend who was in charge of the birds."

"Mr. Prinsen, Mrs. Sloan," Walter Talbot, president of the Phoenix and Maricopa County Board of Trade said. "I hate to interrupt, but with it getting so late, perhaps we should start the meeting."

"Yes, of course," Prinsen said.

Walking to the middle of the room, Prinsen called for attention. "Ladies and gentlemen, I want to welcome you here tonight to discuss what we can do to secure a permanent water supply for our valley."

"I hope this comes to something beyond just talk," Benjamin Fowler said. "We've about discussed this subject to death. It's time for more work and less talk."

"I agree," Prinsen said. "I think we all agree."

"And heaven knows we can't depend on the government to do it," Fowler continued. "There may be something proposed at some time, but we can't afford to wait. What has to be done needs to be done now, and it needs to be done quickly."

John Norton held up his hand to speak. "We don't want the government involved if we can come up with something ourselves. We're the ones who will benefit from this water project, and we're the ones who should build it. But more to the point, we're the ones who should own it. We need to have control over this water ourselves."

"Here, here," someone agreed.

"What I want to know is," Ben Fowler interrupted, "has anybody actually determined whether or not this whole idea is even feasible? What

I mean is, is it possible to control the Salt River water in such a way that it'll provide irrigation for all of us any better than what we already get from the canals?"

"Captain Hancock should address that," Walter Talbot said.

"Very well," Prinsen said. "I believe everyone knows Captain Hancock. He's of riper years, but there's no truth to the rumor that he, personally, welcomed Coronado to Arizona."

After polite laughter, Hancock stood up. "I'm going to speak to you as an old resident of the territory and as one of the longest residents of the valley. The question that has brought us together is of vital importance to everyone, be it man, woman, beast, or bird.

"Now, to get directly to Mr. Fowler's question, let me say that, yes, we do have a sufficient amount of water; it's just a matter of controlling it. Our catchment basin is twenty-seven times greater than the area of land we want to irrigate. The catchment basin gets an average precipitation in rain and snow of fifteen inches per annum, and a runoff equal to one-fifth of that. That's three inches per annum from the watershed. That, times twenty-seven, is eighty-one acre-inches of water for our land."

"Wait a minute," Fowler said. "Are you telling us that we're going to get eighty-one inches of water per acre? That's not possible. Why, with water like that, we could grow a jungle and have monkeys swinging through the trees."

The others laughed, including Captain Hancock.

"Well, that's what we'll start with. We'll lose half of that by evaporation and other sources, but that leaves us with about forty inches of water for our land. This is a good showing for us to make if we want to raise funds."

"Raising funds, yes, and that brings up the big question: How much is such a thing going to cost?" Fowler asked.

"My estimate is five million dollars."

"Five million dollars?" A. C. McQueen stood up. "We may as well go home now. We can't come up with that kind of money."

"I agree with A.C.," Norton said as he put on his hat.

"Don't go yet," Prinsen said. "Christian, you've been listening to this talk. Do you have any ideas?"

"Look, Prinsen, I respect you, but why would you think your houseguest would have any ideas that'd bring us any closer to raising five million dollars?" McQueen asked.

"I daresay that everyone in this room has heard of Cecil Rhodes, have you not?" Prinsen asked. "Well, Christian's worked for Rhodes for close to ten years, and he knows a thing or two about putting capital together. Wouldn't you say that's correct, Christian?"

"I've done a fair amount of negotiating in my time, but I no longer work for Rhodes. However, I believe I could offer a suggestion."

"Go ahead and tell us what's on your mind," McQueen said.

Christian stood and looked out at the faces that were fixed on him. For a moment his gaze lingered on Mrs. Sloan. He found her an uncommonly attractive woman.

"Well, what is it?" someone asked, calling to Christian's attention that perhaps his gaze had lingered too long on the face of a married woman.

"As I understand the situation, the land under the present canal contracts amounts to approximately 275,000 acres," Christian began. "The people who own these lands are the ones who would most benefit from the construction of the reservoir; therefore it is from them that we must get the initial funds."

"Look, Mr. De Wet, it isn't an abstract *them* you're talking about; it's us," Fowler said. "And I think I can say without fear of contradiction that our aggregate worth doesn't equal five million dollars."

"You'll have to borrow the money."

"Why didn't we think of that," McQueen said sarcastically.

"You would need to show the lender that he has a reasonable expectation of profiting from the loan. I suggest you draw up a contract with the people who own the land to the effect that they or their successors will pay the company ten dollars an acre for the land that they own."

"That's sixteen hundred dollars!" Phoebe said

out loud. "I can't possibly come up with that much money!"

"You wouldn't have to come up with the entire amount, Mrs. Sloan. You'd only have to come up with one hundred and sixty dollars, because the assessment would be payable at one dollar per acre per year. And, because this'll also benefit the townspeople, they, too, must be a part of it. All owners of city or town lots within the region to be irrigated should be asked to pay five percent of the value of their lots, which would also be payable over a ten-year period. This would give your company a sum of 275,000 dollars raised from the assessment on the land, and possibly as much as 100,000 dollars more that'd be raised from the town lots. This would mean an immediate infusion of 375,000 dollars within the first year. In addition, you'd agree to pay the company ten cents per acre-inch for the water actually received and consumed, and this could be paid at the end of each month. I know these are rough figures, but this amount of money would enable your company to leverage a bond for twenty years at five percent interest. I believe if you took this kind of proposal to an investor, you'd be able to raise the five million dollars immediately, and under this structure, you should be able to pay off your bond in twenty years."

When Christian finished speaking, the room was quiet.

"What do you think, gentlemen, and ladies?" Prinsen asked.

"Yhomas, if your friend can come up with that idea off the top of his head, what do you think he can do if he really thinks about it?" Captain Hancock asked. "I propose that our reservoir committee hire this gentleman as our financial adviser."

"I second the proposal," Fowler said.

"Wait a minute," Prinsen said. "It's well and good to make the offer, but first don't you think we should ask Christian if he's agreeable to such an arrangement?"

"I appreciate the offer. But I have a responsibility to July."

"July? Why, that's months away," Captain Hancock said.

Prinsen chuckled. "Christian, suppose I hire July to work for me? Would you be disposed to accept our offer then?"

"I'll have to discuss it with him. I believe he's anxious to get home, but as for myself, I wouldn't be opposed to staying."

"You won't be sorry, Mr. De Wet. If you bring this through for us, I can promise you, there will be a mighty big paycheck waiting for you," Captain Hancock said.

3

M r. Prinsen and Christian stood at the door as everyone was leaving. Most were enthusiastic about the prospect of actually getting something started, and they continued to thank Christian for his suggestion.

"It looks like you made quite an impression, my boy," Prinsen said as he slapped Christian on the back. "Besides, if you went back home, you'd have to take sides. Would you fight with the Boers and please Marie, or with the Brits to please Cecil?"

"I really don't know. Maybe this is a godsend. It'll give me a legitimate reason to stay here."

"Yes, and if you can put this together, you'll not only make a fair bit of change, you'll also be doing the valley a real service."

"I get the impression you really like it here.

But what about the ostriches? This is a long way from the Little Karoo."

Prinsen smiled. "That's where your efforts come in. If you can figure this out and we can have a dependable water supply, I can grow more lucerne, and the ostriches won't know if they're in Arizona or South Africa."

"I suppose that's true. What difference does it make if you call their food alfalfa or lucerne? It's all the same to the birds."

"I actually think the Salt River Valley is more conducive to ostrich domestication than either the Cape Colony or Natal. I've not shared my ultimate goal, but I intend to monopolize the feather business in all of America."

"That's a lofty enterprise, but what'll the other ostrich farmers think when they find out what you have in mind?"

"They know I want to get bigger, Christian, and I believe they support me. Right now there are only three other producers in Arizona, and they know if they decide to give up, I'll buy their birds."

"I guess that's a fallback position for them, but I can't believe anyone would really want to raise ostriches."

"It boils down to money. You should ask Mrs. Sloan what she expects to reap this year from, originally, only six pairs of birds."

"Mrs. Sloan—that was the redheaded woman at the meeting? I didn't have a chance to speak to her. Did she leave with the others?"

"She may have slipped out the back. I feel sorry for her. She's by herself and she's got that little tyke, but her biggest problem is her husband's family. Every time she thinks she's about ready to make a profit, her father-in-law puts a fly in the ointment. He owns one of the local banks, so I personally invited him to this meeting tonight, but I knew he wouldn't show up."

Just then they heard a commotion in the kitchen. "I'll bet Phoebe's with the women. Let's see what's going on back there."

Adeline Bucknell was taking the last pan of cookies out of the oven when she tripped over Will Sloan's foot and fell. She lost control of the pan and hot cookies went flying everywhere.

Will caught one, but fell himself and crushed several of the crisp cookies. "Oh, no. We have to make some more, Mama. We can't go home."

"You've made lots of cookies." Phoebe knelt to help gather the crumbs. "It's late, and you know we have things to do before we can go to sleep."

"You go by yourself. I can stay and play with Hannah and Adeline. Isn't that right, Miss Gwen?"

"They can't play anymore," Gwen Bucknell said. "The girls have to go to sleep, too. Anyway, if you stayed here, who'd help your mama find her way home?"

"Here you are," Yhomas said as he and Christian came through the swinging door leading into the kitchen. "Phoebe, has it come to this? You have to eat crumbs off the floor?"

"We're not there, yet"—Phoebe rose from the floor—"but if we don't get any water, we may all have to resort to that."

"You heard Christian." Yhomas indicated the man standing beside him. "He'll have the money put together by Christmas."

"Were you at the same meeting I just attended?" Katie turned toward Christian. "I'm sure you're quite talented, but I don't think you're a magician." She said to her husband, "Nor did he make any claim to be, even if he is your countryman."

"Mr. De Wet, I must say I was quite impressed with your presentation. Were all those figures really off the top of your head?" Phoebe asked.

Christian flashed a dazzling smile, exposing perfect white teeth that contrasted against sunbronzed skin. "I'm afraid you've caught me, Mrs. Sloan. Yhomas provided some of the pertinent information before the meeting started, so I'd given some thought to a solution."

"I catched a cookie," Will said. "Did my mama catch you, mister?"

"No, no, Will. First of all it's 'I caught a cookie,' but Mr. De Wet said—"

"He said you caught him. I heard him."

Phoebe rolled her eyes. "I'm sorry. I believe it's time to gather my son and head home."

"Phoebe, it's late. You can't go home now," Katie said. "Let Trinidad or Cornello take care of your birds. That's why you pay them."

"They're not there," Gwen said.

"Oh, dear, have you fired them?" Katie asked.

"It'd be good riddance if you did," Yhomas said. "If you had somebody who really knew how to handle your flock, you could make a lot more money."

"You're probably right," Phoebe said. "But, no, I didn't fire them. Sunday is Independence Day, and I've given them the week off."

"Independence Day? I thought the American Independence Day is in July," Christian said.

"It is, but this is Mexican Independence Day. And I'm afraid the fiestas last a little longer than the Fourth of July picnics and parades," Phoebe said.

"Well, if they're not at your place, I'm not going to let you go home by yourself," Yhomas said. "I'll saddle my horse."

"Is it far?" Christian asked.

"No, it's about seven or eight miles from here," Yhomas said.

"Then why don't I ride back with her?" Christian asked. "If it's that close, I won't get lost on the way back, and you can write up the minutes of what went on tonight."

"Would you mind, Phoebe?" Yhomas asked.

"No, she doesn't mind," Gwen said. "I think it's a wonderful idea. Will, help me make up a package of cookies for you to take. Then, when you get home, you can invite Mr. De Wet in and have cookies and milk before you go to bed."

"Nope. Can't do that," Will said.

"Why not?"

"We don't have any milk."

"Well, then, girls, you'd better take Will to the summer kitchen and get some milk."

After Christian and the others left the kitchen, Gwen turned to Phoebe.

"What do you think?"

"I think you and your daughters are spoiling my son. It's already past his bedtime, and now he's going to insist on cookies and milk before bed."

Gwen let out an exaggerated sigh. "That's not what I meant and you know it. What do you think about Mr. De Wet?"

"He had some very good ideas. If he can put this together, it'll help all of us."

Gwen stomped her foot. "Sometimes you are the densest person I know. What do you think about Christian? Isn't he the most handsome man you've ever seen? And his English accent—don't you think that makes him even more mysterious?"

"I will grant you, he is an attractive gentleman, but that's all I'll say."

"I won't let you stop there. Don't you think he'd make a good husband?"

"Gwen, don't even think that, let alone say it. If people thought it was above my station when I married a banker, what do you think the talk would be if I went after an international financier?"

"You don't know that's what he is. He's been here for two weeks, and he's been one of the most accommodating guests Mr. Prinsen's ever had.

Buck says he and the man he brought with him are willing to help do anything. Just the other day they helped build new plucking boxes. Now, you tell me, would a financier do that?"

"You heard Mr. Prinsen say he worked for Cecil Rhodes for ten years, and everybody knows Mr. Rhodes is one of the wealthiest men in the world," Phoebe said. "So, by extrapolation, I would say Mr. De Wet is both well educated and well-off."

Gwen shook her head. "Phoebe, don't sell yourself short. Just because Frank Sloan browbeats you all the time, don't listen to him. You have a lot to offer a man."

"Thanks, Gwen, you're a dear friend, but I know who I am. There are days when I'm so weary I want to walk right up to Mr. Prinsen and sell every bird I have and leave. But then I go talk to Edwin and I know I can't. Raising ostriches was my dream, and I believe I can make a living for Will and me. If I walk away, every piece of Will's life with Edwin will be gone."

Gwen took Phoebe's hands in hers. "Someday, you've got to stop blaming yourself for Edwin's death. It wasn't your fault."

Just then Hannah came into the kitchen. "Miss Phoebe, Mr. De Wet is out front with your buggy. He's ready when you are."

"Thanks, Hannah, where's Will?"

"He's with Adeline. He's afraid you won't let him take all the cookies."

"All the cookies? Well, he's right."

"Let him do it. Not counting the ones that fell on the floor, there weren't many that made it into the oven," Gwen said. "And if you have a guest . . ."

"You never give up." Phoebe shook her head and followed Hannah out the door.

When Phoebe approached her buggy, the running lamps had already been lit, and the mirrored reflectors were casting twin beams in front of them. She could see Will hugging his bundle of cookies, while Adeline had the pail of milk.

"I believe this young man is ready to get going," Mr. Prinsen said. "I wish I was going home with you, because I know these cookies are going to be good. Maybe Mr. De Wet can bring me one when he comes back."

"Wet? Is that his name?" Will asked.

"Come, Will, get in the buggy. You've had a long day," Phoebe said. "Thank you, Mr. Prinsen, for inviting me. I have a good feeling about this meeting."

"I'm glad you could come. I only wish W.F. would've accepted my invitation."

Phoebe raised her eyebrows at the reference to her father-in-law, but didn't comment.

Adeline put the milk in the buggy and then started to lift Will.

"No. I want to ride with Wet. My daddy always let me ride with him."

"You need to be in the buggy. Who'll keep the milk from spilling?" Phoebe asked.

"It won't spill. It's in a cream bucket with a top. And I want to ride with Wet on the horse."

"Ma'am, if you don't mind, I'm perfectly fine having him ride with me."

"Goodie, goodie, I get to ride a horse!" Will dropped the cookies and ran to Christian.

Phoebe chuckled as she retrieved the package. "Well, I can't fight both of you."

Christian picked Will up, sat him in the saddle, then swung up behind the boy. Phoebe said her good-byes, hugging the two girls and Gwen, then climbed into the buggy and started out, the light beams showing the way.

"My daddy used to let me hold the reins," Will said.

"He used to? He doesn't anymore?"

"He can't. Mama says he's in heaven."

Christian glanced toward Phoebe and knew she hadn't heard the comment. "I'll bet you miss him a lot."

"Not as much as mama. Sometimes she talks to Daddy in his grave." Will hesitated. "But I don't think he can hear her," he added in a whisper.

"Sure he can, if he's in heaven."

When Will put his hands on the reins, Christian didn't stop him.

The ride from Prinsen House to Phoebe's farm took about half an hour. When the buggy turned into the drive, the light beams fell on a small white building.

Suddenly, Phoebe stilled. "The lights are out!"

Phoebe set the brake on the buggy and jumped down. Removing one of the lamps, she started running toward the building.

Christian dismounted, then, carrying Will, ran after her.

"What is it? What's wrong?"

"It's the brooder house. The eggs are about to hatch and the incubator lanterns should be on," she said as Christian and Will caught up with her.

She flung open the door, and when she did, the light of the lamp spilled into the building.

"Oh, no," she cried in anguish. "The eggs. They're gone."

The top to the incubator was standing open and not a single egg was still inside.

"Do you think an animal could have gotten into the shed?" Christian asked as he put Will down.

"It could've been. With Trinidad and Cornello away, I shouldn't have gone to the meeting."

"Mama, what's this?" Will brought a lifeless chick to her.

A lump formed in Phoebe's throat as she looked behind the incubator and found a pile of shattered eggshells, the dead embryos still inside. Tears began to swell in her eyes. "I don't think this was an animal."

Without even thinking, Christian put his arm around her and pulled her closer to him. She didn't resist.

"Why don't you leave me the lantern and you and Will go on to the house? I'll take care of this. He doesn't need to see this in the morning."

"You don't have to do that." Phoebe stepped back.

"I want to. Besides, I have to earn my cookies some way. Isn't that right, Will?"

"Mama, I forgot." Will took Phoebe's hand. "Come on." He started pulling her toward the door.

"Go on. I'll unhitch your horse before I come in," Christian said. "Put a light by the door and I'll find you."

Phoebe was glad for the distraction as she went about plating the cookies and finding glasses for the milk. She thought about sitting at the dining room table, but quickly dismissed it. She and Will always ate at the little farm table in the kitchen, and she wouldn't change just to make an impression on a man.

The lantern was lighting the way up to a porch as Christian approached the house. The door to the kitchen was open and he could see Phoebe putting cookies on a plate. When she turned around, Will took one and began eating it, a simple thing that any child would do. Christian thought Will could be about four or five years old, close to the age Christian must've been when he was put in an orphanage.

When Phoebe came back to the table with the glasses, she saw that a cookie was missing. She said something Christian couldn't hear, but she kissed the boy on the top of his head and put another cookie on the plate. The simple act was so natural, and yet it made Christian melancholy. Never in his life had he ever had anybody who loved him unconditionally.

Mrs. Van Koopmans cared for him—he never doubted that—but her feelings were based on her vicarious pride in his achievements. When he wasn't yet in his teens, he was invited into her salon, where she held her own with the leading political men of South Africa. Her friendship with Rhodes got Christian his education and his position. But never once could he remember the old and gentle lady placing a kiss on him. This snapshot of Phoebe and her son suddenly made him sad.

"I see him. I see Wet."

"Honey, his name is Mr. De Wet." Phoebe moved to the door.

"Wet works," Christian said as he stepped into the little kitchen. "Are there any cookies left? I saw one find its way into someone's mouth when his mother wasn't looking."

Will reached for a cookie and put the whole thing in his mouth, a mischievous grin crossing his face.

Christian snatched a cookie and did the same thing, causing Will to giggle uncontrollably.

Phoebe shook her head as Will climbed onto a chair. "Have a seat."

Christian and Will continued to play little games with the cookies and milk, and even though Phoebe was anxious to discuss what had happened in the brooder house, she didn't broach the subject.

She knew who was behind the vandalism. When Mr. Prinsen said he'd invited W. F. Sloan to the meeting and he'd declined, it made perfect sense. She hated to think what else she'd find in the morning.

"All right, little man, it's time for you to clean your teeth and get ready for bed." Phoebe stood.

"No, I want to play with Wet."

"You've had enough playing for one night. Tomorrow when I need you, you'll be so sleepy, you won't be able to do anything."

"Will you sleep here?" Will asked Christian.

"No, I have to go back to Mr. Prinsen's house."

"Why?"

"That's it, Will," Phoebe said. "When you're ready for bed, you can say good-night. Run and get your pajamas on."

The boy jumped down and disappeared through a door off the kitchen.

"Thank you for being so understanding. He's a very energetic little boy."

"I can see that, but he seems to have a good sense of humor."

Phoebe smiled. "He gets that from his father. Edwin was always joking with him."

"Edwin is your husband?"

"Was." Phoebe swallowed. "He died last year."

Just then Will came into the kitchen and ran to Christian, putting his arms around his neck. "Are you going to be my daddy?"

Christian glanced toward Phoebe as she closed her eyes and bowed her head in an obvious effort to hold back tears.

"Nobody can ever take the place of your daddy, but can I be your friend while I'm here?"

Will nodded. "I like you. Do you like Wet, Mama?"

"Yes, I do, but now you have to go to sleep."

"Can Wet put me in my bed like Daddy used to do?"

"I think that's a good idea. Where do you sleep?" Christian asked.

"Mama sleeps in there, but I'm a big boy. I sleep upstairs all by myself."

"Then let's find your room."

When Christian came down the stairs, the kitchen was empty, but the back door was standing open.

He stepped out and found Phoebe in a porch swing. "Do you mind if I join you?" Phoebe moved to the end of the swing, and Christian sat beside her. "Will's all tucked in. It's not every kid who sleeps with an ostrich chick. Where'd he get that?"

"Gwen and her girls made it for him." Phoebe's voice began to quiver. "What kind of madman would deliberately kill little chicks? They would've been hatched in another week. Were any of the eggs left unbroken?"

"No. If I were guessing, I'd say they were hit with a hammer. You know how hard an ostrich egg is. Do you have any idea who did this?"

"Yes," she whispered.

"Your father-in-law?"

Phoebe jerked around, causing the swing to swerve. "What made you say that?" Phoebe challenged.

"It was just a comment Yhomas made. He said you had the beginnings of a prosperous troop of birds, but every time you come close to getting ahead, your father-in-law, as the saying goes, puts a fly in the ointment."

"He does do that, but it's his son who's the most unbearable."

"Then why do you stay here?"

"I've asked myself that same question many times. If the moon is just right, it'll cast a shadow on a tree up on that little knoll. That's where Edwin is buried. If I leave, Will will have no connection with his father, and as much as I dislike my in-laws, I wouldn't take that away from him."

"You should think about yourself." Christian reached for her hand. He began to massage her palm, feeling the rough texture of calluses.

Phoebe withdrew her hand quickly. "I think you should go, Mr. De Wet. Mr. Prinsen will be expecting you."

"I'm sorry, I shouldn't have done that."

"There's no need to apologize; you didn't do anything." After a moment she began to speak again. "After Edwin died, I had a procession of prospective suitors, and I didn't like it. I don't have time for it, and I like my life just the way it is."

"I understand."

"If I'm going to be your friend, do I call you Mr. De Wet, or Wet, or do you have another name you'd like to be called?"

Christian paused. He'd like to tell her his story—how he'd been known only as Jacktar for the first ten years of his life, how he seldom allowed anyone to get close to him. He sensed in her the same defenses, the same walls that were meant to keep out the pain of the past. He knew there had to be more to her story. A young woman had to have a reason why these exasperating birds meant so much to her. Why she'd work like a farmhand just to hold on to this land. Yes, there had to be a reason.

"My *given* name is Christian, and I'd be honored to have you call me by that name."

"All right, Christian it is. And I'm pleased to have you as my friend."

"Good. Now that we've established our parameters, it brings two friends back to the problem at hand. Is there anyone here to help you?"

"Yes, I have two men who work for me."

"But they aren't here now."

"No."

"Then, as your friend, I'm going to stay here tonight."

"You can't. You can't do that," Phoebe said in panic.

"I think I should. You say you have an idea as to who might've done this, but what if you're wrong? What if the person who came here knows your men are gone, and that person also knows you're defenseless?"

"I have a gun, and I know how to use it," Phoebe said defiantly.

Christian laughed. "I'm sure you do, but I'm still not going to leave you. You don't know what you'll find in the morning. What if there's more damage other than the eggs? What if your grown birds have been killed? How will you explain that to Will?"

"Oh, dear, I hadn't dared think of that."

"All right, then it's agreed, I'm staying. Do your men have a bunkhouse?" Christian rose from the swing.

"They do, but it's not kept up very well. They are both old men, and I think neatness is not something they are very concerned about. If you're going to do this, you'll stay in the house. I have five bedrooms."

"All right. Which room is mine?"

4

After showing Christian to his room, Phoebe put on her nightgown and climbed into bed. It was unsettling to listen to Christian's footsteps in the room above her. She heard the springs of the bed when the footsteps stopped. His boots came off with two distinct thuds. Holding her breath, she waited. She'd invited a man—a stranger— into her house, and now he was in the room adjacent to her sleeping son's.

He'd suggested that someone might want to prey upon a defenseless woman, but what if he'd said that just to get her to let her guard down? What if he came down in the night and tried to assault her? She thought about setting a chair under the doorknob, but then what would happen if Will had one of his nightmares and came down to her room?

There was only one thing to do. As quietly as she could, she made her way to the dresser and withdrew Edwin's Colt .44 from the top drawer. She'd told Christian she knew how to use a gun, and technically that was true. Less than a month ago she'd shot a rattlesnake coiled on the bank of the irrigation ditch.

With trembling fingers, she withdrew a shell from the ammunition box. After the snake incident she'd unloaded the gun, but to be on the safe side, she pulled the hammer back, to check the cylinder. Seeing no bullet, she fully expected to hear the relatively quiet snap of the hammer falling on an empty chamber.

To her complete shock, a muzzle flash lit up the room, accompanied by a loud report of a gunshot.

Phoebe screamed. What had she done?

Christian had just stripped down to his drawers when he heard the shot. Without bothering to pull on his pants, he bolted out of the room. Bursting through Phoebe's door, the acrid smell of cordite burned his nostrils. In the darkness he couldn't see.

"Phoebe, where are you?"

She didn't answer.

He moved, hoping to find some way to light the room. He heard a loud bump that sounded as if something had been dropped. Christian's heart began to beat rapidly. Who was in this room? Where was Phoebe?

"Phoebe?"

This time he heard an intake of breath and he knew she was alive. The kerosene lamp had been turned down so that only a small arc of yellow-red outlined the mantel.

"Are you hurt?" As his eyes adjusted to the dim light, he could make out where she was standing. Moving toward her, he took her in his arms, her sobs now uncontrollable.

"What happened?"

"I . . . I'm not sure." Her voice quavered, the words coming between sobs.

"You're safe now." Christian continued to hold her. "Did someone break into the house?"

"No, I did it myself."

"You fired a gun? Why?"

"I wanted to protect myself in case you came to my room."

Christian chuckled quietly, stroking her hair as she laid her head on his chest. "You got your gun to keep me out, but your gun brought me to you."

"Mama, I heard a loud noise, and it waked me up. Can I sleep in your bed? Wet! You didn't go home!" The little boy came bounding toward Christian and Phoebe and grabbed both of them around their legs.

Then Christian remembered he hadn't bothered to pull on his trousers. He was in his underwear holding Phoebe, who wore only a nightgown, and now her son was causing his body to stay in contact with hers. At a time when he shouldn't have had such thoughts, he was acutely aware of their near nude proximity.

Quickly, he released Phoebe, and after adjusting the lamp so there was more light, he turned his attention to Will. "The loud noise scared me, too, but everything is all right." Christian knelt beside Will.

Will saw the gun lying on the floor and picked it up. "Did you have to shoot a rattlesnake?"

"I'll take that," Christian said as gently as he could. He was fearful that in the excitement Phoebe may have cocked the gun a second time and another bullet might be in the chamber.

"You can have it, Wet. It was my daddy's."

When Will handed it over, Christian pulled the hammer back to half cock and spun the cylinder, checking it. Every chamber but one was empty, and he was certain this must've been the one that had discharged. Pulling the shell casing out, he saw that it was, indeed, spent. Satisfied that the revolver was now empty, he turned to Phoebe. "Where shall I put this?"

Phoebe pointed to the dresser, and Christian put in on top, not wanting to invade her privacy by placing it in a drawer.

"Come on, Will, with all this excitement I'm hungry again. Did we eat all your cookies?"

"I don't think so." Will turned to his mother. "Can we have some more?"

Phoebe nodded.

"Then let's go find them." Christian scooped up the boy and went to the kitchen.

Phoebe was still visibly shaken, but she moved to her dresser to put the gun away. She looked around the room to see where the bullet had hit, but was unable to find any trace of it.

She needed to say something to Will, to comfort him. He'd been present when his father had died, and he often had nightmares about it. When she looked in the kitchen, she saw Christian and Will sitting at the table. Will was giggling about something and seemed to have forgotten the gunshot that had awakened him.

"Did your horse go home?" Will reached for a cookie.

"No, he's still here."

"What's his name?"

"You know, I don't know. He's Mr. Prinsen's horse and he didn't tell me."

"I think his name is Poongie."

"Poongie? What kind of a name is that?" Christian asked. "I think his name is Sissy."

"Sissy—that's a girl's name. I think his name is Booby."

Will continued to come up with nonsensical syllables to name the horse, and Christian interacted patiently, all the while allowing Will to eat as many cookies as he wanted.

Phoebe should've joined them but she couldn't. This was the first time she'd had the chance to really look at Christian. As he sat at the table with her son, still clad only in his underwear, she was amazed at how comfortable he seemed.

His eyes were light blue and his face was bronzed, but his upper body and his bare legs were not. Phoebe reasoned that a businessman wouldn't be inclined to shed his shirt and work in the sun as Edwin had often done. She knew Christian was taller than Edwin because her head had lain on his shoulder while he comforted her. Edwin was more portly, even having what some would call a potbelly, but Christian didn't seem to have an extra ounce of fat on his body.

All at once Phoebe caught herself. She had been ogling Christian as if he were an animal she intended to buy. All that was lacking was looking into his mouth and counting his teeth!

She turned quickly, hoping that Christian hadn't seen her staring. The most troubling thing was that mentally she'd been comparing him to Edwin, and Edwin was coming up short.

She was sure that Christian would work on the reservoir project for a few months only and then he'd go back to South Africa. That was how it should be.

Phoebe wouldn't allow herself to get entangled with another man whose station was obviously so far above her own. She'd never again be put at the mercy of a W. F. Sloan, who would not let her forget her place. After all, she was the house-keeper who got pregnant and snared the master's son.

This ostrich farm had been her idea. Every-one, including Edwin, thought it was a crackpot idea at first, but she'd convinced him it could be successful. Now she considered this enterprise to be a way to prove to the Sloans—and everyone else—that she wasn't a gold digger. She'd make it on her own, without any help from anyone else. She owed that to Edwin's memory and she owed it to Will.

"All right, little man, it's time for us to go back to bed." Christian stood.

"No, no, one more cookie." Will grabbed another.

"That's it." Christian picked Will up and threw him over his shoulder.

"My teeth. What about my teeth? Mama makes me clean my teeth."

"Not tonight. Let's go."

When Phoebe went back to bed, she felt guilty she hadn't joined the two in the kitchen and was relieved when Christian extinguished the kitchen lamp and she heard them clomping up the stairs to the bedrooms.

She thought it odd how easily Will had taken to Christian. Because he spent so much time with her, he usually had difficulty relating to a man. Of course, the only men he saw regularly were Rueben Bucknell, Andy Patterson, and Trinidad and Cornello. Frank Sloan came often enough, but his visits were always punctuated with strife. Will's reaction to him was either to hide someplace or cling to Phoebe, making his behavior one more thing for Frank to criticize.

The very thought of Frank made her cringe. And now he'd done yet another thing that caused her stress. She wanted to believe destroying the eggs wasn't his doing—that he wasn't that cruel—but he was the most logical culprit, probably at his father's urging.

She lay back on her pillow, not yet turning down the light, and then she saw it. A bullet hole in the ceiling.

Christian was awakened by a crowing rooster, and when he opened his eyes, he saw the red-orange orb of the sun, barely two disks above the eastern horizon. It took him a moment to realize that he wasn't in his room at Prinsen House, but rather in the house of a woman he'd met only last night.

Last night! Last night had been busy. The gunshot had more than startled him, it had frightened him. Fortunately it was just an accident, and as frightening as it was last night, this morning he could smile about it. With a yawn and a stretch, Christian got out of bed and reached for his pants . . . the pants he now realized he'd failed to put on when he'd hurried down to Phoebe's room. He put on his shirt, pulled on his pants, then reached for his boots.

When he tried to pull the first boot on, his foot hit something inside; curious, he turned the shoe upside down.

It was the bullet!

Surprised, Christian examined the boot and found a hole in the sole. The bullet Phoebe had shot had passed through the ceiling of her bedroom and the floor of the room where Christian was staying. It had gone through the sole of his boot before it was finally spent. He poked his finger through the hole, then pulled on the boot. He needed a cup of coffee.

Phoebe awakened to the smell of freshly brewed coffee. She smiled in her half sleep, thankful that Edwin had started breakfast.

She bolted upright in her bed as she clutched the quilt to her chest. Someone was in her house. Who? Then the recollection of the night before came to her. Christian, the gunshot, and the destruction of the eggs.

Quickly she rose and began to dress. She grabbed one of her two old blue chambray dresses that she wore on most days when she was working with the birds, but then thought better of it. Instead she chose a yellow gingham that she often wore when she went to town. Brushing her russet hair, she secured it with side combs, allowing her ringlets to hang down her back.

"Good morning," Christian said, looking around from the cookstove when Phoebe stepped into the kitchen. "I wanted to make you some breakfast, but I was afraid I'd make too much noise and wake you up."

Phoebe was at a loss for words. Gwen had asked if she didn't think Christian was a handsome man, but she wasn't prepared for her reaction to seeing him standing here, in her house. He was dressed in the same cream-colored shirt he'd worn the night before, but his shirt was open at the collar, far enough down for her to see a strong neck, and just the suggestion of what she already knew was a broad chest.

Christian hadn't combed his hair this morning; it was somewhat disheveled, a few ringlets falling across his forehead.

"You don't have to fix breakfast. I can do that." Phoebe went to the cupboard to take down some flour. "Do you like flapjacks?"

"Flapjacks?"

"Pancakes."

"Yes, I love pancakes."

"All right. You can carve the bacon if you'd like. It's in the icebox."

As Phoebe began preparing the batter, Christian started carving slices of bacon. She glanced over at him a moment later. "Heavens, how many slices are you cutting?"

"I don't know. There's you, Will, and me. I figured three collops apiece."

Phoebe laughed. "I'm not familiar with a collop, but I'll eat one piece of bacon, and Will won't eat any."

"Oh, then that means I'll eat"—Christian began counting—"five collops, and you shall have one." He self-consciously chuckled.

Christian put the knife down, and as he moved, he felt the floor through the hole in his boot, reminding him of the incident the night before. Smiling, he reached into his pocket. "You lost this last night." He withdrew his hand. "I found it in my boot." He laughed and opened the palm of his hand.

Seeing a bullet, Phoebe gasped and put her hand to her throat. "God in heaven! You found that in your boot?"

Christian turned around and lifted his foot, showing the hole in the sole.

"Oh! That's the bullet I . . . What if . . . ?"

Christian had thought to make light of the situation, but from her expression he saw she wasn't taking it as a joke. "Phoebe." He stepped to her quickly and pulled her into his arms. "It's all right."

She leaned against him for a long moment, until finally she realized what she was doing and stepped away, although the disengagement was more gentle than abrupt.

"I'm so sorry. I could have . . . Oh, Christian, what if you'd been standing in that very spot where the bullet came through?"

"Well, the important thing is I wasn't. But now we're about to have another catastrophe." He inclined his head toward the stove, where smoke was beginning to rise as the pancakes curled in the skillet.

"The pancakes! I forgot!" Phoebe rushed to the stove, grabbing the handle without benefit of a cloth. Immediately, she dropped the hot pan, making a loud clatter. "Damn."

"Mrs. Sloan, did I just hear you curse?" Christian's facial expression clearly showed he was jesting.

"I'm sorry. I shouldn't have . . . It's just that I am so discombobulated this morning. You must think I'm a real scatterbrain."

Christian snapped off a piece of an aloe plant that was on the windowsill. "No, Mrs. Sloan, I don't think you're a scatterbrain." He took her hand in his and began rubbing the soothing liquid over her burn. When he'd finished, he lifted her hand to his lips and kissed it. "There. That should take care of you." He didn't drop her hand as his gaze held hers.

Just then Will came bounding down the steps and into the kitchen.

"Wet! You're still here. . . . You stayed all night with us. Yippee!"

As Will ran toward them, Christian dropped Phoebe's hand and caught him with one arm, lifting him into the air.

"Are you ready for breakfast? I've made something special and I know you're going to like it." Christian set the boy on a chair and turned to get a piece of bacon that was cooling on a plate.

Will wrinkled his nose. "Yuck! I don't like bacon."

"Oh, but this is something different. This is a collop." Christian popped a piece of bacon into his own mouth.

Gingerly, Will imitated Christian, and a wide grin crossed his face. "Mama, collops are good. Why don't you ever make some?"

"I'll have to do that." Phoebe glanced toward Christian. "Mr. De Wet has a lot of tricks up his sleeve."

"Someday I'll have to show you a few more." Christian flashed a smile toward Phoebe.

She felt an unexpected warmth radiate through her body. "I'm sure you will . . . someday." She tossed it right back to him with the same challenging smile. She was pleased to see, by the quick blink of his eyes, that he knew she knew exactly what this exchange was about.

Phoebe brought the platter of pancakes over to the table, then put a couple on Will's plate and several on Christian's.

"Mama, you know what you did?"

"What did I do?"

"You gave Wet a whole bunch of pancakes. Do you remember when you used to give Daddy a whole lot of pancakes?"

"Yes, Will, I remember." Phoebe felt a flush in her cheeks, which she hoped Christian didn't notice.

As Christian began to eat, he thought about how much he was enjoying this breakfast. It wasn't just the food, though the pancakes were quite good. He was enjoying the ambience of a family meal, something he couldn't remember having experienced before in his entire life. Though Mrs. Van Koopmans had been good to him, he'd never considered himself to be a part of her family, nor had she ever encouraged it. This was something entirely new for him, and he was enjoying what this meal represented much more than he would've thought.

Then, as if unwilling or unable to carry this fantasy any further, Christian pushed his chair back from the table.

"The pancakes were delicious." He took a last swallow of coffee. "I am most appreciative."

"And the collops, Wet. Don't forget the collops," Will added.

"I could eat that many pancakes and more, but we've got work to do. Are your nesting birds close by? I think I should check on them."

"I dread to think what you might find. I only have my original six pairs of adult birds, and if they're gone, I'll . . ."

"Let's hope all is well. Are they in paddocks?"

"Yes, if that's what you call their pens. You'll see them when you get to the rise."

"What about Wapi?" Will picked up one of the crisper pancakes. "Can Wet give this old pancake to him?"

"No, honey, we don't need to encourage him. Anyway, isn't taking care of Wapi one of your jobs?"

Christian's eyebrows rose. "Should I know something about . . . Wapi?"

"He's an orphan chick. One of my nests was washed away by a thunderstorm, and Will insisted we rescue the eggs and put them in the incubator. Only one hatched, and now he's become sort of a pet, or a nuisance, depending on how you look at it."

"Now, how do you know Wapi is a boy?" Christian asked. "I've always heard it's hard to tell the sex of an ostrich until it gets through the hobble-dehoy stage."

Phoebe laughed. "Are you calling our birds awkward? Never. The Sloan birds are the best in the valley. Isn't that right, Will?"

"Yes, ma'am."

"Well, I'd better go make the acquaintance of this fine flock," Christian said. "Where's your tackey?"

"Tackey? I don't know what that is." Phoebe's brow furrowed.

"Don't tell me you go out among the birds without a stick," Christian said, astonished.

For an instant, a scene flashed across Phoebe's mind when, yes, she had gone among the birds without a stick. "It's by the gate," Phoebe said, her voice devoid of emotion as she quickly turned away.

Christian was confused by her reaction, but didn't question her. "Give me a pancake, Will, and if I get to meet Wapi, I'll give it to him."

When Christian reached the first enclosure, he found several sticks that had thorns still intact. Picking what he thought was the strongest one, he opened the gate and went in search of the nesting birds.

Phoebe was busy in the kitchen mixing up bread dough. She was thinking about the $600 Mr. Prinsen would've paid her for her hatchlings, but the loss, while distressing, hadn't devastated her.

She credited that to the comforting support she'd received from Christian De Wet.

Hearing the screen door open, she said, "You're back. Please tell me the nests and the birds are safe."

"Were the birds in danger? I hadn't heard that."

"Frank!" She dropped her spoon on the floor. Picking it up, she turned toward him.

"I heard about your difficulties. I thought I'd come out here and see if there's anything I could do."

"And what did you hear?"

"That you lost all the eggs in your brooder. Surely, you know that."

"The question is, how do you?"

"My handyman was out and he ran into Cornello this morning, and Cornello told him how bad it was."

"Cornello told Rojas?"

"Yes. He said not a single egg was spared. He said it looked like they may have been hit with a hammer. I wouldn't put it past that old man that he might do something like this himself."

"Yes, who's to say." Phoebe clenched her jaw.

"Finally—after all this time, you're making some sense. Get rid of those two old men, sell these damned birds, and move into town." Frank moved toward her. "You won't have to work so hard."

"And how do you propose I support myself?"

A revolting expression crossed his face. "It's

interesting that you use the word *propose*. You've heard my proposal from the day you tricked my brother, and I'm running out of patience. You may think you don't have to submit to me, but so help me, when I'm through with you, you'll be begging to come to my bed."

"Are you threatening me?" Phoebe raised her chin defiantly.

Frank crooked his finger under her chin. "No, my dear. It's not a threat. It will happen. The eggs are just the beginning."

Just then, Christian came into the kitchen, having come through the parlor. "Is this man bothering you?"

Frank whirled around. "Mister, I don't know who you are, but you can't just walk into my brother's house and get away with it." Frank pulled a small-caliber revolver from his pocket and pointed it at Christian. "I think you'd better get on your horse and ride out of here before I put a bullet through you."

Christian laughed. "It wouldn't be the first time I've been shot at in this house."

Frank looked toward Phoebe. "What is this man saying? Do you know him? Has he been bothering you? Whatever it is, I won't allow it."

Just then Will came bounding into the kitchen. Seeing Frank with a gun pointed at Christian, Will hurried to Phoebe and buried his head in her skirt. "Don't let Uncle Frank shoot Wet. Get your gun, Mama, and shoot Uncle Frank."

Phoebe picked Will up and held him in her

arms. "No one's going to shoot anyone. Frank, I think it's time you left."

Christian came to stand beside Phoebe and took Will from her. The boy wrapped his arms around Christian's neck and buried his head on his shoulder.

A menacing smile crossed Frank's face. "I'm beginning to get the picture here. Will, my boy, does Wet sleep here?"

"Yes, sir."

Frank nodded. He turned and, without saying a word, stomped out of the kitchen.

"I take it 'Uncle Frank' is your brother-in-law."

"One and the same. You've just met Frank Sloan."

"Seems like a pleasant fellow," Christian said sarcastically. "From what I heard, it doesn't sound like there's much familial congeniality between you two. I'm glad I came in when I did."

"Oh, the birds," Phoebe said, concerned. "I forgot about them. Are they still alive?"

Christian laughed. "Your birds, and their eggs, I'm happy to say, are just fine, but I must say, you've got a couple of feisty ones out there."

"Did you see Wapi? Did you give him the pancake?" Will asked.

"I did, and he asked about you. He told me to give you his best."

Will laughed. "That's silly. Wapi's an ostrich, and ostriches can't talk."

"Oh, but they can, if you know how to listen to them."

"Mama, Wet can talk to ostriches. I'm going to make Wapi talk to me."

Phoebe laughed. "Don't get into an argument with him."

"If I do, I'll win," Will called over his shoulder as he hurried outside.

Christian waited until Will was out of earshot before he turned back to Phoebe. "You can tell me it's none of my business, but I'm concerned about what I just overheard. Is there something you'd like to tell me?"

Phoebe drew a short, audible intake of breath. She clenched her hands and closed her eyes. "He wants me in his bed," she said frankly.

"Since you're his brother's widow, maybe he feels an obligation toward marrying you. In some cultures, that's the expected thing to do, but I'd think he'd try to develop a better approach than what I just overheard."

"You don't understand; he's not interested in marriage. He has a wife, but he wants me to be his concubine."

"It seems to me that you were quite specific in your response. I'd think it's only a matter of time before he gives up."

"Frank Sloan will never quit trying."

"Of course he will. No man is going to continue pursuing a decent woman once she's turned him down. Not any man of character, that is."

Decent woman. Those words were stinging. In Phoebe's mind, she wasn't a decent woman. If Christian knew what she'd done, how she'd become pregnant before she and Edwin were married, would he condemn her for her transgression? Now was the time to tell him if she wanted any kind of relationship with Christian, but she couldn't.

Whom was she kidding? The term *relationship* hardly described what was happening between them. Yesterday was the first time she'd ever laid eyes on the man, yet she'd seen more of him than she had seen of any other man except her husband. Now would be the time to blurt out, "I was pregnant before I got married," but what if Christian wasn't a forgiving man? What if he was like Frank?

No, she wouldn't say anything—at least not about her own history.

Finally she spoke. "Frank isn't a man of character. If he were, would he have broken all my eggs?"

"You're sure he's the one who did this?"

"He didn't admit to it in so many words, but he said Cornello told Rojas, and there's no way Cornello would know what happened. I've not seen him since the fiesta began, and I can't believe he'd leave the dancing to come all the way out here just to destroy his livelihood."

"I know Cornello works for you, but who's Rojas?"

"He works for the Sloans."

"Do you think your men will be back today?"

"Probably not. I'm sure the celebration has a few more days before it's over."

"Then that settles it. You need another man. Someone who can look out for your birds and for your safety, too."

Phoebe looked down. "Trinidad and Cornello have been with us from the very beginning and I trust them. I can't bring in someone else."

"But you need someone who knows ostriches."

"Are you volunteering for the job?" Phoebe laughed to cover her embarrassment. "Anyway, won't the water project occupy most of your time?"

A suggestive smile crossed Christian's face. "As much as I would love to be your man, it's not me I'm offering. I brought a good man with me from home, and now that I've agreed to stay in America for a while, he won't have much to do. I think he'd very much welcome the opportunity to be gainfully occupied."

"I appreciate your offer, Christian, but quite frankly, I can't afford someone else. It's all I can do to come up with the money I pay Cornello and Trinidad. And now that there won't be any chicks to sell, it'll be harder than ever."

"I understand, but you won't have to pay July anything. His salary is already taken care of, and like I said, he'll be anxious to have something to do. I'm going to ride over to the Prinsens' and bring him back. And I won't take no for an answer." Christian ameliorated his absolute declaration with a smile.

5

"**W**ell, if it isn't Mr. De Wet," Gwen Bucknell said. "If I'm not mistaken, we missed you last night."

Christian was in the stable unsaddling his horse and was surprised to meet the farm manager's wife. "Mrs. Bucknell, it's my pleasure."

"I'm sure it has been." A smile crossed Gwen's face. "I believe the last time I saw you, you were riding out of here on your way to Phoebe Sloan's house."

"That's right. I spent the night with her."

"Oh?" Gwen lifted an eyebrow.

"I suppose I should revise that," Christian said when he saw Gwen's expression. "When Phoebe and I—that is, Mrs. Sloan and I—got to her house last night, we found her brooder house had been broken into, and every egg broken. They were not only broken, it was apparent that they'd been cracked deliberately."

"Frank Sloan." Anger crossed Gwen's face. "It's just like that no-good scoundrel to do such a thing. He's out to ruin Phoebe."

"I met the man briefly this morning, and I share your opinion. At any rate, I thought it best not to leave Phoebe alone last night after we found the broken eggs."

"I agree, and under the circumstances, spending the night was absolutely the gentlemanly thing to do."

"Mama, don't you have your horse saddled yet?" Hannah asked, coming into the stable. "Papa says we should get started before it gets too hot."

"My daughters and I are going to be away for a while, but before we come home, we'll stop by Phoebe's place," Gwen said. "I hope nothing else has happened."

"I'm sure she'll appreciate that."

Christian went in search of Yhomas. He wanted to tell him what had happened at the Sloan place and also tell him of his plan to have July work for Phoebe. When he reached the library, Yhomas was conversing with Benjamin Fowler.

"There you are, Christian," Yhomas said when he saw him. "You remember Ben."

"Of course. As you're the chairman of the Water Storage Committee, I assume I'll work for you—that is, if you still want my suggestions."

"We very much want to hear what you have to say." Benjamin Fowler extended his hand. "I'm in contact with a California lawyer who thinks we can get the government to pay for all of this, and with your experience with Cecil Rhodes, you undoubtedly have some insight."

Christian rubbed his chin as he weighed his thoughts before he answered. "I'll say this: I respect Rhodes for his foresight and intentions. I believe he thought he was doing what was best for South Africa, but from my vantage point, I know that some of the people he took into his confidence were unscrupulous. My advice to you would be to make certain that anyone involved in this project is thoroughly vetted and proven to have the utmost integrity."

Yhomas Prinsen began clapping his hands as a wide smile crossed his face. "My dear friend Marie Van Koopmans couldn't have said it better!"

"I can assure you George Maxwell is an honest man," Fowler said, somewhat taken aback by Christian's comment, and Yhomas's reaction.

"I'm sure he is," Yhomas said. "It's just that Christian has seen firsthand what corruption can occur when private enterprise colludes with government dollars."

"Then that's an even better reason to have him on our side," Benjamin said. "I'm wondering, Christian, would you be available to accompany a group of men who are going up to the Tonto Basin? Maxwell thinks we should form a cooperative and get total control over the dam site before we try to get Congress to authorize federal funding."

"What would this group be doing?" Christian asked.

"They need to make some preliminary surveys. They'll be boring in the bedrock to see if Tonto would be the best site. Also, someone needs to estimate some costs before we try to raise capital."

"When would this expedition begin?" Christian asked.

"As soon as we can get Frederick Newell here from Washington. He's supposed to be the government's best hydrographic surveyor, according to Maxwell."

"Do you think the team could use a good mechanical engineer?" Yhomas asked.

"Of course," Benjamin said. "Who do you have in mind?"

"A friend of Christian's. Christian, do you think Clarence could leave Albany?"

"Clarence Woodson? Why him?"

"From what you've told me, he may be one of the most innovative men I've ever heard about. You said he helped invent a long gun out of nothing, and he devised a water system that kept Kimberley alive during the siege. If he's not doing anything, I think he'd be an ideal person to help us out."

"You may be right," Christian said.

"Then as a member of this committee, I'm

suggesting we bring him out here . . . and I'm suggesting he bring his family with him. You wouldn't mind renewing your friendship with his daughter, would you?"

Christian laughed. "Now I understand what you're saying. It would be good to see Ina Claire again. But seriously, I do believe Clarence Woodson would be a valuable addition to any organization if he's available."

"Well, then, send for this fellow," Fowler said. "I'll let you know when Newell is expected. Perhaps they can coordinate their travel."

"I'll take care of it," Yhomas said.

"Good."

Gwen Bucknell and her two daughters were tying their horses to the hitching rail in front of Phoebe's house when a lone ostrich came running toward them.

"Get ready, here comes Wapi," Gwen said.

When the bird reached them, he began extending his gangling neck under Hannah's arms, trying to take the sack of peppermint sticks she'd brought for Will.

"Get away," Hannah scolded as she tried to fend off the six-foot-tall bird. "What's Miss Phoebe going to do with this thing when he gets full grown?"

"I don't know," Phoebe said with a little laugh as she and Will stepped out onto the porch. "Girls, see if you and Will can get him back in his pen. You may have to give him a little of your candy."

"You need someone to build a pen that would keep him in," Gwen said. "I hear you had a little trouble last night."

"I suppose Mr. De Wet told you."

"Since you two spent the night together, don't you think you should call him Christian?"

"Gwen!" Seeing the humor in Gwen's eyes, Phoebe laughed. "You're awful. You know it wasn't like that."

"I know. And given the circumstances, I'm glad he stayed with you."

"Did he tell you I took a shot at him?"

"What?" Gwen gasped.

"I put a hole in his boot."

"My Lord, Phoebe!"

Phoebe laughed again, then took Gwen inside and led her into the bedroom. She pointed to the hole in the ceiling. "Evidently his boots were sitting just over where the bullet came through."

At that moment, there was a knock at the door. "Senora Sloan?"

"That must be the boys." Phoebe went to the front door. "Good morning, Cornello, I'm glad you're back. Where's Trinidad? Did he go to check the incubator?"

Cornello lowered his head and removed his hat. "No, ma'am, that is why I am here."

"Oh, dear, has something happened?"

Cornello cleared his throat and looked away before he spoke. "*Sí, he is in la cárcel.*"

"He's in jail?"

"Yes, ma'am, Judge Johnstone put him in jail when he not pay his fine."

"What did he do, Cornello? Tell me, no matter how bad it is."

"He had his gun with him, but he did not show it."

"You mean he had a concealed weapon," Gwen said, overhearing the conversation. "Everybody knows you can't do that."

"Yes, ma'am." Cornello nodded. "He needs fifty dollars to get out of *la cárcel*. He say to get it from you, senora."

"Fifty dollars! I don't have fifty dollars. Trinidad will have to stay in jail if he thinks I can come up with that kind of money. How long has he been there?"

"This his second day."

"His second day? Cornello, do you know if either you or Trinidad has seen Rojas Montoya?"

"Yes, ma'am. I see him at the fiesta."

"What did you talk about?"

"Bad things. He say lots of damage. He say we go."

Phoebe's brow furrowed. "What kind of bad things?"

"Lots of people die. Rojas brother . . . my sister—they both live in Galveston. We go see if hurricane"—Cornello made a swirling motion with his hand—"blow them away."

"I'm so sorry, Cornello. Of course you should go. I have five dollars. Will that help you?" Phoebe turned to go back in the house before Cornello could answer. When she returned, she handed him the money. "If you see Trinidad, tell him I can't help him."

"But who will help you, senora? The eggs—don't forget to turn them."

"I will." Phoebe didn't want to tell Cornello what had happened because she thought it was important for him to go to his sister in Galveston. The papers had been full of accounts of the mounting death toll, now numbered in the thousands, and by comparison twenty-five eggs was a small loss. Phoebe hugged Cornello. "I hope you find your sister well."

"Yes, ma'am." Cornello put on his hat and turned to go.

Phoebe and Gwen watched the old man walk away. "He won't be back," Gwen said.

"I think not. Did you hear him remind me to turn the eggs? That proves he knows nothing about what happened, so he couldn't possibly have told Rojas, which means Rojas couldn't possibly have told Frank. The only way Frank could've known about the broken eggs is if he's the one responsible."

"From the moment I first heard, there was no doubt in my mind as to who broke them. But what are you going to do now? With Cornello gone and Trinidad in jail, who's going to help you?"

"Christian suggested he might bring over a friend who came with him from South Africa. Maybe I should take him up on his offer."

"That would be July."

"It seems like a strange nickname."

"I don't think it's a nickname. I think it's the only name he has—not even a last name."

"No last name? How can that be?"

"He's a Zulu."

"Oh?" Phoebe's eyes opened wide.

Gwen laughed. "He's a most endearing man, and I'll say this. If July comes to take care of you, no one, not even Frank Sloan, will dare cross you."

"Why do you say that?"

"He's a big man—practically a giant. July will make an excellent bodyguard for you, and besides, Buck says he knows a lot about ostriches."

"That's good. I hope Christian was serious, because it sounds like July is just the person I need right now."

"Yhomas said you could keep the horse over at Mrs. Sloan's place for as long as you need it," Christian said as he and July saddled their mounts. "You're sure you don't mind doing this?"

"Does Mrs. Sloan know that I'm . . ."

"A black man?" Christian chuckled. "Now that you bring it up, I don't think I mentioned it. What I said was that you're a good man. And right now I'll feel better knowing there's a good man over at her place to look out for her."

"Why don't *you* stay there, then?"

"I thought about that, but I don't think it'd look right."

Now it was July's turn to laugh. "You think in America, where you and I couldn't stay in the same hotel, it'll look better if a black man stays with this woman than it will if you stay with her?"

"You won't be there by yourself. She has two men who work for her, but I don't expect they know too much about raising ostriches. Maybe you can teach them a thing or two."

"Maybe, if they'll listen to me."

When they arrived at Phoebe's place, Will came running out to meet them. "Wet! You've come back!"

"Yes, but I can't stay very long." Christian and July dismounted.

Will looked up at July in awe. "Are you a giant?"

Christian smiled, pleased that what Will had noticed first about July was his size.

"Will, this is my friend July. And if July is my friend, and I am your friend, that means July must also be your friend."

Will smiled. "Do you want to see my pet ostrich?"

"Would that be Wapi?" July asked.

Will's eyes opened wide. "How do you know his name?"

"Well, when we rode by, Wapi told me his name." July smiled. Christian had told July all about Will and Wapi.

"Wapi can talk to you, too?"

"Yes, indeed."

"Let's go find your mother, then you can take July on a tour of the place," Christian said.

• • •

When the two men entered her home, Phoebe was overwhelmed by July's size.

"I take it you agree that July will be welcomed here."

Phoebe extended her hand to July. "I'm Phoebe Sloan, and of course you're welcome here. I'm sorry for staring, but I do believe you may be the tallest man I've ever seen."

"My people are tall."

On the ride back to the Prinsens, Christian felt better knowing July would be overseeing Phoebe's operation. He knew she'd be safe as well, because July's size could intimidate her brother-in-law or anyone else who tried to bother her.

Phoebe had said that Frank Sloan was married, and yet he'd openly said he wanted her in his bed. What kind of man would insinuate such a thing, especially to his brother's wife? If Phoebe were his sister-in-law, he'd do everything he could to take care of her. If Phoebe were his wife . . .

Christian quickly put the thought out of his mind. Women were an enigma to him. He was soon to be thirty years old, and while he wasn't a virgin, he'd never before met a woman who excited him. But he'd be lying if he didn't confess that last night when he held Phoebe, she in her thin nightgown and he in his underwear, the close contact between them had generated prurient ideas.

He thought of Ina Claire Woodson, and wondered if, by having such thoughts of Phoebe, he was being untrue to Ina Claire. He and Ina Claire had grown quite close during their time together while Kimberley was under siege.

He'd never had such thoughts about Ina Claire; he'd thought of her more as a good friend than anything else. But, to be fair, the time he'd spent with Ina Claire didn't lend itself to such thinking. They were too busy surviving the siege to let salacious thoughts enter the picture.

Perhaps Yhomas was right. If she came with her father, he might be able to kindle a real relationship with her. That'd be better than pursuing any kind of relationship with Phoebe. Why was he even thinking about Phoebe? He knew little about her, and she knew even less about him. At least Ina Claire knew his past.

When Christian rode into the lane, Yhomas and Reuben Bucknell were standing beside the paddock that contained the feather birds. These were ostriches between six and eighteen months old, and at this age their feathers were a dingy drab color with just a hint of black. As they matured, the males would develop glossy black plumes and the females a soft gray, both having white wings and tails.

"Christian," Yhomas said when he saw him approach. "Did you leave July over at the Sloan place?"

"I did. I think he's going to fit in fine over there. Will seems to be quite taken with him already."

"We're going to miss that big fellow when it's time for the plucking," Buck said. "I was counting on him, but I suppose he'll be more help to Trinidad and Cornello. I don't know how much longer those two can work for Phoebe, but she's too loyal to get anybody else to come in and take their places."

"It may be that she *has* to get somebody else," Christian said. "She said Cornello is going to Galveston—his sister lives there and he wants to check on her to see if she survived the big hurricane."

"I can understand that, but what about Trinidad? He didn't go, too, did he?" Buck asked.

"No. According to Phoebe, he's in jail. It seems he did something during the fiesta, and he can't raise the money for his bail."

"So you left July over there with Phoebe alone?" Buck questioned.

"Yes, I did. I think he'll be the best bodyguard she'll ever find, and he'll be able to take care of her troop as well."

"That's true, but . . ." Buck looked toward Yhomas.

"What? What is it?" Christian asked.

"What Buck is trying to say is that America isn't quite as enlightened as England, or even parts of our own country, where skin color is concerned Arizona doesn't have a Marie Von Koopmans or a Mohandas Gandhi leading peaceful protests against the evils of discrimination. You and I both know that July is as honorable a man as walks the earth, but there are those who would raise a ruckus if it was found that a black man was alone with a white woman," Yhomas said.

"That's ridiculous, July is no threat to Phoebe," Christian said indignantly.

"We're not saying he is," Buck said, "but that's not to say someone else wouldn't say it. You've not met her son-of-a-bitch brother-in-law. If he went out there and found July with Phoebe, he'd have a lynch mob formed before you could say Jack Robinson, and it wouldn't be pretty."

"I have met him," Christian sighed.

"Then you know what he's like. July can't stay there with Phoebe," Buck said.

"But she needs him. Who's she going to find who can do the work as well as he can? Nobody."

"I don't think there'd be a problem if there were two men there—one white and one black," Buck said.

"And who are you suggesting that white man should be?"

Yhomas lifted his eyebrows. "It seems to me like you and July make a pretty good team. And besides, you're just in the way over here."

"Is that how you really feel?" Christian asked, but then he saw both men were smiling and knew they were putting him on. "Have you forgotten? I have a job to do. Mr. Fowler asked me to go up to the Tonto Basin with the survey crew. Who will do that?"

"What about this crack engineer you've got coming? Can't he take your place?" Yhomas asked.

"You mean Clarence Woodson? I suppose he could bring me the data and I could put my figures together."

"You'll have plenty of time," Buck said. "This thing is just getting started and it'll drag on for years."

"How can that be? The people need water and there's a way to make that happen," Christian said.

Yhomas laughed. "Now you're thinking like Cecil Rhodes. For all his faults, he gets things done, but here it's different. There will be lots of arguments and committee meetings. Then Congress will take up a bill and it'll probably fail, and then there will be another one and another one after that. That's just how it is."

"You go on over to Phoebe's and take care of her," Buck said. "You'll see, as soon as the rains start, this reservoir won't be nearly as important as it is today."

"I'll go, but I don't understand. Don't these people ever think about tomorrow? If they've had a drought for three years, who's to say it won't last four? They need to get this project started, and soon."

"Oh, they'll get it done," Buck said, "but who knows when? I'd feel better if Garret Hobart was still on McKinley's ticket, but this fellow he's got now—Teddy Roosevelt: he's got a lot of bluster, but who's to say what he'll do if McKinley gets elected again?"

"They say he's a naturalist," Yhomas said.

"And what does that mean?" Buck asked. "We knew Hobart was a water man and he could get the president to act, but now that he's gone, will this young Roosevelt do anything at all? We'll just have to wait and see."

Christian left Yhomas and Buck discussing politics in America. Everyone looked to the United States as the standard upon which other countries should be measured, yet it definitely had its faults. He had to wonder why the War Between the States had been fought if the people it was supposedly fought to free really weren't free. It'd never occurred to him that July would be in danger.

He began gathering his things to go to stay at Phoebe's place, assuming she'd be amenable to this. He had no idea how long his presence would be required. Surely her man would be out of jail soon and would return to his position. With that thought, Christian decided to leave most of his belongings at the Prinsens. He packed a small satchel with a few clothes and some books, and of course his rifle.

He thought about not taking his copy of Gibbon's *Decline and Fall of the Roman Empire*, but it was hard to break old habits. The book had been a gift from Cecil. No matter how short the stay, Rhodes always took this book with him, and Christian had begun to do that as well. He put the book, bound in red Moroccan leather, in his satchel, but the thousand-page tome took up too much space. He removed it and instead looked through his collection of books.

He smiled when he picked up a couple he'd enjoy reading to Will. *The Jungle Book*, as well as a book of short stories that included "Wee Willie Winkie" and "Baa, Baa, Black Sheep," were both autographed by Rudyard Kipling. Rhodes had built the Woolsack, on the side of Table Mountain, specifically for Kipling's use when he visited Cape Town.

Christian closed his eyes. Cape Town was so far away, and he wondered: Would he ever see his homeland again? Would he ever see Mrs. Van Koopmans or even Cecil Rhodes? Why had he agreed to stay in America? And now he'd been asked to, in essence, be a nanny for a woman he hardly knew.

This water project couldn't be as much trouble as both Buck and Yhomas described. Christian made up his mind. He'd stay until Christmas—three more months—and then he'd go back home.

That is, unless Ina Claire Woodson changed things. Christian smiled when he thought about her. In hindsight, he was sorry he hadn't been more aggressive in establishing a lasting relationship with her. She was pleasant and would make a suitable wife. Yhomas had teased him about her coming with her father, but perhaps Yhomas was right. When she got to Arizona, he should talk to her father and see if Clarence would permit him to court his daughter.

And then he thought about Phoebe Sloan. He definitely liked something about her. He knew she was plucky because he'd seen that firsthand and could already tell she was determined almost to the point of being muleheaded.

She was attractive in an unaffected way. Christian liked the way her ginger-colored hair often fell in uncontrolled ringlets while freckles sprayed across her nose. When he thought about it, he wasn't sure what color her eyes were. Near the center, he recalled, they were light brown, but the color radiated out until the outer edges were a dark green.

How could he know these things about Phoebe? Was it only last night that he'd met her for the first time?

Christian tried to visualize Ina Claire in contrast to Phoebe. He had spent a part of each of the 126 days that Kimberley was besieged with her, yet he couldn't say what color her eyes were. He knew she wore her hair in a bun but couldn't remember the exact color.

Phoebe was different. In that instant, Christian was jealous of her dead husband. She clearly honored his memory, and more than likely she was still very much in love with him.

Love. In his whole life Christian had never known anyone he could honestly say he loved. He admired Mrs. Van Koopmans, he respected Cecil Rhodes, and he was friends with July, and now the Prinsens and the Bucknells.

What about Ina Claire? Perhaps if he worked

hard enough, she could become a reasonably good companion. But could he ever actually love her?

"This is ridiculous," Christian said aloud as he put the books in the satchel. "What's happening to me? I'm still Jacktar and I don't need anybody."

6

When Christian arrived at Phoebe's farm, he saw July and Will stretching woven wire between some recently set posts. July was holding a staple while Will was trying to wield a hammer hard enough to drive the staple into the post. Wapi was standing inside the wire, his big, expressive eyes following every move being made.

"Wapi doesn't have any idea how much his life is going to change when you two get your work done," Christian said as he dismounted his horse.

"Wet!" Will called happily and, dropping the hammer, ran toward Christian. "We're making a yard just for Wapi, so he can play whenever he wants to."

"It looks to me like you're doing a fine job. I'll bet Wapi won't get out of this pen."

Will got a mischievous look on his face. "He will when I open the gate."

"Oh, oh, will your mother like that?"

"She likes Wapi, but not as much as she likes you."

Upon hearing the child's comment, July laughed uproariously. "Sounds to me like this bird isn't the only one whose life is going to be changing."

Christian shook his head. "Not you, too. Everybody's trying to push me into something I'm not looking for."

"Then tell me, why do I see your travelin' bag on the back of that horse? Are you plannin' on going off somewhere, or are you moving in with me?"

"Goodie!" Will clapped his hands. "I'm going to go tell Mama you're going to live with us!"

Will took off running toward the house, and July said, without looking up from his task, "Did Mr. Prinsen send you over here?"

"He did."

"He didn't think it'd be right for me to stay here by myself?"

"Yes. I don't understand it. In Cape Town there's a clear delineation between blacks and whites, but there doesn't seem to be the fear, or the animosity. Look at all the black men who live with Mrs. Van Koopmans. She thinks nothing of it."

"That's Cape Town, but look at Rhodesia. You can't say everything is peachy for the black man there."

"I know."

At that moment Phoebe and Will came out of the house. "Will said you've come to live with us."

Christian studied her face and listened to her voice to see if he could determine her reaction to the news. Was it favorable, or did it reflect some anxiety?

What a cool character she is, he thought. No matter how hard he tried, he was totally unable to read how she felt about it.

"You needn't be concerned," Christian said, though she exhibited no concern at all. "July and I will be staying in your bunkhouse."

"That's not necessary. This house has five bedrooms and you'll both stay in the house with me."

"I don't know that that's such a good idea."

"I can understand your concern, but I promise, I won't shoot you again." Phoebe smiled broadly.

Christian laughed. "Well, if you guarantee that July and I won't be shot, I suppose we can stay."

"Shot? I do not understand." July furrowed his brow. "Are we going to be shot?"

"Mama shot Wet," Will said, his eyes wide.

"Oh, I did not." Phoebe laughed nervously.

"Yes you did, Mama. He has a hole in his foot."

"He has a hole in his boot, not in his foot."

"That's true." Christian, smiling, removed his boot and poked a finger through the hole in the sole.

"You're never going to let me live that down, are you?" Phoebe challenged.

"Nope. If we both live to be a hundred, I'm not going to let you ever forget it."

Christian's aside implied that he and Phoebe could know one another for a long time, but there was no further comment.

"I think it's time to go in," Phoebe said. "July's such a big man I made plenty of food, so there should be more than enough supper for you, too."

Will picked out the rooms where Christian and July would stay, and when it was time to go to bed, Will followed July to the bunkhouse to get his things. Christian was in the same room he'd occupied before, while July was in the room adjacent to Will's.

Christian was preparing for bed when he heard a light knock. He'd already taken off his shirt but, remembering the night before when he had gone down in his drawers, he grabbed it before he opened the door. He was disappointed when he found Will and not Phoebe.

"You forgot. You're supposed to put me in my bed."

"Of course I am." Christian picked the boy up and threw him across his shoulder. "Let's get you to bed."

When he set the boy down on the bed, Will wouldn't loosen his hold on Christian's neck. "I love you."

"I'm glad."

"You're supposed to say, 'I love you, too.' That's what my mama says."

"Then I'll say it, too."

"You can't just say it—you have to mean it."

"Is that what your mama says, too?"

Will nodded his head as he lowered his arms, his eyes now heavy with sleep.

Christian brushed the child's hair off his face. "Good night, little man." He rose, intending to leave the room, as Will's eyes were now closed.

Instantly, they popped open. "You can't go. You didn't say it."

"I love you, too."

Satisfied, Will turned over and was asleep before Christian got to the door.

Christian was unduly affected by the exchange with Will. He was lying in his bed with his hands laced behind his head, staring up into the darkness. In his entire life, he'd never had anyone say he or she loved him, and he himself had never uttered the words to another person.

"You can't just say it. You have to mean it."

Will attributed that quote to his mother. Christian felt there was more to Phoebe Sloan than what she was disclosing. It'd be interesting to discover just who she was.

Then in the darkness he saw a spot of light on the ceiling. For a moment he was puzzled as to its source; then he realized it was light shining through the hole Phoebe had made when the gun went off.

Her room was directly below his, and in the stillness he could hear her moving around—a drawer opened. More than likely she was getting out her nightgown. He wondered if it was the same one she'd worn last night. Closing his eyes, he tried to visualize what it looked like. He couldn't picture it, but he could certainly recall the feel of her body next to his as he held her in his arms.

He lay in the bed until the spot on the ceiling disappeared. What was it about Phoebe that caused him to be so aroused? Because he could not arrest his thoughts, he sat up, thinking he should have brought *The Decline and Fall of the Roman Empire*. If anything could put him to sleep, it was reading that book. The next time he went to the Prinsens' he'd make sure to bring it back with him.

Christian laughed. He wondered if Cecil Rhodes had ever used the book to get his mind off a woman.

It had been a fitful night for Phoebe, and she awakened with the first rays of sunlight. With a sigh she sat up, swung her legs over the edge of the bed, then stretched and yawned.

Getting up, she walked over to look out the window. She liked this time of day—the way the soft morning sun turned the leaves on the olive trees to a gleaming gold. She saw that a nearby nesting ostrich was dutifully sitting on the eggs as he waited for his mate to take the day shift. Phoebe was always fascinated at the routine the pair followed as they shared the responsibility of hatching their eggs and then raising their young, the black-feathered males sitting on the nest all night, the females all day. Both of them turned the eggs, something Phoebe had to do with the eggs in the incubator.

Except no eggs were in the incubator now, thanks to Frank.

She turned away from the window and, when she did, saw her reflection in the mirror. Phoebe had just turned twenty-four, but she thought she looked much older. Too much exposure to the sun had increased the number of freckles on her face, and her hair was constantly a mess. But it didn't matter; Will loved her no matter how she looked.

After Edwin's death she'd withdrawn into herself, her only joy in life being her son. Everything she did was geared toward making Will's life as normal and carefree as she could.

And everything the Sloans did was geared to making her life as difficult as possible. After Edwin died, his father had tried to influence the court to take Will away from her, but Judge Johnstone had ruled in her favor, saying the boy should remain with his natural mother. But Judge Johnstone was up for reelection in November, and W. F. Sloan had let it be known that he'd see to it the judge wouldn't be reelected. Phoebe never doubted that this powerful family could get that accomplished. And if she left Arizona, she had no doubt that someway, somehow, they'd follow her and she'd lose Will forever. She had no choice. She had to make this ostrich farm a success.

But today was a different day.

Sitting in front of the dresser, she picked up the silver-backed brush and began running it through her hair, trying to coax some semblance of order into her unruly locks. Even as she was doing this, though, she was aware that had this been any other day, she would've given her hair little more than a few cursory strokes.

What was she thinking? This was an ordinary day. And like on any other ordinary day, she had chores to do. It was good she was up so early because she'd need to fix an extrabig breakfast for her houseguests. Phoebe smiled. She'd cooked breakfast every morning for Cornello and Trinidad, but, for some reason, cooking for Christian and July pleased her.

She thought about putting on another one of her town dresses, but chose her old blue chambray instead. She couldn't pretend to be somebody she wasn't. If Christian noticed her, it'd be for who she was, not for what she looked like.

In the quiet of her bedroom, she felt her face flush. For one irrational moment, she felt a sense of guilt in even thinking that Christian would notice her. It was as if she'd betrayed Edwin.

But that was nonsense. She'd done nothing to betray him, not by thought, word, or deed. And besides, Edwin was gone. How could a woman betray a husband if he was dead?

Those thoughts were tumbling through her mind as she started, not for the pens, but toward the little grave on the hill. She opened the gate to the low white fence, then went inside and sat down on the grass beside the grave. A cluster of desert baby blue eyes was growing on top of the grave and she reached for them, intending to pull them as she did all the weeds that grew inside the enclosure. But she decided to leave the little splash of color.

"They're blue, Edwin. I wish they were orange; I know that's your favorite color. But the blue looks nice, so if you don't mind, I'll just leave them here for now."

She pulled a few other weeds around the runners of the morning glory–like flowers.

"I suppose you know a man has spent the last two nights with me. But of course you know: you're right here, you've seen everything. And you know nothing untoward has happened.

"I hate to bring this up again, but it's Frank." Phoebe sighed. "He's doing what he can to break my spirit." Tears began streaming down her cheeks. "For the life of me I can't understand how he could be your brother. And he . . ." She closed her eyes and bowed her head as her sobs overtook her. When she could cry no more, she sat with her legs bent and her arms encircling them, resting her head on her knees.

"Mama?"

Phoebe blew her nose on her handkerchief and turned to see Will calling from the steps of the porch. "Here I am, Will," she called as she got to her feet and stood by the grave.

"You have to come quick. July's hungry."

"I'll be right there."

Standing at the window in his bedroom, Christian had been watching Phoebe for at least a half hour. A lump formed in his throat. How could one man be so lucky that he'd found a woman who loved him so much that her love transcended the grave?

Again Christian felt a twinge of jealousy.

Will and July were sitting at the table when Phoebe returned to the house. July was playing a game with Will that July called trap. He encircled Will's wrist with his thumb and forefinger, and Will tried to pull his hand free. When he was successful, his laughter seemed to bubble. It was good that he was so engaged that he didn't notice his mother's puffy eyes.

"How about eggs and bacon?" Phoebe asked, keeping her back to the two.

"No, no, Mama, I want collops," Will said. "Mr. July, do you know what that is? It's much better than that old bacon."

July laughed. "I've heard of it. If you say it's good, I'll give it a try."

Phoebe liked the sound of July's voice. It was deep and melodious, with an accent she couldn't place. Some words were said with a decidedly British accent, while others tended to sound more like German. She'd be interested to learn his story.

When the eggs were cooked and the bacon fried, she cut off an enormous slab of bread and placed it before July. "I'm afraid I don't have any butter, but I've got some preserves if you'd like."

"Am I too late for this feast?" Christian came into the kitchen. His hair was damp and a few beads of water were on his forehead. Without thinking, Phoebe wiped the water off his brow. Christian smiled.

"Oh, I'm sorry," Phoebe said, clearly embarrassed. "It's just that . . ." She turned away, but Christian caught her hand.

"Look." Will pointed to his mother's hand. "Wet knows how to play trap, too. You have to try to get away, Mama. That's how you play it."

Christian tightened his grip on Phoebe's hand as his gaze sought hers. Neither said a word as the moment extended. Finally, Christian released her hand. His expression was empathetic, hers guarded. She turned away quickly and began cutting another slice of bread.

"Mrs. Sloan, is there anything in particular you'd like me to attend to?" July asked.

"First of all, if I can call you July, then you should call me Phoebe. When I hear 'Mrs. Sloan,' I think of my mother-in-law." She made a face, clearly indicating a problem with that.

"Yes, ma'am."

"I think the most important thing is to make sure the plucking boxes are in order. I've got forty feather birds that were plucked about eight months ago. I know that's a little soon, but I need to generate some money now that I won't be selling Mr. Prinsen any young chicks."

"I'll look at them and see what I think. Where are your plucking boxes?"

"I know," Will said. "Can I show him?"

"I don't know," Phoebe said. "I'm not sure Mr. July wants you at his elbow all the time."

"I do need somebody to show me where things are, and I think this young man would be about the best guide I could hire. Shall we get started?"

Will jumped down from his chair, grabbed July's hand, and started pulling him toward the door.

When they were gone, Phoebe came back and poured two cups of coffee.

"It looks like you've lost your job as potential father." Phoebe sat down opposite Christian.

"I'm not sure I like that. Will is an endearing child."

"You didn't mention his mother—you know if he got a new father, I'd have to be a part of the bargain."

Christian nodded his head. "I could accept that."

"You know, we've been sidestepping this issue from the moment I met you. Gwen Bucknell thinks you'd be the perfect man for me."

Christian laughed. "A matchmaker. Is she Peruvian by any chance?"

"Peruvian? I don't know what you mean."

"In Cape Town, there was a group of people

who came from Russia on a ship called the *Peruvian*. From then on, many people who followed the same religion were called Peruvians. Those people were experts at finding mates for people."

"If Gwen is a matchmaker, she has her work cut out for herself where I'm concerned."

"Why? You're a very attractive woman." The tone of Christian's voice changed. Up to this moment most of the conversation had been in jest, but now he was dead serious. "You have a lot to offer a man."

"Don't tease me, Christian." Phoebe's voice was barely above a whisper.

Christian rose and circled the table. He helped Phoebe to her feet, and with a hunger in his eyes and his hands on her shoulders, he pulled her to him. Lowering his head, he kissed her.

At first the kiss was tender and hesitant as Christian tested her reaction. She held her emotions in check for as long as she could, but he knew the instant she surrendered. Her pliant body melded to his as she wound her arms around his neck and deepened the kiss.

Christian held her to him, feeling the emotion between them as he felt the swelling of his member.

Phoebe felt his arousal and put an end to this sensual torment. She drew back. "You shouldn't have done that."

"Why? You and I are both mature enough to know when we want something."

"You don't understand." Tears gathered in

Phoebe's eyes. "If anyone found out that I care for you . . ."

"Phoebe, it's not 'anyone' you're talking about, is it? It's your in-laws. What do they have on you that makes you so afraid?"

"They'll take Will away from me."

Christian shook his head. "They can't do that. You're his mother."

In the recesses of his mind he saw a four-year-old boy, a boy exactly Will's age, being wrenched from the arms of a young woman. And he never saw or heard from her again.

After a long, pregnant pause in the conversation, Christian broke the silence. "I saw you this morning."

Phoebe looked toward him, a quizzical expression on her face.

"At your husband's grave."

"I guess you think that's silly." Her chin jutted out in defiance.

"No, I don't. I'm not here to judge you on anything."

"I'm sorry, I shouldn't have snapped at you, but I find comfort in visiting Edwin." She chuckled. "I tell him everything. I wonder what he'll think when I tell him I kissed you?"

"I think you have that wrong. It was I who kissed you."

"No, Christian." She shook her head. "We both know that is wrong. You just said we were mature enough to know when we want something. Well, from the night you sat at this table entertaining

Will, I've wanted you. But it cannot be. I'm going to have to ask you to leave."

"Phoebe, that doesn't make sense. You have an ongoing operation, and no matter how strong or tough you think you are, you need help. July is the logical person to help you, and both Buck and Yhomas know he can't stay here by himself."

"Then I'll find someone else who'll stay with me until Trinidad gets out of jail. But no matter what, you can't stay."

"Will you at least let me stay until you find this other person?"

"All right, but you have to promise me we'll never be together alone."

Christian's body tensed as his eyes narrowed. "Yes, ma'am." He gave her a mock salute, turned on his heel, and strode out of the kitchen, banging the door behind him. When he was clear of the porch, he kicked an empty bucket, causing a loud clatter.

As Phoebe watched Christian head for the barn, an ache began to build in her chest. What had she just done? Why was she so afraid?

Inside, she knew the answer. The undying love she had for Edwin was all a sham. She'd allowed him into her bed the night they'd conceived Will because she was so miserable. She had no one in Arizona and no one in Illinois to go home to.

Edwin was likable enough, and when she discovered she was pregnant, she told herself she could learn to love him. After Will was born, she'd tried, but Edwin was never interested in her. It was all about Will, an heir for W. F. Sloan, and as long as Frank and Myra remained childless, Will was in line to inherit a considerable fortune.

Outside, Christian was fighting his own battles. He'd fully intended to return to South Africa by Christmas. But now he was feeling a strong pull to stay here.

To stay here and do what? Marry Phoebe?

Even as that question popped into his mind, he thought of Ina Claire. He hadn't ever actually considered marrying her, though she'd been the only other woman in his life he could have considered in such a way. He found himself comparing the two women, placing each in her own position.

Ina Claire was a good, decent woman whom he had shared danger with. She was intelligent, resourceful, and dutiful, and would no doubt make someone a fine wife.

Phoebe was spontaneous, effervescent, sensual, and . . .

And what?

Christian was not without sexual experience. While he was in London, an older woman had introduced him to carnal pleasures, and there had been a cabaret dancer in Paris, a diplomat's daughter in Berlin, and others he couldn't remember. He'd never bedded Ina Claire, nor had he ever wanted to. He told himself it was because she was a "good" girl and the daughter of a friend.

But now he knew better. He'd never bedded

Ina Claire because she'd never inflamed his senses the way Phoebe . . .

"Christian?"

He realized July was talking to him and had been calling his name for some time now. "Yes?"

"We need to repair the plucking box."

"Oh, yes." Christian laughed self-consciously. "I'm afraid I was doing a bit of woolgathering."

They'd just finished the box and were gathering their tools when Will came running, looking distressed.

"It's Wapi—something bad's wrong with him. Wet, you have to save him!"

Abandoning their tools, the two men ran after Will until they reached Wapi. The bird was weaving about and bobbing his head, appearing to contort his neck into a letter *S*.

"What do you think it is, July?"

July immediately diagnosed the problem. "He's swallowed something. If we don't get it out, it won't be good."

"And how do we go about doing that?"

"We cut it out, and then we sew it up."

"All right, but I'm not sure I understand how we're going to do that." Christian pulled his knife out of his pocket. "I don't think Wapi's going to stand still for this."

"He's not. Will, run and tell your mother to bring us the strongest thread she has and a big-eyed needle. Can you remember that?"

"Yes, sir." Will turned and started running toward the house.

"Do you think we should try to get the bird into the plucking box?" Christian asked. "That would contain him."

"We can't do that. Even though this is a tame bird, an injury tends to make even a young ostrich mad. Now, help me get him down, and whatever you do, make sure you don't get in front of him. Oh, and grab the tackey stick in case you need it."

Christian grabbed the stick, and between the two men they managed to guide Wapi into a corner of the pen. Even though the bird was less than a year old, he was six feet tall and weighed over a hundred pounds. If he'd been full-grown at seven to nine feet tall and weighing as much as three hundred seventy-five pounds, two men could not have corralled him. As it was, it was a tussle to get him to the ground.

July was careful to stay behind. When Wapi felt him, he spread his wings, which was exactly what July wanted him to do. July got his arms under the wings and wrapped around the body. Then he lifted Wapi a foot into the air and went down with him. Once July had him on the ground, he trapped Wapi's legs with his own and rendered the bird almost completely immobile. By that time, Phoebe had come out to join them.

"What in the world?" she asked, concerned by what she was seeing. "What're you doing to Wapi?"

"Do you have the needle threaded?" Christian shouted.

"Not yet."

"Well, get it ready. I expect we'll need it in a minute."

Wapi was flopping his head around, and Christian got into position to put his knee on Wapi's neck. When he had control of the big bird, Christian found the bulge in Wapi's throat. Just above it, he made an incision, and blood began to gush out. Once he'd made the cut, he stuck his finger into the wound and found one of the large staples that had been used to construct Wapi's pen. It was lodged crosswise, and Wapi's contortions had driven the sharp ends into the flesh.

Being careful not to make the situation any worse, Christian extracted the staple. Then, keeping the neck still, he said to Phoebe, "Now sew it shut."

Phoebe offered the threaded needle to Christian.

"It has to be you, Phoebe. Just whip it shut at first, and then you'll have to go back and make some interrupted stitches."

"I can't do that."

"Of course you can. Just pretend you're mending a tear in Will's pants."

"Do it, Mama, please," Will begged. "Don't let Wapi die."

"All right." Kneeling beside Christian, Phoebe began sewing the wound shut, somewhat hesitantly and experimentally at first, but quickly getting the hang of it. Completing the task relatively quickly, she then went back and put in tacking stitches in several places so that the wound wouldn't burst open if the long chain was somehow broken.

"Good job," Christian said. "No, not a good job, a great job."

Phoebe beamed under the praise. "I should've brought some antiseptic."

"All right, all three of you get out of the pen before I let him up," July said. "But leave me the tackey. Who knows what he'll do when he's free."

Christian, Phoebe, and Will left the pen, then watched as July let go of the bird and rolled a few times on the ground to get away.

Wapi got up quickly, and Christian watched anxiously, concerned that he might attack July, but no such attack came. Instead Wapi, perhaps concerned that his neck might be cut again, ran to the opposite side of the pen, running hard into the wire fence. Taking advantage of Wapi's departure, July hopped up and hurried out through the gate.

"Why did he do that?" Will asked.

"I think he's just confused," July said.

"Is Wapi going to die?" Will asked, frightened.

"Are you kidding?" Christian replied. "Wapi will be around to pull on your whiskers."

Will laughed. "I don't have any whiskers!"

"But you will someday. And when you do, Wapi will be here to pull on them."

"How did you know what was wrong with him?" Phoebe asked.

"July's the one who recognized the problem, and he's the one who told me what had to be done."

Phoebe laughed. "And the brilliant thing you did was listen to him."

"That's it."

Phoebe wiped the blood off her hands onto her apron and then took July's hand in hers. "I can't thank you enough." She looked up at the big man. "If we'd lost Wapi, Will would've been devastated, and I guess I would have been, too."

Just then they heard the approach of a horse. "Hello! May I join in this gathering," someone called.

"Mr. Prinsen." Phoebe smiled a welcome at their visitor.

"My goodness, what happened?" Yhomas came toward them. "Has there been an accident."

"Wet cut Wapi's throat," Will said.

"What?"

Christian chuckled. "It wasn't anything sinister, I assure you. Wapi got a staple caught in his throat, and we had to get it out."

"Ah, that's right, I know Wapi. He's one of your birds."

"He's *my* bird," Will said resolutely.

"Indeed." Yhomas nodded. "I think I've heard

about that bird. Is he the one that likes to eat peppermint?" He withdrew a stick from his pocket and handed it to Will.

"Thank you. Do you want me to share it with my bird?"

"You can do whatever you want. I have some good news to share." Yhomas withdrew a telegram and handed it to Christian.

Christian read it quickly, and a big smile crossed his face. "I didn't think he'd do it."

"What is it, Christian, if I may ask?" Phoebe asked.

"A friend of mine—an American who worked in South Africa—is coming to help do the engineering survey for the Salt River project."

"That's wonderful. I'm sure you'll be pleased to have an old friend here to work with you."

"I am. Clarence Woodson is an innovative man. If anybody can get this water project started, it's Clarence."

"I hope you're right." Yhomas swung up into his saddle. "We never see you anymore, Phoebe. When you get a chance, why don't you come over and spend some time with us? Katie and Gwen could use some company."

"Thank you for the invitation. Maybe I can get over some afternoon, but you know how busy this time of year is."

"Isn't that true? I just got fifty-five chicks from Watson Pickrell. He didn't want to sell them, but when I knew I wasn't going to get any from you, I offered him a price he couldn't refuse."

"I'm not completely out of the business, Mr. Prinsen. The eggs in the nests are hatching now, and if enough survive, I may have some chicks to sell you after all."

"I'll be glad to take them anytime. Phoebe, you know my offer still stands. I'll buy your whole herd anytime you're ready to sell."

Phoebe smiled. "I know, but now is not the time."

After going back inside, Phoebe walked over to the kitchen window and watched as Christian and July rode out to check the nesting birds. She smiled when she saw Will sitting proudly in front of Christian, his hands on the reins. Edwin had never been as attentive to Will. Christian seemed to have endless patience with the child.

Phoebe took a deep breath and turned away from the window. She was worried about Will. What would he do when it was time for Christian to leave? Even though Christian had been with them such a short time, Will was certain he was going to be his father. At first she was a little embarrassed by his insistence, but Christian seemed to take it in stride.

And who was she to say he couldn't be Will's father someday?

Phoebe gasped, then chuckled. Where did that thought come from?

To get her mind off such an improbable scenario, she turned her thoughts to her ostrich farm. She was determined to make it profitable.

If Yhomas Prinsen thought there was money in ostrich feathers, then Phoebe Sloan could make money from them as well. If she could just hang on, she might be able to provide for Will without help from anyone.

It'd be a dozen years before Will would be old enough to make a decision about the path for his life. She hoped he'd choose to be educated so that he'd never know the hardship her father had endured as he worked in a coal mine. But if he chose to be a rancher or a storekeeper or an ostrich farmer, she wanted that to be by his free will.

But what about herself? She was twenty-four years old. What would happen to her? Absently, she ran her hand through her hair. A knot formed in her throat as she began to feel sorry for herself. If she admitted it, she was jealous of her son. He got to be with Christian whenever he wanted, but since Christian and July had come, she was excused from doing many of her outside chores.

Why couldn't it be her sitting in front of Christian? With that thought, she felt her face flush. She knew sitting in front of Christian on a horse would lead to his arousal—the same arousal she had felt the day he had kissed her.

Well, right now what she wanted was the company of a man.

What was wrong with her?

Good, decent women didn't have such prurient

thoughts. With Edwin, sex was on a schedule. He didn't think it was wholesome to have sex more than three times a month, and if she tried to initiate it, Edwin accused her of being immoral. The words *make love* were never uttered. The purpose of sex was to conceive another child, and on one occasion, she'd done that. When she miscarried after three months, Edwin deemed her unfit to carry another child and never came to her again.

Now Frank was constantly badgering her. He wanted to take her to his bed, and though he kept tolling her it was just a matter of time before she gave in, she knew she would never do that.

Having Christian around was causing more confusion. She knew he'd be a willing partner. When he kissed her, he said they were both mature enough to know when they wanted something, and she had to admit, she wanted him.

She closed her eyes and lowered her head. These thoughts were so wrong. She was the mother of a four-year-old child and she had a reputation.

Oh, yes, she had a reputation. After all, she had gotten pregnant before she was married. So what difference would it make if she had sex with a man who would be half a world away by the end of the year?

"I can't believe this. Do something, just do something productive," Phoebe told herself as she opened the cabinet and began sifting flour from the bin. Her thought was to make bread, but it was too late in the day for it to rise sufficiently.

A pie. That was what she'd do. She'd make a pie.

A full day of hard work was good for Christian because it kept his body and mind busy. Wapi seemed to be recovering, but he was much more subdued than usual, and Will kept running back and forth to his pen to make certain he was all right.

"I don't know how that boy does it," July said. "Does he never get tired?"

"Of course he does," Christian said. "I'll bet he's asleep before the kitchen is cleaned up."

"After what we've been through, I'll be right behind him."

Just then the dinner bell rang, and the three headed for the water barrel. "Come on, Will, time to clean up. What do you think your mom has for us tonight?"

"Nothin' special. Just some old soup."

When the three entered the kitchen, the meal was indeed soup.

"See, I told you." Will sat down next to Christian.

Christian began to sniff. "My nose says there's something else—something with cinnamon."

"What is it, Mama? What is it?"

"It's a surprise. After you eat your soup, we'll find out."

When the meal was over, Phoebe withdrew the freshly baked apple pie from the pie safe.

"Yippee!" Will said. "I want the biggest piece."

"And you'll not get it. July is the biggest, so he'll get the largest piece, and besides that, he earned it. After all, it was July who knew how to save Wapi."

"But I'm the one who told him Wapi was sick." Will's eyes were wide.

"Yes, you did," Christian said, "so you should get the next-biggest piece."

"You spoil that boy." Phoebe hit Christian on the arm.

"There's nothing wrong with that," Christian said with genuine tenderness.

After the pie was finished, Christian helped Will get ready for bed. When he had his pajamas on, Christian picked him up and carried him off to bed.

"The little tyke is worn-out," Christian said when he returned to the kitchen. "Where's July?"

"He's calling it a night, too. Would you like another piece of pie?" Phoebe opened the door to the safe.

"No. Ask me tomorrow. You mentioned that we should've put some antiseptic on Wapi. Do you have some sort of ointment or something?"

"Oh, dear, is he not doing well?"

"When we left him, he seemed a little lethargic. I didn't want to say anything, but 'cutting his throat,' as Will called it, is a bit drastic, wouldn't you say?"

"Of course. Let me see what I can find." Phoebe

went into her bedroom and returned with a jar of carbolic salve. "Will this work?"

Christian took the jar and opened it. "It'll do; that is, if we can get it on him. Do you feel like doctoring an ostrich for the second time today?"

"I don't think we have any choice." Phoebe grabbed the lantern and lit its wick.

A few minutes later they were standing outside Wapi's pen. Wapi was in one corner with his head resting on the ground, his large eyes shuttered.

"Oh, no, he's dead." Phoebe placed her hand on Christian's arm. "What am I going to tell Will?"

When Wapi heard Phoebe's voice, he raised his head but didn't stand.

"Thank goodness." She opened the gate.

"Wait, we'd better use the tackey, and we should probably have a hood. Wapi's not going to take too kindly to us touching his neck again."

"You're right." Phoebe went into the barn and returned with a black piece of cloth that was put over a bird's head when it was being plucked. "Shall I put it on, or you?"

"Let me. You keep the stick handy, and use it if you have to. Let's hope Wapi remembers that he's a pet."

The hooding went easily, and while Phoebe held the lantern, Christian applied the salve liberally.

"That'll have to do." Christian removed the hood. "I don't think he'll let us near him again."

Christian waited while Phoebe returned the

hood to the shed, then they walked back to the house together.

"Would you like to sit in the swing for a few minutes?" Phoebe invited when they reached the porch. "No, wait, I guess that was pretty unthinking of me, as hard as you and July worked today. July was as tired as Will."

"I'd love to sit with you. That is, if the night doesn't end the way it did the last time we did this."

"What are you talking about?"

"The gunshot. The night you almost killed me. That evening started out just like this."

"How long are you going to hold that against me?" Phoebe asked with a little chuckle.

"Phoebe, the only thing I want to hold is you."

"Oh?" Her voice was inviting more.

Christian moved toward her, the light of the lantern shining in his eyes.

Phoebe knew he was going to kiss her, and when his lips touched hers, she held her breath. She wanted this kiss, but she wasn't sure of herself enough to take it beyond this gentle brush. She needn't have worried, because the kiss deepened and caused her stomach to spiral into a wild swirl.

He pulled her to him, and his hand began to knead her back as he pressed her against his chest.

Finally, Christian drew away and stared into her eyes. "Phoebe, this is as far as I go. You're a grown woman; you're answerable to no one but yourself. If you want this to go any further, the next step is up to you." He kissed her one last time, then rose from the swing.

Phoebe sat there for a long time, dazed by what had just happened. She was as ready for sex as she'd ever been in her life, the dampness between her legs affirming that. But what kind of wanton woman went to a man's bed? If she did, wouldn't she be the same as a prostitute?

With much trepidation Phoebe lay in her bed, her eyes wide open, looking at the moon shadows on her bedroom wall. In the past, after Edwin had chosen to abandon her bed, in frustration she'd found a way to satisfy herself. Moving her hand to the junction of her legs, she felt the moistness. She withdrew her hand quickly as if she'd been burned. She'd not even thought about doing this since Edwin had died, and she wouldn't do it now. She willed herself to sleep, to forget that an extremely handsome man was in the room above her—a man who'd openly challenged her to come to him.

As she tossed and turned, she heard the hall clock strike twelve and then one. She wondered if Christian was lying in his bed, listening to the same chime. Or had he fallen asleep instantly, just as Edwin always had?

He had told her that if she wanted this to go further, it was up to her.

"Yes, I do want this to go further, Mr. De Wet."

Phoebe got out of bed. She didn't bother taking her robe—she wouldn't need it for what she had in mind.

Leaving her bedroom, Phoebe climbed up the stairs, treading quietly, then walked down the hallway to the door that led into Christian's room.

She reached for the doorknob, turned it, and pushed the door open slightly, then stopped.

What was she doing? This was so foolish. Without doubt, this could be the most foolish thing she'd ever done in her life.

Closing the door as quietly as she'd opened it, she turned to go back down the hall, then was startled by the door's being pulled open from within the room. Christian stood in the doorway, visible in the silver moonlight that spilled in through the hall window. He was clad only in his underwear.

"Christian, I . . ." she started quietly, but she was unable to finish because Christian pulled her to him and silenced her by putting his mouth over hers.

Christian's first thought was that July or even Will might see them. He pulled her into the room, then closed the door behind her.

He covered her mouth with his, and deep down he knew this was wrong, that he was violating his best intentions by compromising Phoebe while he was staying with her. He hadn't expected this to develop so quickly, and he was torn between two conflicting emotions: the one to avoid taking unfair advantage of this woman who'd opened her home to him, and the other to explore the parameters of this kiss, to see how far she'd allow him to go before she asked him to stop. Or would she ask him to stop at all? Was she as caught up in this maelstrom of sensations as he was?

But she'd come to his room, he hadn't gone to hers. With the soft, inviting curves of this beautiful woman pressed against him, he was powerless to resist his own sense of propriety. When he felt her lips part under his and felt her tongue dart into his mouth, he knew there'd be no turning back.

What was she doing? The thought so filled her mind that Phoebe was sure she'd spoken the words aloud. She had been so adamant that the attraction building between them, bubbling up just beneath the surface, not come to fruition, yet here it was, and she'd been the instigator.

The feel of Christian's mouth on hers was exquisitely pleasurable, so pleasurable that she felt she'd die if he stopped. But there didn't seem to be any danger of his stopping, as his kisses grew deeper and more demanding.

Phoebe wanted more, and when his hands lifted her nightgown to caress her bare skin, she let out a trembling sigh that was both relief and surrender.

She ran her own hands over his body, feeling his broad shoulders, the musculature of his arms, and though it thrilled her, it quickly became clear to her that even this wasn't enough. An aching was within her, a yearning hunger for what she had gone without for so long. She wanted not merely to see and kiss and touch Christian, she wanted to be one with him.

He showered kisses on her throat. She shut her eyes and could feel his hands busily lifting her nightgown over her head. Reciprocating, she began to tug at his underwear, and they came together again, but this time naked flesh was against naked flesh.

Then Christian did something totally unexpected. He literally swept her off her feet, picking her up, then carrying her to his bed. Being physically carried by this man so aroused her that she thought she'd scream with pleasure. And even as he was carrying her, she kissed him again, sending her tongue probing deep into his mouth.

Once he laid her down on the bed, his mouth roamed over her body, sucking at her nipples and driving her wild with pleasure. Then his hand dipped down across her stomach, onto her thighs, and finally to that spot that yearned most for fulfillment. His fingers dipped into the crevice, slickened by the juices of her arousal. His hands and fingers continued to caress and tease her as his lips stayed at her breasts, drawing first one nipple into his mouth to be titillated by his tongue, only to surrender that breast and move to the other.

"Christian," she moaned. "Oh, Christian!"

Her hand moved down until she found what she was looking for; wrapping her fingers around him, she could feel the heat, and the pulse of it. She guided him to her, and as she gasped with delight, he closed the connection with a long, deep plunge.

Phoebe was engulfed in pleasure as she felt him slide in through her moist cleft. She'd thought she was experienced, but compared to what she was experiencing now, she may as well have been a virgin. She matched her movements to his, lifting her hips to receive each thrust.

As they made love, his tongue dipped in and out of her mouth, matching the thrusts below. Absolutely nothing in her past had prepared her for what she was experiencing now.

As his strokes grew stronger and faster, the sensations grew, heightened, then spun out of control, bursting through her like a bolt of lightning.

Never had she felt anything that compared to this, and even as she was basking in the glory and wonder of it, from somewhere deep, deep inside a new convulsion of sensation arose, sending her into more paroxysms of pleasure. She knew the instant Christian was ready and felt his body tense as he emptied himself inside her.

For an instant she was frightened. It had taken only one time with Edwin for Will to have been conceived. What would she tell Frank Sloan if this, too, resulted in a child? Closing her eyes, she forced the thought out of her mind. She'd deal with that if and when it occurred. For this one night, this was her pleasure.

The two lay side by side, allowing the sensual gratification they had each experienced to recede. This room, which during their lovemaking had been their own private world, was now invaded by outside sounds: the lonesome whistle of a distant train, the haunting answer of a coyote, the hooting of an owl, and, more immediate, the two chimes of the clock that echoed from downstairs.

Was it but an hour ago that Phoebe lay in her own bed?

She sat up.

"What is it? What's wrong?"

Phoebe swung her legs over the edge of the bed. "I should go downstairs."

"Why?"

"I think it'd be better."

Phoebe put her nightgown on in the darkness and started toward the door.

"Please don't leave."

"I have to."

Christian closed the distance between them and embraced her, holding her close against his nude body. He nuzzled her hair with his lips as his hands explored the curves of her back. "I want to say thank you, Phoebe. The gift you've just given me means more than you can know."

He kissed her gently as he opened the door for her to leave. "I can't wait for tomorrow."

When Phoebe reached her own room, she didn't go to bed but stepped up to the window as she'd done many nights before. She never tired of the beauty of a star-filled night sky. When she saw the tree that guarded Edwin's grave . . .

"What have I just done?" She spoke barely above a whisper.

She continued to stand at the window for a long time, her mind a jumble of emotions. When she'd allowed Edwin to come to her bed that first time, it was because she'd been miserable and alone. But what was her excuse now? She wanted—no, needed—Christian De Wet. In her mind she'd used him to bring her pleasure. From this night on, her relationship with him would be changed. Christian's parting words had been "I can't wait until tomorrow." Hers should be "I hope tomorrow never comes." How could she face him after what she'd done?

8

Phoebe was awakened the next morning by the smell of breakfast cooking, and by a tune someone was singing. Dressing quickly, she went into the kitchen, where Christian was standing at the stove. Seeing Phoebe, he turned and, with a smile and an extended arm, improvised the lyrics of the song.

> Phoebe, Phoebe, give me your answer do,
> I'm half-crazy, all for the love of you.
> It won't be a stylish marriage,
> I can't afford a carriage,
> But you'll look sweet, upon the seat
> Of a bicycle built for two.

With a laugh, Phoebe responded:

Christian, Christian, here is my answer true,
You're half-crazy if you think that that
    will do.
If you can't afford a carriage,
There won't be any marriage
'Cause I'll be switched if I'll get hitched
On a bicycle built for two.

"Oh, that was funny, Mama!" Will said, coming into the room. "Sing it again."

"We can't sing it again," Phoebe said. "If we do, Wet will burn the collops, and we don't want burned collops, do we?"

Then July came into the kitchen. Taking his place at the table, he was unusually quiet.

"Did you hear Mama and Wet singing?" Will asked.

"I did. My people can hear things that others don't." He looked pointedly at Christian.

Phoebe lowered her face as she grasped the meaning of his statement.

"It wasn't his fault," she said, so low that she wasn't sure July heard her comment.

"It doesn't matter. It happened, and I don't intend to be a party to whatever you two have in mind—that is, until you make it right." July placed his hand on Will's head. "Have you given any consideration to this child?"

"A party? We're going to have a party?" Will smiled up at July.

"Maybe so," July said, "but now I need you to help me clean out the bunkhouse. Can you do that?"

"Sure. Then when Cornello and Trinidad come home, it'll be all clean."

"I'm not sure they'll ever come back," Phoebe said, "but it may be best if Wet and July stay out there."

"No! Don't make them do that!" Will grabbed hold of July's leg. "I like it when there are daddies in the house."

Christian spoke for the first time, looking first at Phoebe and then July. "It won't happen again."

July turned to Will. "Come on, let's go see how Wapi is doing this morning."

"But you didn't eat your breakfast," Will said.

"I'm not hungry."

When Will and July were gone, Christian turned to Phoebe with a sheepish smile. "I never thought it'd be July who made me get a conscience."

"Do you think what I did was so terrible?" Phoebe's eyes glared and her chin jutted out. "If you do, you can just go back to the Prinsens, because I don't need you. July can take care of us."

"What will the Sloans say?" Christian asked, confused by her comment.

"No more than what they said when I slept with Edwin." She threw down a dishcloth and stormed into her bedroom, slamming the door behind her.

Christian watched her go, helpless to say or do anything. Last night had been nearly perfect for him—a woman whom he cared for had come to him, a woman who clearly wanted him. He'd told her he was looking forward to this day, and he meant it. After she had left him, he'd lain awake a long time, envisioning what it'd be like to stay in America married to Phoebe. When he had finally drifted off to sleep, he'd convinced himself that he was through with South Africa.

But now that had all changed.

Cleaning the quarters proved to be quite a chore. The floors hadn't been swept in a long time, cobwebs were in every corner, the mattresses on the two bunks had to be aired, and the single window was so dirty that it was practically opaque.

When the quarters were clean, Christian and July began moving their personal belongings from the house.

"What will you do when Trinidad and Cornello come back?" Will asked as he followed Christian back and forth from the house.

"We'll all live together," Christian said.

"Don't you like us anymore? Did you forget? You said you loved me."

Christian knelt down to the child, seeing in his eyes a sadness that was heartbreaking. "I'll tell you what. When I get all my belongings moved, would you like to go for a ride?"

"Oh, goodie. Wait till I tell Mama."

As Will ran pell-mell toward the house, Christian looked on with a glum face. He was going to miss this little guy, but he felt he had to leave Phoebe alone after what had happened between them. Setting his bag inside the bunkhouse, he withdrew his Rudyard Kipling book. This would be the time to read to the boy.

Christian and Will rode for quite a while, going down the lane that separated the ostrich kraals, and Christian smiled. In his mind, he had thought the word for *pen* that was used at home.

He thought of home and wondered if, perhaps, he should tell Yhomas that he'd decided to go back home right away. That might be the best thing for him and Phoebe, before they let this thing between them get any further. Right now he could see even more problems down the road if they continued, problems that might prove insurmountable. That could only lead to heartache for both of them. Besides, if Yhomas was correct, the water project could take years to complete. The committee didn't need Christian to explain how they could get private capital when it seemed to be the consensus among the members that the government should pay for the project.

But then he thought of the Woodsons. It'd be loutish if he wasn't here when they arrived—especially after the note he'd written to Ina Claire. He didn't think ho'd been too personal in the letter, though he had written it in a way that could be interpreted as suggesting more than he intended.

But that was before he'd gotten to know Phoebe Sloan.

When they got to the Grand Canal, Christian and Will dismounted and, for a while, threw rocks into the water.

"Did you bring a fishing pole?" Will asked.

"No, I didn't. Is that something you like to do?"

The little boy shook his head. "I don't like to fish."

Christian laughed. "Then I'm glad I didn't bring a pole. Do you like to read?"

Will scrunched up his nose. "Don't you know I haven't had my birthday yet? I can't read."

"Well, then, let's go sit under that tree over there and I'll read to you." Christian took out *The Jungle Book* and found a comfortable spot to sit down. Will climbed up on his lap and lay his head on Christian's shoulder, and he started to read:

Mowgli's Brothers

> It was seven o'clock of a very warm evening in the Seeonee hills when Father Wolf woke up from his day's rest, scratched himself, yawned, and spread out his paws one after the other to get rid of the sleepy feeling in the tips.

"Do you ever get a sleepy feeling in your tips?" Christian asked, but when he looked down, Will's eyes were already closed. Christian laughed gently as he repositioned the child and held him tight against his chest. "I guess we won't find out what happened to Mowgli's brothers today."

• • •

The two sat for a long while as Christian let his thoughts wander. He was disheartened to see how small the trickle of water was in the canal. It was a shame. The potential for the Salt River Valley was so immense if only the committee would get the reservoir project started immediately.

He thought back to Kimberley, a town in the Karoo; yet, thanks to his power and money, Cecil Rhodes had built the suburb of Kenilworth to the north of the diamond mines. Rhodes had demanded that anyone who lived in the community should plant trees—not just any tree, but those that Rhodes personally approved. Consequently the town had an abundance of orange and lemon groves, as well as orchards containing apricots, peaches, pears, apples, and quinces, and of course grapevines were growing everywhere.

Christian thought that an orange grove would be much easier for Phoebe to handle than the obstreperous ostriches.

Christian decided what America needed was a man who had the strength of character to lead the country to make decisions that would benefit all the people. From what he'd read, President McKinley, who was running for reelection, didn't have that trait. Neither did William Jennings Bryan, the man running against him. But Christian liked what he'd heard of McKinley's choice for vice president. Christian believed that, if given a chance, Arizona would come to appreciate the young Teddy Roosevelt.

After almost an hour, Will began to move. He raised his head. "The brothers, what happened to them?"

"I think they went home to see their mama, and I think we should go find your mama, too."

"She's not worried. She knows I'm with you." Will turned and hugged Christian. "I'm so glad you didn't leave us."

"I'm glad, too." A knot formed in Christian's throat. "Now, let's find our horse and get out of here."

On the way back to the house, Will sang little songs that his mother had obviously taught him. He tried to get Christian to join him, but they were songs Christian had never learned. When they arrived, Christian rode up to the porch and lowered the child to the ground.

"There you are. I was beginning to think you'd kidnapped my son." Phoebe laughed nervously. "Did you have a good time?"

"Wet read me a story. It was about a wolf."

"Oh, dear. What was that about?" Phoebe frowned at Christian.

"The wolf went to sleep and then he came home to find his mama," Christian said.

"It sounds like a good story. By the way, the bunkhouse is going to be a little crowded. Trinidad came home while you were gone."

Christian pursed his lips. "I guess that's my cue to ride out of here."

"No! I don't want you to go!" Will yelled as he moved toward Christian.

The horse, frightened by the sudden movement and noise, reared up, his hooves thrashing at the air in front of him.

Phoebe screamed as she pulled Will out of the way.

The horse was bucking wildly as Christian tried desperately to get the animal under control. When he did, he jumped down to find Phoebe lying still on the ground. Will was sitting beside her, not reacting at all.

"She's dead." Will's eyes were wide. "Your horse killed her."

Christian was confused by the child's reaction, but he knelt beside Phoebe. He saw a big lump forming on her forehead as he checked to see if she had a pulse.

"You have to help me," Christian said as he picked up Phoebe. "You have to get me a cloth with some cold water. There isn't any ice anywhere, is there?"

Will didn't move.

Christian ran toward the house carrying Phoebe. When he looked back, Will was still sitting in the exact same spot as if he were in a trance. As loud as he could, Christian yelled for July, hoping he was within hearing distance. He knew he shouldn't leave Will, but Phoebe needed him more.

He carried her into her bedroom and laid her on the bed. He felt for her pulse, and when he found it, he uttered a silent prayer. Her breathing was shallow, so he knew she was alive, but she'd been knocked unconscious.

Leaving her on the bed, he went to the kitchen and found a cloth. Taking it out to the cistern that was beside the house, he began to pump, but no water came.

"July!" he called. "July, I need you now!"

July came running. "What's wrong?"

"It's Phoebe. The horse kicked her in the head and she's been knocked out. Now I can't get this damned pump to work."

July leaned over and picked up a small container of water. He began to pour it down the top of the pump. "Now try it."

Christian pumped harder, yet no water came. "Why does she stay here? Nothing works the way it's supposed to."

"You pour. I'll pump." Within an instant the water was coming. "There it is. The leathers just had to get wet."

Running back into the house, Christian hurried to Phoebe. He placed the cool cloth on the bump looming on her forehead.

"Christian?" July called as he came into the house. "Where are you?"

"In Phoebe's bedroom."

July hurried into the bedroom, where Phoebe was lying on the bed. Her face was ashen and she lay motionless. "Is she alive?"

"Right now she is. Did you see Will?"

"Yes, he's outside."

"Go take care of him. Phoebe needs to see a doctor, but I don't think we have time to get him out here, so I'm going to take her to town. She said this Trinidad is back. Have you seen him?"

"Yes, I met him."

"Well, tell him to hitch up the buggy. No, I'd better take the buckboard so I can lay her down in the back."

"All right." July hurried out of the room.

"Phoebe? Phoebe?" Christian said softly.

Phoebe groaned and opened her eyes. She tried to move her head but squeezed her eyes tight as she grimaced. "What happened?" she mumbled. "Where am I?"

"You're in your room right now, but I'm going to take you to see a doctor as soon as Trinidad gets the buckboard hitched up."

She lifted her hand to her forehead, and when she touched the bump, she winced in pain. "What happened?"

"You were kicked in the head."

"By an ostrich?" Her voice rose in fear as she tried to get up.

"Not an ostrich, a horse."

"How . . ."

"It was an accident." Christian mopped her forehead with the cloth. "You were trying to save Will."

Her eyes shot open and she grabbed Christian's hand. "Is he dead? Is my baby dead?"

"No, honey, you saved him. He's with July."

"July? Why isn't he with Edwin?"

Christian was swept with compassion when he heard her question. He knew that sometimes head injuries resulted in delusions, and he wanted to choose his response carefully.

"Because Edwin isn't here."

A scowl crossed her face. "He never takes care of our baby." Just then a wave of nausea hit Phoebe. She tried to sit up, but she stopped and put both hands on the bed.

"Stop it! Stop spinning me around, stop, please stop!"

"Lie back down. Then you'll feel better."

"Oh, the room. It won't stop." Phoebe's fingers clutched the bed. She closed her eyes and Christian sat beside her, trying to comfort her until Trinidad came in.

"The buckboard's ready."

"Thank you. You must be Trinidad." Christian extended his hand. "I'm Christian De Wet. Can you drive the buckboard into town? I want to get Phoebe to a doctor."

"I thought that's what you would want. I made a bed in the back."

"That's good."

Christian lifted Phoebe from the bed and carried her out to the waiting buckboard. He saw Will sitting in the same spot where the accident had occurred. July was with him.

"Hold up a minute," Christian said after he

had put Phoebe in the wagon. "I need to tell Will what's happening."

Christian walked over to where Will was sitting. He knelt down to him and tried to hold him, but Will's body stiffened.

"I'm going to take your mama to town to see the doctor, but you're going to stay here with July. He'll need you to help him take care of Wapi. Then, when your mother gets back, you'll know how to take care of her."

Will did not acknowledge Christian's words. He turned to face him with a look that was beyond the child's years.

"She's going to be all right. I know she is because she has people like you and me who love her. We'll take care of her." Christian took Will in his arms, trying to offer him what comfort he could give him, but the child was unreceptive. "July, I have to go. Has he said anything?"

July shook his head. "Not a word. He's just been sitting there, staring straight ahead."

"He saw the whole thing, so I'm sure he's scared to death. Stay with him and try to get him away from this spot. I hate to leave him but I have to go."

"I know. I'll do my best."

Christian got into the back of the buckboard and sat so that Phoebe's head was cradled in his lap.

"All right, Trinidad, let's go. Drive as fast as you can but try to avoid the rocks. I don't want Phoebe to be jostled any more than she has to be."

Trinidad slapped the reins against the back of the team and they started out with a jolt.

July watched the buckboard until it disappeared down the road.

"Don't you think we should go inside?"

Will didn't answer.

"All right. Let's go up to the porch. We can sit in the swing while we wait for your mother to come back."

Will still didn't answer, but he didn't protest when July scooped him up and carried him to the house.

July tried to engage Will by picking up some of the wooden animals, but Will sat silently.

"I think you need a new toy." July stepped out into the yard. He found a piece of wood and brought it back. "What do you think I should carve? A cow? A dog? A lamb? I know what I'll carve. You'll have to tell me if you know what it is."

For the next hour, July carved on a piece of wood, gradually shaping a giraffe, all the while keeping up a one-sided conversation with Will.

Seeing a cloud of dust billowing up from the road, July thought at first that it was Christian returning, but when it got closer, he saw it was a buggy. It stopped in front of the house and a man stepped down. He ignored July completely and addressed the child.

"Get your mother. I have some papers for her to sign."

Will didn't move.

"Did you hear what I said, young man? When I tell you to do something, you do it." Frank walked toward the porch. "Now, get your mother, like I said."

"She's not here," July said.

"And how would you know that?"

"She was in an accident."

"An accident? What kind of accident?"

"She was kicked by a horse."

"Is she dead?"

July didn't answer.

"So where is she?"

"She was taken into town to see a doctor."

"And she left this boy alone."

"No, sir. I've not left his side."

"Humph. In my opinion, she did leave the boy alone. Who are you, anyway?"

"Julius Van Koopmans." July used the name Christian had given him.

"And what are you doing on my brother's property? Surely you haven't been hired by my sister-in-law."

"No, sir, I came with Christian De Wet."

Frank cocked his head and squinted his eyes. "De Wet? Is that the man who is bedding my sister-in-law?"

Again July was silent.

"Your failure to answer my simple question is all the answer I need. Come on, boy, you're coming with me." Frank advanced toward Will.

July put out his arm, putting Will behind him. "I wouldn't do that if I were you. His mother will expect him to be here when she returns, and I intend to see that he is."

"Do you have any idea who I am? I'm the boy's uncle, and I have no intention of leaving him here alone. Now, Will, you're coming with me."

"He's not going." July reached down to pick up Will.

"You can't keep me from taking my nephew who's been abandoned by his mother—left in the care of some black man with an uppity accent. Now, I'm going to demand you give me my nephew."

Will, who had been passive through this whole exchange, threw his arms around July's neck and buried his head on his shoulder.

"I think Will has spoken," July said. "I'll not let him go with you."

"If you don't let him go right now, you'll find out what it's like to rot in an Arizona jail—that is, if you don't wind up swinging from a rope. Now, for the last time, give me my nephew."

Frank reached out for Will, but as he did so, July wrapped his hand around Frank's wrist and began to squeeze.

"Just keep that up, you son of a bitch! I'll add assault to your list of crimes."

July squeezed harder, and Frank went down to his knees in pain.

"Trap," Will said, speaking for the first time.

"Let me go!"

"Trap," Will said again.

July released Frank's arm and he got up, then

backed away, wrapping his hand gingerly around his wrist. "I think you broke my wrist."

"I don't think so. If I had wanted to break your wrist, you would've known it. Now I'll tell you what's going to happen. Will was left in my care, and he's going to stay with me until his mother returns. Whatever business it was that brought you out here can be discussed when she gets home."

"We'll see how big you are when I come back with the sheriff," Frank said angrily as he turned and walked back to the buggy. "He'll have a warrant for your arrest, and an order making you turn the boy over to me as his lawfully appointed guardian."

Still favoring his wrist, Frank got into the buggy and drove away.

July watched until he was some distance down the road. "Come, Will. I think you and I need to go visiting this afternoon. Maybe Miss Gwen will have some cookies."

"How long was she unconscious?" the doctor asked.

"I'm not sure. Maybe five or ten minutes."

"Has she been nauseous?"

"Very much so." Christian thought of the ride into the town. "I would say . . . I don't know how to explain it . . . but explosively so."

"Projectile vomiting. It's quite common in concussions."

"How serious is that?"

"It can be serious if there's bleeding in the

brain, but I would add that, in most cases, there is full recovery." The doctor shook his head. "Of course that wasn't true for her husband. God rest his soul. You know he was killed by one of those damned birds?"

"I didn't know that. Did the child see that happen?"

"Oh, yes, poor little fellow. Likely never got over it."

"And now, seeing his mother being kicked as well, no wonder he's so upset. I want to take Phoebe back to the house if that's possible, just so he knows she's all right."

"I don't think so—not tonight anyway. She's sleeping now, but it's still touch and go whether she's out of the woods yet. She could slip into a coma, and if that happens, I want to be nearby. If everything is all right, you can take her home tomorrow."

Christian walked over to the bed where Phoebe was quietly lying. He picked up her hand and began to stroke it. "The doctor wants you to stay here tonight."

"Will?" She opened her eyes and looked at Christian.

"That's a good sign," the doctor said. "She remembers her child."

"He's with July now, and I'm going to him. Don't worry, we'll take good care of Will. You just try and get better. We all need you to be well." Christian leaned over and kissed her lightly.

She smiled and closed her eyes.

9

When Christian and Trinidad returned, Will wasn't there. Instead, there was a note, written in Afrikaans.

Ek neem seuntjie huis waar ons was voor.
Oom het vir hom sal terugkeer met balju.

The note told him that Frank Sloan had come for Will, but July refused to give him up, so Sloan was returning with the sheriff. Now July and Will were over at "the house where they were before."

Christian smiled. July had written the note in Afrikaans so Sloan couldn't read it when he returned. And "the house where they were before" referred to the Prinsens', July using that phrase because, even in Afrikaans, the name would stay the same.

"Where do they go, the big man and the boy?" Trinidad asked.

"They are somewhere safe. Trinidad, I'm going to leave you here by yourself tonight. I'm not going to tell you where Will is because, that way, if Sloan returns with the sheriff, you can honestly say you don't know where he is."

Trinidad chuckled. "It'll be good to fool the sheriff. He kept me in jail because Senora Phoebe did not have the fifty dollars the sheriff said I must pay to get out."

"I'd heard you were in jail."

"The sheriff said I don't wear my gun where people could see. I told the sheriff, 'Why should I wear a gun so people can see? Would that not scare them?' But the sheriff said it is the law." Then the smile on Trinidad's face was replaced by a look of concern. "If I don't tell the sheriff where the boy is, can he put me in jail again?"

"No, Trinidad, it's not the same thing. You'll not get in trouble, the boy will be safe, and Phoebe won't have to be worried."

The smile returned. "Good. This I will do with much *júbilo*."

Yhomas Prinsen met Christian when he rode up to the house. "How is Phoebe?"

"She has a concussion. The doctor thinks she'll be just fine, but he wants to keep her for the night. Where's Will?"

"I think he's in the kitchen."

"Has he said anything yet?"

"He may have spoken to the girls, but I haven't heard him speak."

When Christian walked through the swinging door that led to the kitchen, he was met with the aroma of baking cookies. Gwen and Adeline were animated and talkative, while Will sat on the floor leaning against the wall, saying nothing.

"Christian." Gwen looked worried. "What can you tell us about Phoebe?"

"The doctor says she's going to be just fine. But he wants to keep her overnight, just as a precaution."

"Did you hear that, Will? Your mama is going to be just fine. Do you think we should save some cookies for her? Or do you plan to eat all of them yourself?"

"Mama's dead. Wet's horse killed her."

"No, Will, she isn't dead, I promise you," Christian said.

"Yes she is. Mama's dead, just like Daddy."

"Oh, bless his little heart," Gwen said. "Is that why he hasn't said a word since July brought him here? Did he actually think Phoebe was dead?"

"She didn't move," Will said. "She didn't move and she didn't talk to me. I think she's dead."

Christian sat down on the floor in front of Will and reached out to put his hand on the boy's shoulder.

"Will, have you ever fallen and bumped your head?"

Will nodded, but didn't speak.

"Did it hurt?"

Again Will nodded.

"Well, that's the way it is with your mama. When the horse kicked her, she got a bump on her head and it hurt a lot. The doctor wants her to stay with him tonight, but he said we could go get her tomorrow."

"Why didn't she come home today?"

"The doctor thinks she should rest there instead of coming home in the buckboard." Christian smiled. "You should have seen how fast Trinidad was driving. We were bouncing along and it made your mama's head hurt."

"She won't come home—not ever."

"Yes she will. I know what. Why don't you come with me to bring her home tomorrow? Then, if she wants to lie down on the bed Trinidad made for her, you'll be right there to take care of her. And I'll be careful when I drive the buckboard. We won't bounce around."

Will jumped up and wrapped his arms around Christian's neck. Christian embraced the boy, pulling him even closer.

"Well, now, if Phoebe is coming home tomorrow, I think we need some more cookies," Gwen said. "But I don't know who'll help Adeline and me. Hannah's not here and we need someone to tell us if these are good enough for your mama."

"I can do that." Will wiggled out of Christian's arms.

"I think I can help, too," Christian said, "but we

should try one of these just to make sure they're all right, don't you think, Will?"

"That sounds like a good idea." Gwen handed a hot cookie to Will.

Christian stayed in the kitchen until he was sure Will was engaged. Then he went in search of July.

"There you are," Christian said when he saw July with Buck and Yhomas. "I'm glad you thought to leave me a note written in Afrikaans."

"I'm sorry, Christian. I know it was wrong to leave the birds by themselves, but I couldn't take a chance on the uncle taking Will."

"Don't apologize. You did exactly the right thing. Your note said Sloan was bringing the sheriff."

"Yes, sir. He'd brought some papers he wanted Phoebe to sign, but when she wasn't there, he said he'd bring the sheriff to take Will. I thought I could refuse the uncle, but if he brought the sheriff . . ."

"Sheriff Sturgeon would've taken you in," Buck said, "but if it came to taking Will away from Phoebe, Judge Johnstone would step in. He won't let the Sloans get away with that."

"That is, if he's still the judge after the election," Yhomas said.

"That's right, and here stand three men who can't vote," Buck said.

"Well, what happens if Sloan guesses this is where July would bring Will? What if he brings the sheriff here?" Christian asked.

"If they come here, I'll handle it," Yhomas said. "You have to remember, I was schooled by my father, who hid out in the Drakensberg for many a night during the Great Trek. No one will find that boy if I want to hide him."

Christian chuckled. "Now that you mention it, I could teach Will a thing or two about evasion myself."

Yhomas nodded. "Let's hope it doesn't come to that. You'd better go see how he's faring."

Christian found Will sitting at the kitchen table, playing with the giraffe July had carved for him.

"That is a fine-looking giraffe you have there," Christian said. "Where did you get it?"

"July made it for me."

"Well, you're a lucky young man, then. July has never given me a giraffe."

"I'm July's friend."

"So you are."

"Will's been telling us how the accident happened. It sounds to me like Phoebe is one lucky lady," Gwen said.

"I'd say so," Christian said, "because she has a little boy named Will." He winked at the child and was rewarded with a big smile.

"Wet says I can go with him tomorrow when we get my mama. Do you want to come, too?"

"I think that's a great idea," Christian said. "She'll appreciate having you with us. You can help Will comfort her in the back of the buckboard."

"The buckboard? Why not take the surrey? Don't you think that'd be more comfortable?" Gwen asked.

"She doesn't have a surrey," Christian said.

"No, but Mr. Prinsen has one and I'm sure he'll let us use it," Gwen said. "We can stop by the house and I can get her a more comfortable garment to come home in."

"Does that mean we're going to stay here?" Will asked. "Who's going to take care of Wapi if I'm not at home?"

"You forgot. Trinidad is there and he'll take care of Wapi," Christian said.

For the first time since he had known him, Will began to cry. Christian took him in his arms. "What's wrong? Trinidad won't let anything happen to Wapi."

"I forgot. You won't be at our house anymore, Wet. Don't go away."

Gwen was listening to the child's comments. She raised her eyebrows. "Is there more to this story?"

"No," Christian said, "it's just that, with Trinidad back, Phoebe doesn't need me anymore."

"Yes she does," Will said between sobs. "You can't go, Wet. You can't go. Mama needs you."

"I tend to agree with Will. In view of her present condition and now whatever Frank has up his sleeve, don't you think she does need you?"

Christian let out a long sigh. "This is between Phoebe and me. I'll stay until I'm sure she's stable, but then I need to start studying the Salt River project."

"And you can't do that from her house?" Gwen asked.

Christian shook his head. "Come on, Will. Let's go find a place to sleep."

The next morning, it took about an hour to get away from the Prinsens'. Christian, Will, and Gwen were in Yhomas's surrey, while July followed in the buckboard.

When they reached Phoebe's place, Trinidad came out to greet them, a wide grin on his face. "You were right. The sheriff came out here looking for the boy."

"Was Sloan with him?" Christian asked.

"Oh, yes. I tried to stop him, but he went in the house. He went to Miss Phoebe's room, opened every drawer, put stuff all over the floor. I don't know what he was looking for."

"Well, he obviously wasn't looking for Will. Gwen, why don't you go see if you can put things in order?" Christian asked.

"I'll do that and find her something fresh to wear home. Why don't you come, too, Will? You can help me."

When Will was out of earshot, Christian turned to Trinidad. "Tell me exactly what happened when the sheriff got here."

"He asked me if I knew where the boy was. I said no. Then Sloan says for the sheriff to search the barn while he searches the house. When he came out, he asked where you stay and where the big man stays. I didn't tell, so he searched the bunkhouse. When he found your things, he got mad—came out swearing and kicking. Then they rode away."

"You handled that very well, Trinidad. July, go check the bunkhouse. Make certain my rifle's still there."

"Do you think you might need it?" July asked.

"You never know. I've never had to fire it, but I want it handy just in case."

"I'll do it, and then Trinidad and I will go see how many chicks have hatched out. I'm thinking any egg that's left in the nest is probably not going to hatch by now."

"Good," Christian said. "I don't know what time I'll be back from town. If Phoebe's not better, I don't know what I'll tell Will."

"You'll handle it. You're good with that little boy, and I think you'd make him a good daddy—especially since you seem to like his mother." July slapped the reins on the back of the horse and moved the buckboard before Christian had a chance to comment.

When the surrey pulled up in front of the doctor's office an hour later, Phoebe was sitting in front of the window. Her face brightened when she saw Will coming into the doctor's office. Opening her arms in invitation, she said, "Will!" Happily, he ran into them, and they hugged, then she showered his forehead and cheeks with kisses.

"You're looking none the worse for wear." Gwen smiled. "Except for that bruise on your forehead and your black eyes. Have you looked at yourself?"

"I don't have to see it, Gwen, I can feel it," Phoebe chuckled.

"Well, I'm glad you can laugh about it. What were you doing, standing in front of a rearing horse, anyway?"

"Gwen, I know you'll find this hard to believe, but I don't remember a thing. The last thing I recall was standing in front of the porch, then the next thing I remember, I was lying on the bed with a throbbing headache."

"Well, who wants to remember getting kicked in the head?"

Phoebe laughed. "I'm glad you brought Will with you."

"He was concerned about you," Christian said. "We all were."

"Mama, Uncle Frank came to take me away."

"What?" Phoebe looked concerned.

"And July played trap with him."

"What?" Phoebe's look of concern changed to confusion.

Christian laughed. "When Frank reached for Will, July wrapped his hand around Frank's wrist. Apparently that was enough to dissuade him."

"He played trap," Will repeated.

Now Phoebe laughed as well. "I think July could dissuade anybody."

"He brought Will to our house after Frank came, and it's a good thing he did. Trinidad said he came back with Sheriff Sturgeon," Gwen said.

"Sheriff Sturgeon? Why?"

"No one knows for sure," Christian said. "July said Frank was bringing some papers for you to sign. Do you have any idea what they could be?"

"I'm afraid not, and even if I did, I've forgotten it now." Phoebe reached for her forehead.

"You're going to use this amnesia thing, aren't you?" Christian brushed her hair back from her face.

"No. I'm not going to forget everything that's happened to me." Phoebe looked directly at Christian.

"I know," Christian said. "We'll have to talk about that, too."

For a moment it was quiet, then Gwen said, "Here." She held out a bag she was carrying. "I thought you might want to change clothes before we start back. Christian said you had quite a bout with nausea."

"Oh, Gwen, that's very thoughtful." Phoebe stood up to reach for the bag, then quickly sat back down again. "Oh."

"What is it?"

"It's nothing, really. I just got very dizzy for a moment. The doctor told me I might have these dizzy spells for a couple of months, though they should eventually go away.

"Christian, why don't you and Will wait here while I go in the back to get changed?"

"I'll go with you," Gwen offered.

When the two women stepped into the back of the office, the doctor came out front.

"Is it all right for her to go home?" Christian asked.

"Yes, it's quite all right, and it'll be good for her," the doctor replied. "She's been waiting all morning."

"She just had a dizzy spell. Is that anything to worry about?"

"Well, I wouldn't recommend that she climb up on anything very high for a while. But as long as she's careful about where she is or what she's doing, she shouldn't have any trouble. I'll want to see her again—just to make sure she's doing all right. Let her get plenty of rest, and bring her back in about a month."

"We'll have her here," Christian promised.

When they pulled up in the yard. July and Trinidad were there to meet them.

As Christian handed the horse's reins to Trinidad, he said, "The boss lady is home."

Will hopped down and Christian offered his hand to Gwen. When it came to Phoebe, he lifted her out of the surrey, not releasing her when her feet touched the ground.

"You look as if you've been in a fight, Miss Phoebe. Is this your first black eye?" July asked.

"Indeed it is." Phoebe allowed Christian to still hold her. "I'm glad to be home."

Trinidad shook his head. "When I took you out of here, I wasn't sure you'd come back. All I could think of was that day with Mr. Edwin."

"I thought about that, too. I didn't sleep all that well last night." As Phoebe took a step away from

Christian, a wave of dizziness came over her. She reached out for Christian's arm.

He steadied her. "Are you all right?"

"I think I should lie down."

Without hesitation, Christian scooped her up in his arms and began walking toward the house.

When he laid Phoebe on her bed, she closed her eyes, gripping the side as if she needed to hang on.

"It's awful, Christian. The room is whirling around me."

"You need to stay in bed for a while."

"I can't."

"And why not?"

"Who's going to take care of Will?"

"Maybe he could go stay with Gwen until you feel better."

"No!" Phoebe's eyes darted open and she tried to sit up, but immediately she fell back on the pillow.

"You know Gwen and the girls would love to have him until you feel better."

"Frank was here looking for my son. I won't let him take Will. I won't let that happen."

"I understand. Then I'll take care of him."

"That would mean you'd have to stay here, wouldn't it? I mean, in the house, not in the bunkhouse."

"I suppose it would. Would you be all right with that?"

"I think the question is: Would you be all right with it?"

"Why wouldn't I be?"

"It's just that, last night, I remembered something that happened before the horse kicked me. Didn't you say, 'I guess that's my cue to ride out of here'?" Phoebe asked, repeating the words Christian had said when she'd told him Trinidad was back.

Christian looked down. "I did, but it's not what I wanted to do. Maybe you don't remember what precipitated those words."

Phoebe reached for Christian's hand. "I do remember—I remember it very well, and I am embarrassed by what I did."

Christian smiled. "You mean banning me to the bunkhouse?"

"No, Christian. I was a brazen hussy to come to your room. I'm sorry."

Christian leaned down and kissed her. "I'm not sorry. I'm not sorry at all."

Tears were glistening in Phoebe's eyes as she wrapped her arms around Christian. "I don't know how to act. I've never known a man like you."

"I'm not very good at this either. Why don't we pretend like we're just meeting one another? Phoebe, may I have your permission to start a courtship?"

Phoebe smiled. "That depends. Do you have a carriage or a bicycle built for two?"

"For you, a magic carpet." Christian kissed her again. "I'll let you rest now."

"All right, but don't let me sleep through lunch."

"I won't."

Leaving her bedroom, Christian walked back into the kitchen. "Whatever you're making smells awfully good."

"Will suggested soup."

"Will did that?" Christian tousled the boy's hair.

"I think Mama will like it, but now I'm helping Miss Gwen make noodles to go in the soup." Will dropped a handful of flour into the bowl Gwen held.

"I think that'll be all we need." Gwen mixed the stiff dough.

"If Will is finished here, I could use some help to move my things out of the bunkhouse."

Will looked dejected. "Where are you going?"

"I'm moving back upstairs, unless someone else has taken my room."

"Oh, goodie! You're coming back!" Will began clapping his hands, raising a cloud of flour.

10

"Under the circumstances, I think someone should be in the house with Phoebe," July said when he found out Christian's intentions. "But I'm going to stay in the bunkhouse."

"I understand, but I'm sure it'd be all right if you moved back to your room as well."

" 'See no evil, hear no evil, speak no evil.' I've lived by that maxim for a long time, and I probably shouldn't have opened my mouth yesterday."

"No, you were right to speak up. If something is going to happen between Phoebe and me, it should happen in its own good time."

"Do you want something to happen?"

"Yes, I think I do."

"Do you want this, Wet?" Will came out of the bunkhouse carrying Christian's rifle.

"Let me carry that. It's a little heavy." Christian took the rifle from the boy.

"Do you ever shoot that gun?"

"I've never shot this particular rifle, but I learned how to shoot when I was just a boy."

"Will you teach me how?"

"When you get a little older."

Will's face broke out in a broad smile. "You're going to stay with us a long, long time."

"We'll see." Christian picked up his satchel. "Let's go see if the soup is ready."

"It's good to be eating together," Phoebe said when everyone was gathered around the kitchen table. "July, you have my eternal thanks for doing what you did when my brother-in-law came."

July was abashed by Phoebe's kind words. "I didn't do anything. I just knew that Will didn't want to go with that man, and I said I'd take care of him until you came back."

"And you did that very well," Phoebe said.

"I don't ever want to see Uncle Frank again. He's mean," Will said.

"Honey, he's your daddy's brother," Phoebe said. "Uncle Frank was probably worried about me, and that's why he was so gruff."

Will shook his head. "I don't like him."

"Well, he's not here now," Christian said. "I think I need to go out and see if I can count the new baby chicks. Does anybody want to come with me?"

"I'll go." Will jumped down from his chair, then

stopped. His face contorted. "I can't go. I have to take care of Mama."

Phoebe laughed. "You go ahead. Miss Gwen's here if I need anything, and besides, I'm going to take a long nap. Do you want to take a nap, too?"

"I'll go with Wet."

Phoebe's condition improved slowly over the next few weeks. Although the bouts of nausea and dizziness occurred with less frequency, they were often enough to make it difficult for her to actually tend to her birds. She found herself totally dependent on Christian and July.

She was pleased to see how both men took to Will's insistence that he help them. They never gave the slightest indication that he might be in their way, but included him as much as they could. It was almost as if they were a family, as if Christian was there, not simply because he was needed, but because he belonged. But, Phoebe told herself, this was a temporary arrangement. It couldn't last forever, and she knew that she had to keep the arrangement in perspective in order to keep Will from being too badly hurt when Christian left.

But even as that caution crossed her mind, she knew that she wasn't thinking only of Will.

Christian tapped lightly on Phoebe's door.

"It's open," Phoebe called softly.

When Christian opened the door, Phoebe was propped up against the pillows.

"Hi." He stepped toward the bed. "Do you mind

if I sit here awhile?" He intended to sit in a chair, but Phoebe moved over, indicating that she wanted him beside her. When he sat, he took her hand. "It's been a long day for you."

She smiled wanly. "For you, too. Will can be a handful for someone who isn't used to being around small children."

"He's a good boy, Phoebe. You're an excellent mother."

"That's not what the Sloans think. They think Frank and Myra should be the ones to raise him, and maybe they're right."

"I know you don't mean that. A boy should be with his mother. Believe me, I know."

"That's a strange comment coming from you, a man who's had so many opportunities."

"That's true, I have had opportunities, but I'd trade all of them to have had the love of my mother."

"What happened?"

"It's a long story. I was young—about Will's age, I think—the last time I saw my mother."

"She died?"

"I was taken from her, so I really don't know. I suppose she did, but the people who ran the orphanage never tried to find out anything about her, or if they did, they didn't tell me."

"You lived in an orphanage?"

"For a little while."

"What happened? Were you adopted?"

"Not exactly. Some older boys took pity on me," Christian chuckled. "I guess you can say I was a runaway when I was about six or seven, and from then on I was on my own in the world."

"A seven-year-old can't take care of himself."

"He can if he's determined, and if he has no other choice."

"Oh, Christian, how awful."

"It was a long time ago, and I don't want to talk about it right now. I came in here to see if you needed anything before you went to sleep."

"There is something I need. Is Will in bed?"

Christian nodded. "He's all tucked in and been read to. I started 'Mowgli's Brothers' again, and we didn't get as far as we did the first day I tried to read it to him. If I ever see Kipling again, I'm going to let him know his story puts children to sleep."

"Do you mean the writer Rudyard Kipling? You've met him?"

"I have."

Phoebe sighed.

"Is there something wrong with me having met an author?"

"No—it's not that."

"Then what is it?"

"Last night, I had a hard time falling asleep. I was thinking about us."

Christian smiled. "And that's bad?"

"You have to know that I'm attracted to you. I like you, but you and I are from two different worlds. Nothing can ever come of a relationship between you and me."

"Why do you say that?"

"Do you know who I am? Do you know what I am?"

"I know that you are a very vivacious woman, a woman who enjoys—"

"No." Phoebe put her finger to Christian's mouth. "Don't say that."

"Enjoys life. What did you think I was going to say?" Christian had a mischievous twinkle in his eye.

"Since we are baring all tonight, I think it's time to tell you something." Phoebe repositioned herself. "This could be a long story, so you'd better pull up a chair."

Christian moved to the chair and, taking off his boot, rested his foot on Phoebe's bed.

"You weren't the only one abandoned by a mother, except for me it was different. I was seventeen when Mom went to the Chicago World's Fair, an innocent enough thing to do, but she met a man there and never came home.

"If this man had been someone she fell in love with, I think my dad and I might've understood, but that's not what happened. The man was John Dowie. Have you ever heard of him?"

"I can't say that I have."

"He's a charlatan, and he made my mother into one, too. He goes around the country holding 'divine healings,' but they're all fake. My dad met someone who'd seen one of his services. He said my mother was healed from a different illness every night."

"But, Phoebe, what your mother did has no

bearing on you." Christian lowered his foot and moved his chair closer to the bed.

"It's the reason I'm here. The people of the small town where I grew up made fun of us, and my father thought I'd have a better chance if I left Mount Olive. He put an ad in the *Phoenix Republican*, and the Sloans answered it. I came out here to be their maid."

"Then how did you and Edwin get married?"

"Now, that's the question, isn't it? A maid and the banker's son, they don't go together, do they? That is, unless there's a baby on the way."

Christian's only response was to lift her hand to his lips and kiss her fingertips.

"Judge Johnstone married us before the Sloans ever knew about the baby. When Edwin told them we were married and I was expecting, W.F. disowned him. It's hard to not be bitter when you lose as much money as Edwin thought he'd lost. After a while, as he watched Frank spend the money that Edwin considered his inheritance, he got even more bitter. He resented me and he resented Will."

"Then why would Frank want to take Will away from you?"

"Because Myra hasn't given Frank a child, and now W.F. concedes that Will may be his only legitimate heir. He's willing to forget that the child carries my lowly blood, just to carry on what he considers a dynasty."

"That's ridiculous. He's a banker. That doesn't make his lineage a dynasty. July has more claim to lineage than he does. His father was the son of Shaka, one of the greatest Zulu monarchs in Bulawayo."

"There it is again." Tears welled in Phoebe's eyes. "Who's ever heard of Bulawayo, much less Shaka? You know everything and you've seen so many places. What could I possibly have to offer you?"

Christian leaned forward and kissed her. "You can give me what I want most."

Phoebe sat up and wrapped her arms around Christian, holding him to her as she permitted herself to cry.

Christian climbed the stairs. When he walked by Will's room, he opened the door and walked over to the sleeping child. When he'd started the conversation with Phoebe, he thought he'd tell her about the child of the streets that he'd been, but he couldn't get the words out.

He felt the small scar on his face, remembering the night he woke to find a rat gnawing on his cheek. Phoebe said he'd had opportunities. Yes, he'd had opportunities—opportunities to find scraps of food that others had found unfit to eat, opportunities to pilfer and steal. All of this, he learned when he was little more than Will's age.

Even though Christian had never met Edwin Sloan, he disliked the man intensely. If he understood what Phoebe had said this evening, her husband had turned his back on her and Will because of money.

How could any man do that? Phoebe was fascinating, and Will was entertaining. Christian had seen extreme poverty and extreme wealth. In both situations, Christian had never overcome the feeling of being alone. Being here with Phoebe and Will had made him feel as if he could belong to their family.

Christian bent down and kissed Will on the top of his head. The boy shifted positions in his sleep, and Christian stepped back, not wanting to awaken him.

Tonight, he'd asked Phoebe for permission to court her, and he meant it. But he'd do more than court her. He'd do all that he could to convince her he loved her.

Then, unbidden, the thought of Ina Claire Woodson popped into his mind. Was he being unfair to her? He and Ina Claire had never spoken of love, had never expressed anything more than friendship for each other. But they had brought comfort to one another during that long, terrible siege.

Memories of the war and those times at Kimberley came flooding back to him.

"Ina Claire, you shouldn't be out of the shell-proof."

"Why not? We're all going to die anyway. Either we starve to death, or we get hit by the Boers' big gun."

"You can't give up, not now. We've been here 117 days—the column has to relieve us soon."

"I don't believe the military will ever come. Papa says the shells from their new gun weigh a hundred pounds," Ina Claire said. "Long Cecil can't compete with that."

Long Cecil was the gun that the American engineer George Labram and Ina Claire's father had built, to compete with the heavy siege guns being used by the Boers. The gun was named after Cecil Rhodes.

"You're right, Long Cecil's shells are about a fourth as powerful, but that's not to say he is useless," Christian said. "Think where we were before we had it."

"I know. Papa's just sorry Mama and I didn't go back to America when Mrs. Labram left."

Christian reached out for Ina Claire's hand. "For my sake, I'm glad you didn't. We would never have met had you gone back to Albany. Come on. What do you say we get something to eat before the soup is all gone?"

When they reached the soup kitchen at the De Beers convicts' station, Christian and Ina Claire took their place in one of the never-ending lines. About forty thousand people had to be fed, including about ten thousand indigenous Zulus and Hottentots who, before the siege, had been working in the diamond mines. Now Rhodes had put them to work repairing the damaged streets.

The daily rations were down to a cup of tea for breakfast and for dinner, a soup made with horse flesh, and wizened carrots that looked like corks. Occasionally, a few mangel-wurzels were added, but the extreme heat of the Karoo summer caused the beets to shrivel in the ground. The Boers had cut the water from the reservoir, so the only water came from the seepage in the mines. If anyone was caught watering a garden, the imposed martial law—or Military Situation, as it was called by the civilians—withheld that person's meager rations.

Before Ina Claire and Christian got their tin cups filled with soup, a loud boom sounded. The bugler in the conning tower began to blow the warning, having seen the smoke from the great gun on Kamfers Dam.

Seventeen seconds. That was all the time Christian and Ina Claire had to find shelter, so they ducked into one of the nearby tunnels that had been built in the debris taken from the mines.

The incoming shell sounded like an empty and disconnected railway car rolling down the track. There was no whistle, just a rushing sound, and then the big shell hit with a loud thump.

"Where do you think it hit?" Ina Claire asked.

"I think out in the road somewhere. If it hit a building, I think we would've heard it collapse."

"Yes, that's probably right. But it's so frightening."

Christian drew Ina Claire to him and held her close until they heard no more explosions.

Christian pinched the bridge of his nose to make the memories go away. He wasn't being unfair to Ina Claire, he knew he wasn't. They had shared a genuine camaraderie, but no words of affection had ever been spoken.

Christian stayed with Phoebe for an entire month. She laughed when he and Will attempted to cook or clean or wash clothes, but they did whatever had to be done, letting her rest and recuperate. The dizzy spells still occurred, but were definitely subsiding, and the few that she'd had were much less severe. Even the bruises had faded.

One day, Christian announced it'd be a good time for Phoebe to go to town to see the doctor.

"I want to go, too." Will hurried to put on his shoes.

"Not today," Christian said. "This is going to be a day for your mama and me."

"But I want to go," Will whined.

"Miss Gwen said you could spend the day with the girls," Christian said. "I think she told me that Hannah has a new pony and they want you to go for a ride. Maybe they'll even have a picnic."

"I'd like that," Will said with enthusiasm. He and Christian went to the shed to get the buggy.

Fifteen minutes later Christian and Will brought the buggy around. Christian helped Phoebe in, then disappeared into the house, returning with a small bundle that he laid on the seat.

"What's that?" Phoebe asked.

Will covered his mouth with his hand as he began to giggle.

"Shhhhh," Christian said as he climbed in. "It's a surprise. Don't tell her, Will."

"I don't like secrets," Phoebe said.

"You'll like this one," Christian said. "I know you will."

Releasing the brake, Christian made a clicking sound as he snapped the reins, and the horse started out at a leisurely trot. Will entertained them by singing one song after another. He surprised them both by singing a folk song that July had taught him.

> Baphina obaba
> Ba semazalwini
> Basitshiyel' indubeko
> Indubeko zomhlaba

"Do you know what the words mean?" Christian asked.

"No, I like made-up words," Will said.

"Those aren't made-up words. When July was little, he didn't know how to speak English at all, and this is how he talked."

"Do you know what the words mean?" Phoebe asked.

"I do."

"So what are they?"

"I'm sure he taught it to Will for a reason. It says:

> 'Where are those fathers?
> They are in heaven.
> They left us problems.
> These earthly difficulties.' "

"Not a very joyful song," Phoebe said. "Will, why don't you sing 'Mary Had a Little Lamb'?"

The rest of the trip went quickly and they were soon pulling into the Prinsens' lane.

"Can I tell her now?" Will asked excitedly as Gwen came out to meet the buggy.

"You mean she doesn't know?" Gwen asked.

"No, Wet wouldn't tell her."

"All of you certainly have my curiosity up. What's this about?" Phoebe asked.

"Gwen told me you haven't had a free day since you came to Arizona, and she thought it was a good idea for us to go up to the hot springs."

"I can't do that." A frown crossed Phoebe's face. "Who will take care of Will?"

"The same person who took care of him the night you stayed with Dr. Evans," Gwen said. "Don't worry about him. Just go and have a good time."

"The night? Christian, we're not going to spend the night, are we?"

"If we go, we will. We'll take the train up to Hot Springs Junction, and then we'll catch the stage for Castle Hot Springs."

"But we can't do that," Phoebe sputtered. "What would—"

"The Sloans think?" Gwen finished.

"Yes, they think I'm terrible as it is. What would happen if they found out about this?"

"Phoebe, Castle Hot Springs is a resort. It won't be just you and Christian there," Gwen said. "You deserve the time away. Think of it as a little vacation."

"I didn't bring any clothes."

"The Chicago Store is having a big sale. Have Christian take you there and you can pick out something that you want."

"I can't afford a new dress."

"But I can," Christian said. "Think of it as rent money if you must. I sleep in your bed and I eat your food."

Gwen's eyes rose when she heard Christian's comment.

Christian chuckled. "That didn't come out the way I meant it. I sleep in a bed that Phoebe owns."

"Oh, that's better," Gwen said. "Will, kiss your mama good-bye, and then you two better get going or you'll miss the train. Did you bring him any clothes?"

Will kissed his mother, and then Gwen helped him out of the buggy.

"You be a good boy and make certain you save us some cookies that I know you'll bake. We'll see you tomorrow." Christian said, handing the package containing Will's clothes to Gwen.

11

"**I** feel strange riding off without him," Phoebe said when they were about a hundred yards away.

"You know he'll have fun. Will seems to like the Bucknells."

"It's just that I have a premonition. Something's going to happen."

"Don't think like that. I want you to enjoy this day."

Phoebe rode in silence for a while, deep in thought.

"I've been thinking about the song July taught Will. Is that really the meaning of the words?"

"I think so," Christian said. "I may be off. The first verse is about going over the Limpopo River to work in the gold fields in search of money, but I believe this is the second verse."

"'They left us problems—these earthly difficulties.'" Phoebe's voice quavered. "That certainly is a truism where Edwin is concerned."

"I don't know why you let those people bother you so much. Just live your own life."

Phoebe looked down at her hands and began to pick at her nails. "They think I killed Edwin."

"I thought he was killed by an ostrich."

Phoebe jerked her head toward Christian. "You know that and you didn't say anything?"

"I thought it was an accident—just like when the horse kicked you."

"It was more than that."

Christian was surprised by Phoebe's remark and wasn't sure how to respond. For a long moment the break in their conversation was filled only by the sound of the hoofbeats and the whir of buggy wheels.

Then Phoebe said, "You said the other morning you saw me sitting beside Edwin's grave. And I believe my response was that I find comfort in visiting Edwin and I tell him everything. That's not entirely true."

"Oh?"

"Well, in a way it's true. I find it's much easier to talk to him now than it was when he was alive. I think I should tell you how it was between me and Edwin."

Christian reached over to take Phoebe's hand in hers. "Phoebe, you don't have to tell me anything, especially if it makes you uncomfortable."

"I want to tell you," Phoebe said resolutely.

"Everything is buried so deep inside of me, I need to get it out."

"All right. I'll be a good listener."

"I came to Arizona to be the Sloans' housekeeper. I thought I knew how to keep a house, but nothing satisfied Mrs. Sloan. Whatever I did wasn't right, but that wasn't the hardest part. It was the way I was treated as a person. Other than to demand I do some task, they totally ignored me. They spoke to one another in my presence as if I weren't there.

"Edwin was the only one who showed any kindness toward me at all; then on the night of Frank and Myra's engagement party, Frank"—she paused for a moment to come up with the right words—"tried to take liberties with me. I was startled, and I spilled the coffee on Mrs. Sloan's fine damask cloth. She got very angry with me, and of course I couldn't explain what had happened. When, finally, my work was done, I took to my bed to cry. A little while later, Edwin came to my room."

"He forced himself on you?"

"No, I can't say that. As I said, Edwin was the only one who was ever decent toward me, so when he came to my room, the situation got out of hand. I know it was foolish, and had I said no, he would've left, but I actually felt I owed him something. So I didn't resist."

Phoebe paused and took a deep breath.

"As a result of that one night of indiscretion . . ."

Phoebe paused again, gathering her thoughts before she went on. "Oh, Christian, I was so naïve. I had no idea what went on between a man and a woman, and I certainly didn't know I could get pregnant from just one time, but it happened. After that night, Edwin was different. He was still friendly, but it wasn't the same. I didn't know what was happening to my body, and it was Crecy who suspected that I was pregnant. She was the cook and she saw me in the mornings when I was so sick. Since Edwin was the only one I'd ever been with, I told him I was going to have his baby.

"At first, he was very angry—he told me I'd have to leave, but then he decided marrying me would be a good way to undermine his father. His family never forgave him, nor me. And now they blame me for his death."

"That's foolish. How can they blame you?"

Phoebe struggled at first, but quickly the words came easier and without hesitation. Christian realized that telling the story was cathartic for her. She not only told the story, she relived it—and, through the telling, so did Christian. She began with the last confrontation she'd had with Edwin.

"Edwin, don't you love me?"

"I married you, didn't I?"

"That's no answer."

"Phoebe, do you have any idea what I have to put up with? You were my mother's maid and I did the right thing by you when you told me you were pregnant. I didn't have to marry you, and if I knew then that I was going to lose everything, I wouldn't have done it. After all, there is no real proof that I'm the one who made you pregnant."

"You know Will is your child."

"I assume that's so, but Frank doesn't think he's mine. The truth is, you tricked me into marrying you anyway, and be that as it may, I have, in all respects, treated the boy as my own."

"He is not 'the boy,' Edwin. He has a name."

"You don't have to lecture me. I know that. All I meant to say is that I treat him as my own."

"What about his mother? Do you treat her as your wife?"

"I'm out here on this damn farm working every day just to satisfy you while my brother sits in the bank doing nothing, getting richer and richer. I know he's laughing at me for my foolishness."

"That's not what I mean, Edwin, and you know it. We never act like husband and wife."

"We argue enough—isn't that what husbands and wives do?"

"No, husbands and wives love one another, they do things together. And they sleep together," she added pointedly.

"That's all you ever think about. Why don't you find some man who thinks with the front of his pants? Or, better yet, go get a job where men pay you to lie on your back."

"You bastard! Get out!" Stung by her husband's

words, she slapped him. "Get out! I don't ever want to see you again!"

"Boy!" Edwin called. "Come in here!"

"What do you want with Will?"

Will came into the room rubbing his eyes.

"Come with me." Edwin jerked Will by the arm. "Your mother wants to be by herself."

Edwin, dragging Will behind him, left the house.

"No!" Phoebe yelled as she followed along, pulling at Will. "You can't take him! You can't take my child away from me!"

"We'll see what I can do." Edwin went to one of the nearby pens. He jerked open the gate. "Take these damned birds with you and get off my land." He turned and, with Will in tow, started back to the house.

The commotion had caused the flighty birds to react. The male, protecting his mate, ran out of the pen and headed directly for Edwin. With a swift kick, his sharp claw tore into Edwin's back, causing him to fall as blood poured from the wound.

Grabbing the thorny pole that stood by the gate, Phoebe ran to her husband and son. The ostrich was coming toward his victim again when Phoebe reached them. She poked the stick into the bird's eyes and, temporarily blinded, it turned and ran the other way.

Will was crying and Edwin was lying motionless. Grabbing the child, Phoebe ran in search of Trinidad and Cornello. When she found them, they got the buckboard and loaded Edwin's limp body into the back.

"Cornello, take care of Will. Trinidad, get us to town as fast as you can."

When they reached the doctor's office, Phoebe starting calling for him, and Dr. Evans came out to the wagon.

"He's alive, but not for long," the doctor said after a quick examination. "You'd better go get his father."

Trinidad hurried to the bank, and soon W.F. was running back to the wagon. When he saw Edwin, he took his son's hand.

Edwin opened his eyes and smiled. "I'm sorry. You were right. I should never have . . ." Those were Edwin's last words.

W.F. turned to Phoebe, deep-seated hatred on his face. "You killed him. I'll make you pay for this." He turned and walked away, leaving Phoebe alone with the body.

Phoebe quit speaking then, and though Christian wanted to say something to comfort her, he realized that, for the moment, she needed the quiet.

"Both Frank and his father blame me for Edwin's death. But not because of the argument we had that day. They blame me because they think I tricked Edwin into marrying me. They blame me because he was trying to make a go of it on an ostrich farm, which he never would have done if we hadn't been married. And they've held Edwin's death against me ever since. I've never told that to anyone until now."

"You didn't have anything to do with Edwin getting killed. You said he opened the gate to the pen. It was his own carelessness."

"Yes, and I try to tell myself that. But I keep remembering that one line that plays over and over in my head: 'I don't care if I ever see you again!'"

Christian stopped the buggy and pulled her to him. "Sometimes in our lives we say things we regret, but we can never take them back. I'm sorry this happened, but it doesn't mean you have to blame yourself for the rest of your life. You have Will to consider. He needs a loving mother and I need"—Christian stopped himself before he added *a loving wife*—"you as well."

"Oh, Christian, why couldn't we have met before I ever met Edwin?"

He released her and, after squeezing her hand, picked up the reins. "The important thing is we've met now. And as little regard as I have for Edwin, consider this: if you had never met him, there'd be no Will."

"Yes, that's true, isn't it?"

Just then an electric car rang its bell and the horse jumped. "I'd better watch what I'm doing or we won't get to the doctor's office at all."

When they arrived, Christian helped Phoebe down from the buggy.

"You're looking much better than the last time I saw you," Dr. Evans said when Phoebe stepped into the office. "How are you feeling?"

"I'm doing quite well. I have a few dizzy spells, but they don't last long."

"That's good to hear. You'll probably be having them for a good long while, but they'll get less intense, and further and further apart. Now let me get a good look at you."

Sitting her in a chair, Dr. Evans checked her eyes, then had her cross her legs while he tapped first on one knee, then the other. After that, he had her walk along a straight line on the floor.

"Excellent!" he said when the examination was over. "I can safely say you may resume your normal activity, with moderation. Have your man here handle some of your hard work."

Phoebe was embarrassed by the doctor's pronouncement. She started to explain that Christian was not her man, but she thought it best to let it drop. "Thank you, Doctor."

"Oh, but, Mrs. Sloan . . ." Dr. Evans said as she was rising from the chair.

"Yes?"

"Try to stay out of the way of a rearing horse," he chuckled. "I have a prescription for you. Have some fun in addition to all your work. Now, that's straight from your doctor's mouth, so you have to do it. Do you hear me?"

"I hear you," Christian said, "and I'll try to see that she follows your advice."

The doctor laughed. "I'm holding you to it, son.

This girl's pretty special to us here in Maricopa County."

Christian and Phoebe left the doctor's office and walked around the corner to the Chicago Store.

"Have you thought about what you want?" Christian asked when he saw the window display of women's clothing.

"Yes. I want to go home."

"Oh, no you don't." Christian opened the door. "Dr. Evans all but prescribed an outing for you, and so did Gwen. If you don't pick something, I'll do it for you."

"Good morning," the shopkeeper said when they entered. "We have one of our best sales going on, ma'am. What may I show you?"

Phoebe was surprised to see the number of ready-made dresses in the store. In her whole life she'd never had a dress that wasn't hand-made.

"With this cool weather we're having, you might need one of our new kerseys." The clerk pulled a brown coat off a table. "Just look at this beautiful overstrap stitching on the flared cuffs. With your coloring, this would look perfect on you."

"I don't . . . I don't think so," Phoebe said hesitantly.

"We'll take it, but I think she'd like a gray one." Christian walked over to a rod that contained several dresses. "Look at this one." He pulled off a red taffeta dress with big, puffy sleeves. "What do you think?"

Phoebe laughed. "I'm afraid if I wore that, I'd drive off every bird I have."

"Well, what would you like?"

"If I'm going to get a new dress, I think I'd like a blue gingham."

"No." Christian shook his head as he put his hands on her shoulders. "I want you to have something you've never had before. I agree that the red is too much, but pick out something you think is pretty."

"All right." She began looking around the store.

"What about this one?" Christian pulled out a white organdy. "This would make a good party dress . . . or a wedding dress."

Phoebe's eyes opened wide. "For who?"

"I don't know." A smile crossed Christian's face. "I was just thinking."

Phoebe moved around the store and finally settled on a cream-colored silk waist and a navy-blue pebble serge skirt. "I'll take this."

"And she'll take these." Christian handed a tan walking skirt, a matching cheviot jacket, and the white organdy dress to the clerk. "And you'll need some new undergarments."

Phoebe's mouth dropped open. "You can't say that!"

Christian laughed. "I just did. If we're going to be away for the night, you're going to need some things, aren't you?"

Christian carried the bundle containing Phoebe's new clothes when they left the Chicago Store.

"You were awful." Phoebe hit Christian on the arm. "I was mortified. You know what people will say?"

"Do you care?"

Phoebe thought for a moment. "No," she laughed.

Taking her hand, Christian walked her back to their rig in front of the doctor's office.

Across the street, a woman was watching. When Phoebe and Christian rode off in the buggy, she went into the Chicago Store.

"Hello, Myra, dear," the clerk said when her customer came in. "I thought you might be in today. I have some new party dresses in, and I know how much you and Frank entertain."

"I'm not buying today. I want to know about the man and woman who just left here."

"I don't think I've ever seen them before, but I wish more men took an interest in women's clothing. I'd be selling a lot more clothes if there were more like him. Wasn't he a handsome fellow, though? Seems a shame he's going to marry that woman. But I guess she could be pretty if she'd protect her skin from the sun a bit more."

"I hear some people think she's a ravishing beauty."

"Well, Myra, you seem to be inordinately interested in her. Who is she?"

"She's my sister-in-law."

• • •

"Two round-trip tickets for Castle Hot Springs," Christian said to the ticket officer at the Santa Fe, Prescott and Phoenix Railway depot.

"Very good, sir."

"How long will it take to get there?"

"You'll be on the train for just under an hour and a half, and on the stagecoach for about four hours. You should be there around suppertime."

"Then I guess we'd better get a bite to eat before we leave."

"And we can take care of that, too. Just step around the corner to the Pacific Grotto. They sell box lunches that are right good."

"Thank you."

Christian bought two boxes, one with potted ham and the other with potted chicken. In addition, there were several saltines, some locally grown pears, and a small spice cake.

"This may take a while," Christian said as he sat down beside Phoebe. "Ham or chicken?"

"It doesn't matter."

"Then I'll take the ham."

"Sir, I heard you say you're going to the hot springs," a gentleman said as he approached them.

"We're going; that is, if we get there today," Christian said.

"You will be back by November sixth, won't you? I'd like to ask you for your vote."

"I'd love to vote, period," Phoebe said. "I don't understand why Arizona isn't a state yet."

"And that is one of the main reasons I want to be elected as a territorial delegate to Congress. I'm Governor N. O. Murphy, but my friends call me Oakes. And you, sir, may I count on your vote?"

"I can't vote for you either," Christian said.

"You're a Smith man? Let me tell you why I'm the best person to go to Congress. You know Arizona needs this water project to go through. If I'm elected, I can guarantee that the National Irrigation Congress will find in our favor."

"Well, then the Salt River Committee doesn't need me."

"Wait a minute, who are you? Are you that foreigner from South Africa? The one Ben Fowler hired?"

"I am."

"Whatever it is you do, I hope you can get the job done. This valley needs water. Now, I didn't catch your name?"

"Christian De Wet." Christian extended his hand to Governor Murphy.

"De Wet? Are you against the British?" Murphy screwed up his eyes as he scrutinized Christian.

"I can't say that I am."

The governor moved a rock that held down several copies of the *Arizona Republican*. He picked up a paper and handed it to Phoebe. "Front page, four columns over. Can you read that headline? 'Drubbed De Wet.' If your friend's a Boer, he'd better think about going back where he came from." The governor turned and began addressing another person who was coming into the depot.

Phoebe looked at the front page and found the headline:

DRUBBED DE WET

The Famous Boer Commander Given the Run

The London war office has received the following from Lord Roberts:

"Lt. General Charles Knox successfully engaged General Christiaan De Wet on October 27. During the Boer retreat, Knox caught De Wet in Rensburgdrift. The Boers lost heavily, but due to the treachery of the inhabitants, who admitted Boers to their houses in the night, from which a fire was opened at daybreak, the guerrilla fighters, led by De Wet, escaped. Troops dispatched from Modder River drove off the Boers and destroyed the houses of the treacherous inhabitants."

"Christian, you have the same name as this general. Is he a relative?" Phoebe handed him the paper.

Christian read the article, and immediately his thoughts went to what he'd witnessed. The article said Knox—or "Nice Knox," as the troops called him, because of his civility—had destroyed the houses of the "treacherous inhabitants." Christian knew what that meant. All the farmsteads were burned, the animals were killed, and the women and children, at least those who survived, were rounded up and put in concentration camps. The newspapers didn't report that part of the struggle.

Christian shuddered and put his arm around Phoebe, drawing her close. "I don't know if the general is a relative or not. I don't even know if I'm Dutch or British. Nobody knows who I am or where I came from."

Phoebe leaned into Christian and kissed him lightly. "I know who you are."

Just then the whistle blew, announcing the arrival of the train.

"There it is," Christian said, helping Phoebe to her feet. "Let's decide we're going to forget all the ugly stuff and make the rest of the day—and night—special."

The heavy engine, with its bell ringing, came rumbling into the station, the six large, spoked wheels shrouded by the steam that escaped from the drive cylinders. The engineer, with a pipe clenched between his teeth, was leaning out the cab window, looking back along the train to gauge his position. The train slowed to a stop with a clanking of couplers and the screech of steel on steel as the brake shoes clamped down on the wheels of the five cars.

Phoebe shivered a bit as she stood on the platform watching the train's arrival, though it wasn't from the chilly temperature but rather from the knowledge she'd be spending the night with Christian.

12

The car was warm when she stepped on board, as the small potbellied stoves that stood at each end of the car were being stoked with coal.

"Would you like to sit by the window or the aisle?" Christian asked.

"The window," Phoebe decided as she stepped into the row to take her seat.

A moment later they started forward with a jerk; then came a second jerk as all the slack was taken up in the couplers. Gradually the train began picking up speed. By the time they were out of town, the train was moving so fast, it made her a little dizzy to look straight down and see the ballast whizzing by.

She hadn't been on a train since arriving in Phoenix six years ago. At that time the SFP&P only went to Prescott, and she'd taken the connecting stage at seven in the evening. The thinking was that the stage would travel through the hottest part of the valley during the night, but the eighteen-hour trip with six other passengers had been miserable. Phoebe smiled as she recalled how the only other female passenger had moved from seat to seat, sitting beside one man and then another, Phoebe had pretended to sleep as she listened to the grunts and groans, not wanting to know what was happening as the woman serviced the men.

How naïve she'd been. After her mother had left, there was no one to tell Phoebe how a man and a woman should behave toward each other. She and her friend Selma had discussed what it would be like to lie with a man, but they were both too inexperienced to know for sure.

Phoebe thought back to the night she'd lost her virginity. Edwin, too, was a virgin, and neither of them knew what they were doing. As she recalled, that first time was not unlike the mating of animals. She was sure that something was wrong with her because intuitively she knew that sex could bring pleasure. In the early days with Edwin, she'd fantasized that she was not unlike the woman on the stagecoach, who Phoebe had at the time thought had done what she did for her own satisfaction, and not for money.

She wondered what had made her go to Christian that other night. But he had something about him—perhaps his nonchalance when he'd come to her room in his underwear when the revolver had discharged. She knew he wouldn't judge her for her obvious indiscretion, and had it not been for July's disapprobation, she knew she would've found her way to Christian's bed again.

Even now, all she had to do was close her eyes and she could re-create the feel of his naked flesh against her own, the sensations she'd felt when he took her breast into his mouth, and the heat of his member when she took it in her hands. But the most glorious feeling was the sensation that had begun to course through her body—a feeling she'd never before experienced—when his hand stroked her most private parts.

As she sat on the train, its movement causing a sensation, she began to reexperience the feelings Christian had ignited, and she opened her eyes abruptly. "No!" she said aloud.

Christian took her hand. "What is it, Phoebe? Is something wrong?"

Phoebe withdrew her hand from his and shifted in her seat before she answered. "It's nothing. I was just thinking about something."

"Well, if it was something unpleasant, I hope it didn't involve me," Christian chuckled.

Phoebe smiled and turned to look out the window of the train. She sat in silence for a long time, taking in the desert landscape.

"This is the first time I've been out of Phoenix since I came here," she said to open a conversation. "Some people think this scenery is ugly, but I like it."

"All the cactus fascinates me. It doesn't grow on the Karoo."

"Do you miss your home?"

"A part of me does, but I can never go back to the life I knew before."

"Why is that?"

"Cecil Rhodes."

"I thought he was your mentor."

"He was, but if you don't do his bidding, he turns on you."

"And you walked away from him?"

"I did." Christian smiled. "All because of four long-legged birds."

"Well, I'm glad you came, and I hope you stay a long time."

"I'm glad I came, too, and now I have a question for you. Would you walk away from the Sloans?"

Phoebe turned to look directly at Christian. "It's not the same thing. I have Will to consider."

"It *is* the same thing. If you took Will and left, he'd be happy wherever you went."

"You don't understand, Christian. He'd lose everything that's rightfully his."

"What do you think he'd rather have? Money or love?"

Phoebe couldn't answer. She looked down at her callused hands and broken fingernails from days of hard work. She knew Christian's question wasn't completely about Will.

"Christian, you have so much to offer. You came to this country as a stranger, and just by opening your mouth, you're asked to spearhead a project that's vitally important to this valley. Tell me, what do I have to offer anyone?"

"You really don't know, do you?"

Phoebe shook her head slowly.

"You're the most selfless person I've ever met. From what I can see, you never think of Phoebe first. If someone wanted to fall in love with you, would you let them?"

"Will loves me."

"That's not what we're talking about. After our . . . indiscretion, I asked you if I could court you. Do you remember that?"

"I know you didn't mean that. You were trying to make me feel better after I made such a fool of myself."

A broad smile crossed Christian's face. "Oh, no, Phoebe, if I were trying to make you feel better, I have a much better way of doing that."

"That's what I mean. You're making fun of me again."

Christian's expression turned serious. "I'm not making fun of you, Phoebe. Believe me, I'm not."

For the rest of the train ride, they rode in silence.

"Hot Springs Junction," the conductor called out as he walked through the car. "Stage connecting to Castle Hot Springs, Cave Creek, and Mormon Girl Mine. Layover for Harquahala and points west."

"This is where we get off." Christian began gathering up their belongings.

"I hope Gwen is right about this place." Phoebe looked out the window. "I'd hate to think we came all this way for nothing."

"Don't form any opinions just yet. I think we have another forty miles to go before we get there."

Phoebe screwed her face into a grimace. "That's another four hours."

"But look at it this way. We'll have each other."

His smile was infectious and Phoebe had to laugh. But when they approached the coach, twelve people were waiting to board a vehicle that would normally accommodate nine. Phoebe and four other women were escorted inside. As Christian was one of the younger men, he and two others offered to ride on top of the stage.

Phoebe was disappointed that Christian wouldn't be beside her, but she knew that her emotions would be easier to control with some separation from him.

What would happen tonight? There'd be no child to interrupt them. There'd be no July to condemn them. There'd not be a soul who would know either of their names.

Would she sleep with Christian?

Yes. Without question, that's what she wanted.

Phoebe rubbed her brow; the bruise from the horse's kick was still a little tender.

She wished she had someone to talk to—someone who wouldn't judge her morals—but there was no one. Gwen came the closest, but they could never have this conversation. By encouraging Phoebe and Christian to come to this resort, was Gwen putting her sanction on the possibility of something happening between them?

But did Gwen's imprimatur include acting upon carnal desire?

Phoebe shook her head. No decent woman entertained these thoughts unless she was in love with a man.

Love?

Phoebe recalled Christian's words: *If someone wanted to fall in love with you, would you let them?*

What did it mean to fall in love with someone? Was it about desire or was it about friendship? Or was it about companionship? In Phoebe's case, the answer was yes to all three. She was, undoubtedly, in love with Christian De Wet.

She closed her eyes. She couldn't let him know. She would not entangle another man only to have her accusers claim she'd tricked him.

This was going to be a difficult night.

Phoebe's fellow passengers had been carrying on a conversation for most of the trip, and though she responded pleasantly enough to anyone who addressed her, she remained quiet, either lost in her thoughts or, when her thoughts got too troubling, listening to the others talk. Two of the women were society ladies from back east, and they'd obviously been guests at the resort numerous times. They seemed to know the managers personally and questioned whether "Margaret could outdo herself this year."

After the coach had been under way for a while, it stopped for a moment to, according to the driver, "give the team a blow." Everyone stepped out to stretch their legs as the driver and several of the men disappeared behind some rocks.

Christian approached Phoebe with a grin. "I'd be glad to escort you if you need to take a stroll among the rocks."

"I appreciate the offer, but I'll stay by the coach."

Just then one of the ladies who'd wandered off began to scream. Christian, with Phoebe close behind, ran toward her. When they found her, she was backed up against a rock as a wild burro edged toward her.

"Help me! Begorra, 'n' would someone be for getting this creature away before it kills me!" the woman screamed frantically.

Christian waved his arms, and the burro soon turned its attention to him. Phoebe picked up a few stones and began throwing them toward the animal, and soon it lumbered off.

"'Tis thankful I am that you came." The woman threw herself into Christian's arms. "And what would I have done now had ye not come to m' rescue?"

Phoebe rolled her eyes as Christian contained his laughter.

"Let me help you back to the coach," Christian offered as he eased her out of his arms.

"No, wait. I came out here because . . . sure 'n' could yer wife be for staying with me for a minute?"

Phoebe started, "I'm not—"

"She'd be happy to stand guard. Just yell if you need me again." Christian strode off behind the rock.

"Aye, 'n' 'tis such a ninny," the woman said as she took care of her toilet. "Yer husband is such a dear man."

Phoebe started to correct her, but withheld her comment.

They'd been back under way for a while when an older gentleman pulled out his chain watch. "It won't be long now," he announced as he rolled up the shade on his side of the coach.

Phoebe could see the sun dipping low in the sky, its rays bouncing off the rocky cliffs and crags of the Bradshaw Mountains.

In the gloam of the evening, Phoebe could see the flora begin to change. Interspersed with the saguaro and hedgehog cacti and ocotillo that grew in abundance, she also saw an occasional palm tree. When the coach rounded a bend, before them was a manicured green lawn and a seemingly unending row of palm trees. Excitement caused her heart to beat rapidly as she anticipated what was before her: an evening with a handsome man. Gwen was a dear to be looking after Will, to make this possible for her. Anxious for a glimpse of the resort, she saw it—a large yellow building with a red roof. The first story had a porch with inviting swings, while the upper floor had open balconies.

Just then, Christian opened the door and gathered up her package. "It's a good thing we bought a coat. I think you're going to need it up here in the mountains."

"I think you're right." Phoebe allowed Christian to help her down. When her foot reached the ground, a crone bounded from behind an exceptionally large palm tree. She was wearing a greenish false face with a grotesquely protruding nose, a flowing black dress, and a high-pointed hat that did nothing to control wayward strands of hair that seemed to be starched to maintain its dishevelment.

"Welcome, welcome, my dearies! Hee, hee, hee, hee!" the woman cackled.

"Bridgett, sure now 'n' you've outdone yourself," said the woman who'd been frightened by the burro. "I wouldn't have missed yer Samhain for the world."

Phoebe cast a questioning glance at Christian.

"I think it's a Celtic celebration, but I'm not certain," he said. "Is today the thirty-first?"

"Halloween! That's just what we need to spoil our evening."

"Who knows? Maybe it'll be fun." Christian led Phoebe toward the witch.

The woman addressed as Bridgett stepped out of character and embraced her friend. "Renny, sure now, 'n' did Cullen know you were coming and he just didn't tell me? Himself and Mr. Calhoun left yesterday. Would you be for believing this? He said he didn't want anything to do with my folderol."

"Folderol, is it? Here, now, 'n' if I didn't know Cullen O'Donnell better, I'd be for thinking that never had he set foot on our blessed Eire."

Just then another woman came out to meet the arriving guests. "I see you've met my best friend, Bridgett O'Donnell. If this is your first visit to Castle Hot Springs and the Palm House, it'll be a visit to remember. I'm Margaret Calhoun and I welcome all of you to my home." She stepped aside and, with a sweeping hand, invited her guests to enter a large room lit by dozens of candles, each set in a carved pumpkin. Shadows danced on the wall as cutout paper figures of spiders and bats and black cats swung from the ceiling.

"Before the festivities begin, we need to get everyone settled. Mary Kathleen will see you to yer rooms, since Cullen O'Donnell and Keevan Calhoun had to get to Phoenix in such an all-important hurry," Margaret said. "They told us Governor Murphy needed two more blokes to campaign for him, but Bridgett and I know the only campaigning they'll be a doing is inside Paddy's Saloon."

"Aye, 'n' 'tis the Lord's truth you are speaking there, Margaret," Bridgett said.

A few of the male guests who had converged on the new arrivals raised their drinks in salute as they let out a cheer. "To Paddy. May he be remembered wherever he may be!"

"I'm sorry," Christian whispered as he guided Phoebe toward the desk. "I thought Halloween was for kids."

"You forgot. This isn't Halloween. It's Samhain." Phoebe exaggerated the pronunciation as *sowin*, as she had heard it spoken.

Christian chuckled at Phoebe's mimicry as they stepped up to the desk. "You must be Mary Kathleen. We'd like two rooms, please."

"No, I'm Mary Margaret. Mary Kathleen is standing by the steps and she will see you to yer room and look after the rest of yer bags. Are they on the porch?"

"This is all we have." Christian indicated the bundle Phoebe had from the Chicago Store.

Mary Margaret's eyes widened. "No bags? How can that be? How long do you plan to stay?"

"Only for the night," Christian said. "Do you have rooms for us?"

"I guess we do, but most of our guests stay all winter, or at least a month. Are you sure you came all this way only to stay one night?"

"That's right, we did. Is there something wrong with that?"

"Oh, no, sir, I can find a place for you. What did you say yer name was?"

"De Wet. Christian De Wet."

"All right, Mr. De Wet, I can put you and yer lady in room 205. That has a wonderful view of the falls, and if you leave yer window open, you'll be able to hear it all night."

"I asked for two rooms. Is there another room nearby?"

Mary Margaret looked up abruptly. "Isn't this woman yer wife?"

By this time, Christian was becoming more and more agitated. "No, she is not. Is that a problem?"

A broad smile crossed Mary Margaret's face. "Oh, no, 'tis not a problem at all. Just wait until I tell Bridgett about you two."

"What do you mean, tell her about us?" Phoebe asked.

"Oh, nothing. It's just that you'll be her stars tonight. She gets so frustrated when every year she has to cast her spells over the same people. This year, maybe they'll work."

"Spells?"

"You'll see," the check-in clerk said. "Mary Kathleen," she called. "Would you show Mr. De Wet and his lady friend to rooms 205 and 207, and do make certain their windows are thrown open."

"His lady friend, is it?" Mary Kathleen said with a big smile. "Sure 'n' Bridgett will appreciate that."

"What are you talking about?" Phoebe asked, beginning to get a little piqued by the repeated references to their being unmarried.

"You'll see, milady, when the festivities begin."

Still frustrated by the lack of an answer, Phoebe started to ask another question, but then she thought about Mary Margaret and Mary Kathleen, who were no doubt only paid employees of the resort. Remembering her own experience in Mount Olive, Illinois, as a counter girl for Mrs. Droste's Bake Shop and then as the Sloans' maid, she held her tongue.

Mary Kathleen led them to the far end of the hall, where two rooms were separated from the rest of the rooms on that floor by a reading room. A linen closet was across the hall.

"Here they are." Mary Kathleen opened the door to the first room. She raised the window and placed a stick under it to hold it up. "These rooms are a little out-of-the-way, but they're the closest to the falls, and tonight, especially, you might like that. I'll open the other room before I go down to help with supper. It's served in the dining room and starts in half an hour."

Christian and Phoebe watched Mary Kathleen walk away, and Christian didn't speak until she was out of earshot. "Would you be for tellin' me, lass, 'n' is it to Ireland we've come? I was thinkin' we came by train 'n' coach, but I must've missed the ocean voyage." He perfectly mimicked the Irish brogue.

Phoebe laughed out loud. "Sure 'n' 'tis the divel you be now for mocking them so, Christian De Wet."

Christian laughed as well. "Which room do you want?"

"It doesn't matter."

"It matters to me. I want this night to be perfect for you."

Would it be perfect? Although Phoebe didn't give voice to the question, it sounded loudly in her mind.

Room 207 was the end room, and it had windows on two sides.

Christian walked over to one of the windows and pulled back the crewel-embroidered drapery. "I think this room has the better view. You're facing away from the entrance so you can see the mountains and the waterfall. Come look. You can see where the water cascades out of what looks like a hole in the rock. We'll have to go explore that tomorrow."

Phoebe came to the window and stood beside Christian.

"See?" He pointed to the waterfall.

Phoebe could smell a woody scent with a hint of cloves, or perhaps cinnamon, coming from Christian's face. She smiled. She'd never smelled men's cologne on him before. "You smell good."

Christian turned to her, a grin forming. "I thought I'd better do something to make you notice me when we got up here with all the society folks."

Phoebe nodded. "I suppose you think I'm after one of those old men who raised their glasses to Paddy."

"I don't know. If you take up with one of them, I may have to go after Miss Renny."

"You can't. She thinks you're my husband."

"I see no immediate reason to dissuade anyone of that idea."

"But if they believe that, won't they think it odd that we've taken two rooms?"

"I didn't want to be presumptuous. I'll leave you alone for a bit, but I'll be back in fifteen minutes. We don't want to be late for supper, especially when we're supposed to be the stars of the evening."

Before Christian left, he kissed her on the back of her neck. The mere touch of his lips sent shivers of anticipation through Phoebe.

After the door closed behind him, Phoebe looked around the room. The fireplace had been laid with wood and tinder, ready to be lit if needed to push away the cool of the night. The bed with its canopy atop four posts was as large as any she'd ever seen. Its deep-green velvet coverlet sported elaborate crewelwork as well. She ran her hand over the handiwork, admiring the fine stitches that someone had spent hours completing. Her mother had tried to teach her the intricate stitches, but Phoebe could never satisfy her.

She seldom thought of her mother, but tonight she wondered what she'd think of her daughter. She was in a place where the Rockefellers, the Whitneys, and the Vanderbilts vacationed, yet she, a coal miner's daughter, could stay here as well. She'd never before been anywhere quite as beautiful as this hotel, but even as she was thinking that, she realized that this was the first time she'd ever been in a hotel room anywhere.

Her musings were interrupted by a quiet knock.

"Are you ready?"

"Oh, Christian, I meant to put on one of my new dresses, but now I don't have time."

"I'll wait. Why don't you put on the white one?"

"For Halloween? I don't think so."

13

When Christian and Phoebe reached the dining room, they saw that it was appropriately decorated for the holiday. It had orange and black crepe paper intertwined all around the room. The only light was from the candles set inside carved pumpkins. There were no individual tables, but one long table set with gleaming silverware. Beside each place setting was a hollowed, carved orange that had a small candle inserted as well. On the table were three oversize oval copper trays filled with pumpkins, apples, pears, and clusters of green and purple grapes. In addition, the ubiquitous crepe paper was interspersed with the fruit and connected the arrangements.

"Ladies and gentlemen, I believe our last two guests have arrived," Margaret Calhoun announced when Christian and Phoebe entered the room. "Mr. De Wet, I believe we failed to get the name of your friend."

"My name is Phoebe Sloan."

"Thank you. Mary Kathleen, can you find where Miss Sloan will be sitting?

"Yes, ma'am." Mary Kathleen began scurrying along the table.

"All of you, please find your seats. The place cards are just in front of the orange jack-o'-lanterns."

"Well, now, tell me, Margaret, aren't all jack-o'-lanterns orange?" a man who seemed to have had a bit too much to drink said.

"Of course you're right, Harry. I meant the jack-o'-lanterns made from the oranges."

People began to mill around the table looking for their names, Phoebe and Christian were following Mary Kathleen when a young woman came toward them.

"Mr. De Wet? I believe you're sitting beside me. I'll bet you don't remember me, but I certainly remember you. I'm Helen Hay." She extended her hand to Christian.

Christian shook his head. "I'm sorry, but I don't recall having met you."

"Oh, but you remember meeting with my father, John Milton Hay, do you not?"

"The ambassador, of course, and now I understand he's McKinley's secretary of state."

The young woman flashed a big smile. "Yes, he is," she replied proudly. "I knew you had to be the same handsome man I met long ago. Come. Shall we be seated?"

The ambassador's daughter pointed to a place on the table where her and Christian's name cards were side by side.

"Excuse me"—Christian plucked up the place card that had his name—"I believe this is a mistake. I'll be sitting beside Miss Sloan."

"Oh, but . . . that's not how Mrs. Calhoun had it planned."

Christian smiled a most disarming smile. "Perhaps not, but it is how *I* have it planned. I'll make my apologies to her and perhaps we can speak later in the evening." He put his hand on Phoebe's waist and turned her in the direction Mary Kathleen had gone.

When they found Phoebe's place, the gentleman who'd remarked about the jack-o'-lanterns' being orange was waiting for her.

"I believe I'm to be yours tonight, my dear." He stood and almost tipped over the chair.

"It's Harry, is it not?" Christian asked.

"Yes. Everybody knows old Harry. Harry Hastings."

"There's been a mistake, sir. I believe Harry Hastings is to be sitting by Helen Hay. It's alphabetical, you know."

"Oh, and where is she?"

"That is she on the other side of the table—the one in the yellow dress."

"Thank yo kindly, and, ma'am, I'm sorry you don't get to sit beside me. You would've liked my company."

Phoebe laughed. "I'm sure I would have."

When they were seated, Christian took Phoebe's hand in his. He gave it a squeeze. That simple gesture meant more to Phoebe than she could say, and her eyes began to glisten as she held back her emotions.

Phoebe picked up the hand-printed menu by her place setting and read it over. The first item was Welsh rarebit, and she recalled her introduction to the dish when she was working as a maid for the Sloans. She had shared those domestic duties with a cook named Crecy.

Mrs. Sloan had asked Crecy to prepare the cheese sauce for an after-theater repast to which several dignitaries were invited, including the governor and his wife. It had been a disaster from the very beginning. Frank and Myra had gotten into an argument about something, and Juliet tried to cover for her son's behavior. Crecy had prepared the rarebit to be served at the precise moment Juliet had asked, but when the course was delayed because of the tiff between Frank and Myra, the sauce curdled, the toast burned, and Crecy could do nothing except serve the disastrous meal. Juliet had come to the kitchen, and both Phoebe and Crecy had been hauled over the coals for embarrassing her.

The evening had turned into a complete fiasco. Frank drank much more than he should have, and for the first time in her life Phoebe was confronted by a drunken man. She had no idea what would've happened had W.F. not intervened.

Hindsight told her she should've left the Sloan

household that very night, but she'd just arrived in Phoenix, and she was afraid.

"I'm not all that sure you would have 'enjoyed' Mr. Hastings's company," Christian said, his words bringing Phoebe back to the present. He nodded toward Hastings and Helen Hay, who was obviously being made uncomfortable by the inebriated man.

Phoebe smiled. "Don't you feel guilty now for rearranging the seating chart?"

"Not at all. Do you?"

Phoebe's smile grew broader, and she reached over to put her hand on Christian's arm. "Not in the least."

The meal continued with an orange aspic filled with an oyster timbale that was nestled on a bed of lettuce. Phoebe realized the inordinate amount of time it must've taken someone to form the face of a jack-o'-lantern in the bottom of the mold before the gelatin set. She couldn't decipher what had been used to form the features, but it looked like little black beads. Whatever it was, it had a fishlike taste that she liked.

When she came out of her reverie, she was aware she hadn't been a very engaging dinner companion, but Christian didn't seem to mind. He was speaking with two men sitting across the table while their companions were concentrating on their own food.

Phoebe listened to see if she could interject something intelligent into the conversation, but she soon went back to her own thoughts. She thought it strange to be discussing such sober topics as whether the US military would have to stay on in Cuba, or if the Chinese and the French would reach a peace accord, or how much wealth could be taken out of the Philippines in gold or wood, or if the future for the islands would be in rubber. All of this while women were waltzing around the room dressed as witches and carrying brooms.

Then Bridgett called out to the diners, "Now for the moment you've been waiting for: Let the Oiche Shamhna begin!"

"*Oiche Shamhna shona daoibh!*" many of the diners called out as they lifted their glasses.

Christian turned to Phoebe, lifting his eyebrows by way of questioning what was happening.

Mary Margaret explained, "*Samhain* means 'summer's end,' and they have just wished a happy summer's end. It's like saying, 'Happy Halloween.'"

"Oh." Phoebe flashed a smile at Mary Margaret, who was dressed as a witch as well. "Thank you."

Margaret Calhoun came out carrying a large tray that contained what looked like a fruitcake. She placed it in the center of the table.

Bridgett withdrew a knife from her witch's costume. "As I prepare to cut the barmbrack, 'tis an Irish toast I have for you. May yer neighbors respect you, may trouble neglect you, the angels protect you, and heaven accept you. Sure, now, 'n' may this be the year Renny O'Shea gets the ring."

"Didn't she get the shimble, shimble . . ."

"Here now, Harry, 'n' has demon rum muddled your tongue?" someone called.

The others laughed.

"Thimble," Harry Hastings said triumphantly, finding the word. "Tha's what she got last year, ishn't it? That means she'll be single for life."

"And how many times have you gotten the button, Harry?" another diner asked.

"But I keep coming back. My luck has changed. Look at me now. Am I"—Harry hiccuped—"am I not sitting by the prettiest woman in the room?" He leaned over to try to kiss Helen Hay, but she adroitly maneuvered away from him.

"I believe the ambassador's daughter won't be too happy with you when you two get together later," Phoebe whispered to Christian.

"And why would we be getting together later? Besides, if old Harry hadn't been by her, may I remind you he would've been sitting in my place."

"Yes, but then he would've said I was the prettiest woman in the room."

"That's what I'm supposed to say." Christian kissed her on the nose.

"Here, now." Mary Margaret shook her finger at Christian. "There will be none o' that until the future be told."

At first Phoebe thought the woman was serious, but then she saw that Mary Margaret was trying to contain her giggles.

"May 1900 be the year the barmbrack tells the future good and true." Bridgett lowered her knife and with a thump it split the cake. "There be trinkets in this dish, 'n' for any of ye who have no knowledge o' the meaning of the trinkets, I'll be for explaining them to ye now. If ye get a coin, then that means riches will come to you; but a rag means poverty. A button for a man"—she looked toward Harry—"means unlucky in love. A thimble means single for life. But"—she held up her finger—"the luck o' the Irish will fall upon one here, for if it be yer fortune to bite into a ring in yer barmbrack, sure 'n' that means 'tis romance for you. What think you, Mary Kathleen? Is there romance in the air tonight?"

"Aye"—Mary Kathleen looked directly toward Phoebe and Christian—"for 'tis somethin' I can feel."

Mary Margaret and Mary Kathleen passed the pieces of the barmbrack around, and everyone began eating as people commented to one another, hoping it'd be their luck to find a trinket.

Renny was the first to call out. "Oh, no!"

"What is it? What did you get?" Bridgett asked.

"I got a . . . piece of cloth." The disappointment in Renny's voice was obvious.

Bridgett smiled. "You're already a rich woman, Renny, so ye can laugh at the cloth. Besides, don't ye have all yer good friends, especially Mr. Whitney, who we are missing for the Samhain, but we'll forgive him this year, because he and Andrew have promised to bring Saratoga back to its glory. 'N' when that happens, yer horses will once again run at the front on the nine-furlong track. Sure 'n' the wee bit o' rag means not a thing to Renny O'Shea."

"'Tis fine for you to say, but what about Nora McMullen?" Renny asked.

Bridgett laughed. "And who got the ring last year? Andrew Mellon, that's who. 'N' who did he marry? Sure 'n' 'twas Nora McMullen herself. Don't tell me the barmbrack doesn't tell the future true."

"Ha! It's money for me!" one of the men said as he held up a penny. "I got the coin."

"I got the ring!" Helen Hay said happily, holding the ring aloft for all to see.

"Good for you!" Bridgett said. "And for sure there'll be wedding bells before a year has passed."

"I certainly hope so." Helen flashed a flirtatious smile in Christian's direction.

"Oh, my, Miss Hay not only has her cap set for you, it would appear she now has the 'luck o' the Irish' as well," Phoebe said, needling Christian with a coquettish smile of her own.

"Surely there must be some spell that can ward her off," Christian replied.

"Ladies, you'll be needing a covering," Margaret Calhoun said as she began passing black shawls to each of the women. "Tonight's the night for sprites and fairies, and lest you be covered, they'll carry you away."

"There you go, Christian. All I have to do is jerk the covering from Miss Hay's head, and the sprites and fairies will whisk her away," Phoebe said with a little laugh.

Phoebe and Christian moved with the others outside. All gathered around a big bonfire blazing in a rock cave near the lowest of the three pools of water that came from the springs. A black iron cauldron was suspended over the fire, and just as Mary Margaret, Mary Kathleen, and Bridgett came out of the shadows, a loud boom sounded. The noise startled Phoebe, and, reacting to her quick movement, Christian put his arm around her waist, briefly drawing her close to him.

Without an explanation, Bridgett began in a shrill voice, "Thrice the brinded cat hath mewed."

"Thrice and once, the hedgepig whined," Mary Kathleen answered.

"Harpier cries, ''Tis time! 'Tis time!'" Mary Margaret added, her voice, like those of Mary Kathleen and Bridgett, high and screeching.

"Round about the caldron go; in the poison'd entrails throw." Bridgett threw something into the pot. "Toad, that under cold stone, days and nights has thirty-one; swelter'd venom sleeping got, boil thou first in the charmed pot!"

Then all three joined as one voice: "Double, double toil and trouble; fire burn, and caldron bubble."

"The perfect setting for *Macbeth*!" someone said.

The three women continued Shakespeare's incantation until Bridgett recited the final line: "The charm is firm and good." When they finished, the three witches bowed as everyone applauded.

"With the spirits awakened, 'tis time for the real divining to begin. I'll be for asking now all the ladies who be not wed to come and sit by m' fire," Bridgett said.

Renny O'Shea, Helen Hay, and two other women moved forward and took a seat on stone benches.

" 'Tis one lass that is holding back," Bridgett called. "Sure 'n' I can feel it in m' bones." She reached under her cape and withdrew a string of bones and began to rattle them, then threw them into the pot, where they landed with a splash.

"I think she means you." Christian nudged Phoebe forward.

"I'm not sure I want to do this."

"She called for any woman who isn't married. If you don't go, everyone will think you're either my wife or you're a married woman here for an assignation."

"Christian!" Phoebe laughed as she hit his arm. "Don't say that."

"Then you'd better go take your seat by the fire. After all, she can 'feel it in her bones.'"

When Phoebe was seated, Mary Kathleen gave each of the women two new-crop pecans with instructions that they name the nuts for themselves and their lovers. "If brightly it burns, 'tis for sure married ye shall be before another year has passed. If they sputter and roll away, ye will soon be forgotten."

"Bridgett, do you really believe such nonsense?" one of the men asked.

"Aye, for didn't Cullen O'Donnell 'n' I have our own marriage predicted this selfsame way?"

"Did Cullen know you worked your spell on him?" someone else asked.

The others laughed.

"Bridgett, I'll name one for me, but I'll not be for sayin' the name of the one I want to marry out loud, for 'tis my own secret," Renny said.

"Very well, none among ye need say the name. The fairies will know all the same."

Phoebe looked back toward Christian, who pointed at her, then pointed at himself. She couldn't help but laugh at his antics.

After a moment, Renny's nut caught fire and flared up brightly.

"Here, now, Renny, do ye see that?" Bridgett asked. "Sure 'n' the bit of cloth in yer cake could be not for poverty but for a wedding dress."

"Aye!" Renny said happily. "All the signs are good this year! 'Tis glad I am that I came."

As the others laughed and congratulated Renny, Phoebe noticed that her nuts had both caught fire. The one she had assigned to Christian flared up, as had Renny's, but hers popped once and fell into the coals.

"If they sputter and roll away, you will soon be forgotten," Bridgett had said. But what did it mean if the nut actually jumped? That couldn't be a good omen, could it?

"Clearly the sprites and fairies are against us," Phoebe said when she returned to stand beside

Christian. "Miss Hay got the ring, Renny's pecan flamed bright, and your pecan rolled off into the fire with little more than a sizzle."

"My pecan?"

"Yes. Didn't you hear Bridgett say we were to name one pecan for ourself and one for our lovers?"

Christian's eyebrows rose. "And so you named it for me. But how do you know it was my pecan that fizzled and not yours?"

"Because mine wouldn't dare do that," Phoebe teased.

"And now, gents, 'tis yer turn to test the fates," Bridgett said, interrupting the banter between them.

"I'll show you how it's done," Christian said.

"You think you'll have better luck than I did?"

"We'll see."

"'Tis blindfolded ye shall be, 'n' into a pot of yer own choosing will ye stick yer hand," Bridgette said. "If 'tis clean water yer hand finds, 'tis a virgin ye will marry. But if 'tis dirty water yer hand finds, then yer bride has been bedded before."

The suggestiveness of the statement caused a spattering of nervous laughter.

"The last choice is no choice a' tall, for if the hand finds no water in yer pot, then 'tis a bachelor you'll stay until yer dying day.

"And now, me gentlemen, pick yer spot to learn yer fate." Bridgett put blindfolds on each of the men who'd come forward to sit around the fire pit. "There will be three pots afore ye. I only ask that ye think kind thoughts while the girls shuffle the pots lest ye see the order. 'Tis your own destiny ye hold in yer hand when next ye dip in the druid's pot. Mr. Hastings shall be the first."

"He has chosen an empty pot!" Mary Kathleen said. "There will be nay a bride for Mr. Hastings again this year!"

The others seated on the opposite side of the fire groaned in disappointment. The remaining men, in turn, dipped their hands into the pots, and the joy or disappointment of their choices was shared by all.

"You're the last to go, Mr. De Wet. Will you stay a single man forever or will you pick a bride?" Helen Hay asked.

Christian found the pots and started to dip into the middle one, but at the last moment he moved his hand to the pot on the left.

"Ah, 'n' 'tis the clean water ye have picked. Sure 'n' 'tis a virgin bride for ye." Mary Margaret nodded in Phoebe's direction.

The others looked questioningly toward Phoebe, and she curtsied good-naturedly as everyone began to cheer.

"Remind me not to get into any games of chance while we're here," Christian said when he returned to Phoebe's side.

Despite herself, Phoebe couldn't help but laugh. "Perhaps this string of bad luck is intentional to get us to buy an amulet."

"Ha. If they have one for sale, I'll be sure to buy it."

"And now, 'tis time for the grand finale," Bridgett said. "Go ye all women to the running stream; find a place where three rivulets run together, and at that place, dip your sleeve. Then take yer weary body to yer bed, but 'fore ye drift away, hang yer garment 'fore the mantel. In the dead of night, 'fore the strike of twelve, an apparition you will see as he steals in to turn the sleeve. The face you see upon the wall will be he who is yer lover. And now, my pretties, one and all, I bid you good night."

With a grand sweep, Bridgett and the two Marys disappeared into the cave, leaving everyone standing beside the fire, which had been reduced to glowing embers.

"Do you need me to help you?" Christian asked.

"Help me do what?"

"Find where three rivulets flow together."

"Do you think you can find them?"

"If they're here, I'll find them," Christian promised.

Allowing Christian to take her hand, Phoebe, with a spring in her step and a smile on her face, followed Christian into the darkness, staying close to the bubbling stream as other couples went before them.

"Glory and blessed be all the saints, for I have found it," Renny O'Shea called. " 'Tis here where from three pools the water be joined."

All the women went to the designated spot

and one by one dipped their arms into the water. As they drifted back toward the Palm House, all went to their respective rooms without saying good-night.

Christian escorted Phoebe to their end of the hall. "I brought you here so you could have fun. So tell me, did I succeed?"

"Yes, I had a wonderful time. But I have to say that it was also one of the most unusual nights I've ever experienced," Phoebe said when at her door. "Do you think they really believe that stuff?"

"When I marry, it will be to a woman I love. I'll not be guided by a sprite or fairy." Christian lowered his head as he found Phoebe's lips. The light and tender kiss, the gentle brush of his lips against hers, was enough to cause a quick-building heat to spread through her entire body. "Good night," Christian said, not wanting to let her go. He took a step toward her room and then stopped. Had she wanted him to come in, she would've asked.

When the door was closed, Phoebe leaned back against it. With all her heart she'd wanted to invite Christian into her room, but she'd decided if there was to be any chance of a future with him, she needed to be more conventional, more ladylike. A decent woman had to have some control over her emotions.

She shivered. She told herself it was from the dampness of the sleeve of her waistcoat, which was now actually cold. Taking it off, she hung it on the mantel above the fire lit by the staff—

not to await some fortune-telling apparition, but merely so it could dry.

In his room, Christian stood at the window looking out at the moon over the mountains. Though only in its first quarter, it was big and gold, and the stars around it were as bright as scattered diamonds on black velvet.

Diamonds. It was funny. Diamonds had been such a part of his life for close to ten years, but since coming to America he'd seldom thought of De Beers and his work for the company. Had he wanted to talk to Helen Hay tonight, more than likely he would've been drawn back into that world. He was truthful when he said he couldn't remember ever having met her, but he could remember the endless dinner engagements he was mandated to attend. And he did remember her father.

John Hay had been a private secretary to Abraham Lincoln. Christian remembered having had a long conversation with him when he was the ambassador to the United Kingdom. Hay had said that Lincoln had considered him a surrogate son after the death of his son Willie, and that Cecil Rhodes had confided in Hay that he considered Christian his son.

That conversation had taken place before the war, and though Christian couldn't say that he considered Cecil a father then, he was certainly the closest thing to a father Christian had ever known. He owed much to Cecil, from the time

Cecil found him as a homeless urchin on the docks until he emerged as a polished graduate of Oxford.

Not until the war did Christian see the other side of Cecil, and his unbridled ambition and his ruthless quest for power soured the relationship between them. But that was all a part of Christian's past.

In the room next to him was the woman he wanted in his future. Phoebe had so much to offer a man. She was also one of the most genuine people he'd ever met. She never put on airs, never tried to be someone she wasn't, and she never lusted after the trappings of wealth. He'd fended off more than his share of would-be lovers, but she'd come to him willingly, and the lovemaking they'd shared was remarkable.

Tonight every "tradition" they had shared had turned out to be wrong for them, yet Phoebe had taken it all with good cheer.

Then, as he stood here thinking about her, he knew what he was going to do. He was going to fulfill one of those predictions. He was going to make certain that Phoebe saw her lover before midnight.

Without thinking, he climbed through the window, out onto the balcony.

14

Phoebe was glad Christian had insisted she buy undergarments. She'd selected a new pair of flannel knickers with an interchangeable nainsook lining. In addition, she'd bought a new chemise. The fabric was much softer than her usual muslin, and she was luxuriating in the feel of it against her body as she huddled under the velvet comforter.

As Phoebe lay watching the flames die down, she heard a noise. Her first reaction was to scream, but anyone could be on the balcony, as it was actually a walkway that wrapped around the upper story.

But then she heard someone at her window. She was glad Christian was in the room next door, because if she had to, she'd scream and he'd come to her rescue.

She closed her eyes and feigned sleep, hoping that whoever was at the window was there by mistake. But through lowered lids, she saw that the body coming through her window was Christian himself. With much effort, she kept from smiling.

He quietly crept toward the fireplace. She saw him glance her way, but he continued toward the mantel. He reached for her waistcoat, but the movement caused it to fall. Quickly he turned to see that he hadn't woken her; then, examining the jacket, he turned it around so that the wet sleeve was now on the other side, just as the spell said it was supposed to happen.

This time Phoebe did smile, but she didn't move. Would Christian come to her bed? Would he lie down beside her, or would he kiss her to awaken her? But just as quietly as he'd entered, he headed for the window.

A sinking feeling came over Phoebe. He wasn't going to come to her. She wanted to hop out of bed and run to him, beg him to stay, but she couldn't. That was the old Phoebe—the new Phoebe was trying to control her emotions.

Just as Christian got to the window, he turned back, pleased with himself that he'd been able to enter Phoebe's room and not awaken her. As he put his leg through the open window, he hit his head on the sash.

"Damn," he whispered.

"Is that how an apparition talks?"

Phoebe sat up in the bed, not bothering to cover herself with the comforter.

Christian pulled his leg back through the window. "I didn't want to awaken you." He came over and sat on the edge of the bed.

"I wasn't asleep."

"What? You let somebody come into your room and you didn't scream or yell?"

"Christian, when I saw it was you, I knew I was safe."

Christian smiled. "I just wanted one of these crazy spells to turn out right for you." That was when he really saw her—in a thin chemise, with bows tied across her shoulders. All he'd have to do was reach for a ribbon and the cloth would fall away, exposing her breasts. In the firelight, he'd see her for the first time.

His eyes fixated on her breasts, and he watched her nipples harden as his penis began to awaken. He squeezed his eyes closed in an attempt to lessen his ardor, but when he opened them, Phoebe was looking at him with an expression somewhere between desire and agony.

"Maybe not as safe as you might think," Christian said.

"On the other hand I might be as safe as I want to be."

That response was all it took. Christian reached for her, taking her in his arms, more brusquely than he'd intended. He brought her to him, kissing her with all the pent-up hunger he'd held in check.

He felt her returning his kiss with a passion that matched his own, exhilarating in the feel of her body against his. She ran her hand through his hair as she pressed her lips more fervently to his.

"I didn't intend for this to happen," Christian said when he was able to withdraw from her lips, "but I can't help myself. I don't think you know how much I want this." He kissed her again, this time more tenderly.

Phoebe smiled. "I'm glad you banged your head."

"Would you have let me leave you without saying a word?"

"Yes."

"Why? I know you enjoy this as much as I do."

"I'm trying to be more . . ."

"More what? More enticing, more stimulating, more lovable? Just what is it you're trying to be?" Christian placed a kiss on her nose.

"I'm trying to be someone you'd be proud of—someone more sophisticated. Like this Hay woman tonight. She's someone who could go to parties and dances with you and she'd know exactly what to say or wear or eat or whatever you wanted her to do."

"When I had the chance, did I choose to sit beside her at dinner?"

"You felt sorry for me. You didn't want me to have to sit beside Harry Hastings."

Christian shook his head. "I don't believe we knew Harry was to be your partner. And as far as knowing what to wear . . ." Christian rolled his eyes. "I think I need to give you a lesson right now." His hand went to one of the ribbons that was holding her chemise together. "This bow. It's just not right." When he pulled one end of the ribbon, that side of her chemise fell. "See what I mean? It just wasn't right. I think I'm going to have to fix both of these things."

Phoebe was enjoying the banter, and when both her breasts were exposed, she felt as giddy as a child. "Why, Mr. De Wet, I do believe you are trying to undress me."

"Do you think so?" With that, he began to cup her breasts, rubbing his thumbs over each nipple.

Phoebe closed her eyes and arched her chest, urging him to take a breast into his mouth. When he did so, she dropped back onto the bed.

He threw back the velvet comforter, and when he saw her flannel knickers, he laughed out loud.

"What's wrong?" She sat back up.

"You are the most practical person I've ever known. The next time we buy underclothes, I'm going to pick them out. You're going to have silk that is so sheer I can see you without ever taking them off."

"And what kind of underwear are you wearing?"

A broad smile crossed Christian's face. "I believe you should find out for yourself."

"Sir, I take that as a challenge." Phoebe rose from the bed, her flannel knickers still in place while her chemise went by the wayside. She unbuttoned Christian's shirt, expecting to find a vest much as Edwin had worn, but instead his chest was bare. Her eyes opened wide. "You're not wearing any underwear."

"I wouldn't say that." Christian's voice was deep and husky as he guided her hand to the buckle of his belt. "You're not finished."

Phoebe hesitated. Up until this point, in her mind this had been a game—a sparring match between a man and a woman—but if she opened his pants, there would be no going back. Her hands began to tremble.

Christian put his hands on hers as if to steady them. He bent to kiss her, a kiss so gentle she wasn't sure he had touched her lips. "Shall I?" he asked.

Phoebe's eyes were now as big as those of a doe. There was no question she wanted him. Only two layers of cloth separated her from ecstasy. With deliberate movements, she began to slowly unbutton his trousers. As she did, she watched the bulge in his pants grow harder and harder. When she had the buttons free, she opened the trousers, watching as his underwear strained to contain his manhood.

"God, Phoebe . . . can you go a little faster?"

They began to make love—not a carnal lust that was wild and uncontrolled, but a mutual satisfaction that was more fulfilling than that first stolen night.

Somehow Phoebe knew that this was the way lovemaking was supposed to be, not only the giving and taking of physical pleasure, but the sharing of something much deeper and much more intense. She felt it was a joining of their souls.

When they'd both reached their pinnacles and were coasting down, they lay side by side and Phoebe put her head on Christian's shoulder. With his arm holding her close, she knew she'd never before felt such total contentment. In that moment, with all her being, she knew that this was love.

Phoebe's Farm

The next morning, shortly after breakfast, July and Trinidad were grinding alfalfa for the young birds when Andy Patterson rode up.

"Andy, what brings you here today?" Trinidad asked. "Did you come to help with the plucking?"

"No, I'm looking for Christian. Mr. Prinsen wants him to go into town to get that African engineer and his family."

"What African engineer?" July asked.

"The one Christian knew. Mr. Prinsen told me he built an artillery gun out of odds and ends of metal he found lying around, and it worked."

"Of course. Long Cecil. Everybody knows about

Mr. Labram and Mr. Woodson," July said. "Are they supposed to be on today's train, because if they are, more than likely Christian will be on it, too."

"No, that's just it. They got here yesterday, but Ben Fowler didn't send word," Andy said. "They're staying at the Hotel Adams, and Mr. Prinsen doesn't think that's right. He wants Christian to go pick them up and bring them out to the farm."

"Christian can't go today," July said. "He's not here."

"Of course he's not." Andy hit his head with his hand. "That's why Will's with the Bucknells. Do you know when he and Miss Phoebe will be back?"

"Nobody told us for sure, but we're expecting them today," July said. "I can't imagine Miss Phoebe will be away from Will more than one night, but in the meantime somebody's got to go pick up these folks, and I expect that'd have to be you."

"Me? I don't know these people," Andy said.

"Well, if they're in the hotel, I certainly can't go get them," July said, thinking of his experience when he and Christian first arrived in New York.

"But it has to be you, July. You'll know them if they're from Africa."

July laughed. "They were in Africa—they are not Africans. I think I heard Christian say they were from somewhere in New York."

"It doesn't matter. The only thing I know is that

Mr. Prinsen said to bring them out to the house. Will you go with me to get them?"

"I can go, but I don't know them either."

Ina Claire Woodson was sitting in the window of Coffee Al's Restaurant. This wasn't what she'd envisioned when she thought of coming to Phoenix, Arizona. After the note she'd received from Christian, she'd expected that he would meet them at the train station; but not only was he not there, no one else was either. Her father had sent a telegram to Benjamin Fowler telling him when they were leaving Albany. In truth, her father hadn't told him the exact time of their arrival, but nonetheless it would've taken little research to ascertain they'd arrive in six days.

According to Mr. Newburgh, the desk clerk at the Hotel Adams, the population of Phoenix was just a little over five thousand. It seemed to Ina Claire that if she could personally be acquainted with a large number of the fifty thousand residents of Kimberley, it wouldn't be hard for everyone to know one another in a town this small.

The longer she sat at Coffee Al's, the more aggravated she became. When they were snubbed at the train station, Millicent Woodson had wanted to go back east on the next train; but she and her father had convinced her to stay, whether her father had a position or not. But now Ina Claire was on her mother's side.

Looking out on the street, she saw a white man driving a wagon with a black man sitting beside him. She smiled. It was a welcome sight to see a Zulu.

"A Zulu," Ina Claire said as she slid out of the booth. She paid for her cup of coffee and went in search of the black man. From his size, she was sure he was a Zulu, and if he was anything like the natives she knew, he would know everything about everybody.

When she stepped into the street, the wagon was nowhere to be seen. A couple of older men were sitting on a bench in front of the Valley Bank.

"Excuse me," Ina Claire said as she approached the bench. "Did either of you see a wagon pass by here a few minutes ago? It had two men—a white man was driving and a black man was with him."

"Can't say we saw 'em, but if you say there was a Negro, why, they ain't but about a couple hundert in the whole territory. If you start lookin', I don't reckon you'll have a hard time findin' him; that is, unless he doesn't want to be found."

"Thank you. You've been most helpful."

Ina Claire looked toward the Hotel Adams. She should go and tell her mother what she was doing, but if she intended to find the two men, she should start now.

When she turned the corner, she saw several men gathered around the O.K. Meat Market. They were all looking up to a balcony with a buggy.

"Now, that's something I've never seen before," Ina Claire said aloud.

"You've not been around here for Halloween

much, I'd guess," a man said. "Our young ruffians pulled this off—and right here on Washington Street. You'd think someone would've heard them last night."

"Why did they do this?"

"Just mischief. A place for nothing and nothing in its place. That's what the hoodlums say," the man said. "I had to get my gate out of my neighbor's tree this morning, but at least they couldn't turn my outhouse over. I had it tied down and it was a good thing, because every other one on my block was tipped."

"We've got the block and tackle in place," a man called from the upper balcony. "I think July and I can lift it, but it's up to you men to keep it from falling."

"July?" Ina Claire was sure Christian had mentioned a man by that name in his note. "Is July a black man?"

"He is. Came here direct from Africa not too long ago."

Ina Claire smiled. She was sure this man would help her find Christian.

Christian turned the buggy up the long drive that led to the Prinsen House.

"Christian, do you think they know?" Phoebe asked.

"Know what?"

"Do you think they know what we did?"

Christian smiled. "They'll only know if they can see that my feet don't touch the ground."

"I'm serious. Don't make it into a joke."

"It's not a joke." Christian took her hand in his. "I've never been happier in my life. Waking up with you at my side, and then—"

"Shush." A blush crept over Phoebe's cheeks. "You must think I'm terrible."

"No, no, no—there isn't a man alive who doesn't want his woman to want his body."

"Am I your woman?"

"What do you think?"

A smile of contentment crossed her face as the buggy stopped in front of the house.

"Mama! You came back." Will came running to them with his arms outstretched.

Phoebe chuckled. "Did you think I wouldn't?" She bent over to hug him.

"I knew you'd come back, and I'm glad Wet came back, too."

"Of course I came back." Christian scooped the boy up in his arms.

Will began to giggle. "July does this, too, only he throws me high up in the air."

"July does that?" Phoebe asked.

Will nodded. "He did it today when he brought those people. The lady said July got a wagon down from a roof."

"July did what?"

"A wagon. It was on a roof and July got it down."

"Who told you that?" Phoebe asked

"I Don't Care."

Will's response confused Phoebe. "What do you mean, you don't care?"

"That's the lady's name. Miz Gwen calls her I Don't Care."

"Ina Claire!" Christian said with a broad smile.

"Ina Claire?" Phoebe asked.

"Yes. The Woodsons. Are they here?" Christian started moving toward the house.

At that moment a young woman came running down the steps of the porch. She ran to Christian with both arms open wide. "Christian!" she shouted happily.

Christian took her in his arms, and she leaned into him, then bent both legs so that her feet were off the ground. He swung her around once before putting her back down. Then, made self-conscious by the display in front of Phoebe, he cleared his throat. "Phoebe, this is Ina Claire Woodson. She and I were together in Kimberley while we were under siege from the Boers. She's the daughter of the engineer who's going to help us with the Salt River water project. Is your father here?"

"Yes, my mother and father are both here. He's with Mr. Prinsen and is anxious to see you."

"Come on, Phoebe, let me introduce you." Christian put his hand on her arm.

"No, you go on. Enjoy your friends. Anyway, I need to get home. Wapi needs us."

"Mama, we can't go yet." Will tugged on his mother's hand. "Miz Gwen made a surprise. She'll be mad if I don't help her eat her peach cobbler." Will covered his mouth with his hand. "Oh, no, I wasn't supposed to tell you."

"Now, you can't get Will in trouble, Phoebe.

You have to stay for peach cobbler," Christian said with a disarming smile. "Besides, if you go now, how will I get home?"

How will I get home? Phoebe had been caught by surprise by the unexpected meeting of Miss Ina Claire, and the obvious familiarity between her and Christian. But Phoebe was somewhat mollified by his question.

"All right." She smiled. "I like Gwen's peach cobbler, too."

When they went inside, Clarence and Millicent Woodson were waiting for them.

"Christian, you look absolutely beautiful." Mrs. Woodson stepped toward him, her arms outstretched.

"And so do you." Christian returned her hug.

"Millicent, I don't think a man likes to be called beautiful"—Clarence Woodson extended his hand—"but you do look a heck of a lot better than you did the last time we saw you. It looks like you've put on a few pounds."

"I believe we can all say that," Christian said.

"Well, after 126 days of thralldom, it's a wonder we didn't all die," Mrs. Woodson said. "How we ever endured that man, I do not know."

"After the siege, you know he was promoted," Christian said. "Now he is Colonel Kekewich."

"Promoted? For what? For making us all eat horsemeat?" Ina Claire asked.

Hearing the word *horsemeat*, Will scrunched up his nose. "Yuckie! Wet, you ate your horse?"

"I didn't eat *my* horse, and I tried to not eat

anybody else's either, but sometimes you have to do things you don't want to do. Like when your mother asks you to do something and you don't want to do it."

"Well, right now I think we should all come into the dining room," Katie Prinsen said. "Phoebe, would you mind stepping into the kitchen? I think Gwen wanted you to help her a minute."

"Of course. Come, Will, let's go see what Miss Gwen needs."

"I want to stay with Wet." Will took Christian's hand in his.

"Don't be bothering him now: he has some catching up to do with his friends."

"You go on. Will and I have manly things to talk about." Christian winked at Phoebe.

"So what happened?" Gwen asked as soon as Phoebe entered the kitchen. "Was it the most relaxing night you've ever had?"

"*Relaxing* isn't exactly the word I would use." Phoebe smiled conspiratorially.

"What do you mean, that isn't the word you would use? Phoebe, what happened?"

"Let's just say that the night was very . . . interesting . . . and let it go at that."

"Phoebe, that isn't fair! You know I've been thinking about you ever since you left yesterday. At least tell me if you enjoyed it."

"Yes, I enjoyed it. I more than enjoyed it. And I can't thank you enough for pushing me into going."

"I can't think of anyone who needed that vacation—short as it was—more than you. I'm so glad you decided to do it."

"Ha! It didn't seem to me like it was my decision to make. If it had been, I wouldn't have gone. I'm glad I did, though." Phoebe was quiet for a moment, then nodded toward the dining room, a questioning expression on her face.

"Ina Claire?" Gwen asked.

"Yes."

"She is a delightful person, I'm sure you are going to like her. Even under the circumstances."

"That's what I want to know. What are the circumstances?"

"Apparently Ina Claire, as well as her mother and father, were trapped in Kimberley for several weeks—months, even—while the city was under siege. I'm sure she and Christian became very good friends during that time. Who wouldn't under such circumstances? But I'm equally sure that friendship is all it was. Come, we'd better get dinner on the table."

15

Everyone else had already found seats when Phoebe and Gwen came in with the food. Will was sitting next to Christian, and Ina Claire had taken the seat on the other side of Christian.

"If you will, put the food on the table," Katie said. "I want our guests to partake in our bounty as a part of our family. Gwen, you can't believe what these people have had to endure. I had no idea it was that bad."

"It wasn't all bad," Ina Claire said, her expression filled with adoration as she looked toward Christian.

Seeing her gaze, Phoebe had a sinking feeling in the pit of her stomach. Who was Ina Claire Woodson to Christian?

When the food was on the table, she took one

of the two remaining seats, choosing the one closest to Will.

Yhomas Prinsen asked that everyone hold hands, and then he said grace, thanking God for bringing the Woodsons and Christian through their recent ordeal.

After what seemed to Phoebe a meal that went on forever, Yhomas invited Clarence and Christian into his library.

"Shall we let this man know what you've gotten him into?" Yhomas asked as he put his hand on Christian's back. "Are you ready to go out on a bivouac?"

Phoebe heard Yhomas's comment just before he closed the door. Did he mean Christian would be gone for a while? And if so, would the whole Woodson family go, too?

"Come, ladies, shall we retire to the parlor?" Katie Prinsen asked.

"I'd love to, but I must be going," Phoebe said.

"Nonsense," Katie said. "Will is with Gwen's girls, so he'll be fine. And besides, you should take advantage of this little tête-à-tête among us women."

"Maybe Miss . . . I'm sorry, dear, I don't remember your name," Mrs. Woodson said.

"I'm Phoebe Sloan. Mrs. Phoebe Sloan." She didn't know why it was important to add the *Mrs.*, but she did.

"I didn't know you were married," Ina Claire said.

"She's a widow," Gwen said.

"I'm so sorry," Mrs. Woodson said. "My daughter was acting quite the quidnunc when she made her comment, and I apologize for her."

"Mama! I didn't mean anything by my question. I hardly think I was gossiping."

"Of course you weren't, my dear," Katie said. "It was an honest inquiry, and I'm sure Phoebe wasn't offended."

"I was not," Phoebe said. "After all, I have a son."

"A son who idolizes Christian," Gwen said. "Tell me, ladies, how did you find South Africa?"

"It was easy to find: we just got into a ship and sailed southeast for a long time," Ina Claire quipped.

Phoebe laughed. While she and Ina Claire were possibly going to be rivals for Christian's attention, Ina Claire obviously had a sense of humor.

"Ina Claire, there's no need for you to be so flippant," Mrs. Woodson said.

"I'm sorry, Mrs. Bucknell. Please forgive me for being"—Ina Claire paused and looked at her mother—"flippant."

"Nonsense, there's nothing to forgive. And I'm not 'Mrs. Bucknell,' please. I'm 'Gwen.' "

"And I'm 'Phoebe.' But I am interested in Katie's question. What did you think of South Africa?" Phoebe wasn't just being nice. She really did want to hear Ina Claire's opinion of Christian's homeland.

"Cape Town is an absolutely beautiful city," Ina Claire said. "Most of the people we met were quite wonderful, both the Brits and the Afrikaners. And the indigenous people were friendly and hardworking—at least, those we knew at Kimberley."

"What took you to Kimberley if Cape Town was so beautiful?" Gwen asked.

"Diamonds," Mrs. Woodson said. "My husband is an engineer and he worked with George Labram at the De Beers mine. George was a brilliant man. He was killed one week before the siege was lifted."

"He was an American, too, so we were very close to him," Ina Claire said.

For nearly an hour, Ina Claire and her mother held the ladies spellbound with tales of the ordeal of living in South Africa in the middle of a war. They told of how everything was controlled by martial law, how they could not take a bath or water a garden, how the food was rationed from the beginning, and how the bombardment went on every day except Sundays.

"Oh, that sounds awful! How did you ever get through all that?" Phoebe asked.

"I'm not sure that I could have gotten through it if Christian hadn't been there."

"Yes, from what I know of Christian, he'd be just the type of person you would want at a time like that," Phoebe said.

"We had diversions. We read a lot and played cards when we could, and when the candles had to be put out at nine o'clock, we looked for balloons," Ina Claire said.

"You looked for balloons at night?" Gwen asked.

"Yes," Ina Claire laughed. "But they weren't real. Often in the afternoons there were observation balloons aloft, and when we saw them, we'd get our hopes up, thinking that the British column was coming—but it never did. Then at night some joker would come rushing out with his field glasses and yell 'Balloon!' and like lemmings we would come out and stare at the sky.

"We'd all grab our blankets and go to our usual spots, searching the heavens, trying to find the star that most resembled a balloon. You had to choose a star and fix a steady gaze on it for ten minutes. If it moved, you knew you were looking at a planet. Venus made a nice balloon, but Jupiter and Mercury had a lot of people who thought they were the nicest. Christian liked Mars. He used to tell me he thought it was inhabited, and we decided it had to be the British who got there first. And then there was the Southern Cross, with its five unmistakable stars.

"Sometimes, while we were lying together on the debris heap, Christian would tell me about the places he'd been and the people he'd met and the things he'd done. And for that little piece of time, he made me forget that I was so hungry, I could quite literally eat a horse." Ina Claire laughed again. "He used to say someday we would laugh about everything we were going through, and he was right."

"He was wonderful," Mrs. Woodson said. "We were so disappointed when he couldn't come see us when he was in New York, but now fate has brought us together again. We're so happy to be in Arizona."

"And we're very happy that you're here," Katie said.

Phoebe didn't comment. She couldn't. A lump had formed in her throat that was so large, she thought it'd take her breath. In one evening, any hope of a future with Christian had disappeared.

The library door opened and the three men emerged, the smell of cigar smoke emanating from the room.

"Yhomas, were you smoking a cigar?" Katie asked.

"Yes, that's what a library is for—a place for gentlemen to enjoy one another's company, imbibe a good glass of spirits, and smoke some aromatic tobacco. And what has been happening in the parlor? I daresay you ladies have been chatting a bit."

Yhomas put his finger to his chin and cocked his head. "Do you think the Empire front and princess back looks better, or how about the princess front with the Watteau back? Which is best?"

"Yhomas! I can't believe you." Katie's cheeks began to color.

Yhomas laughed. "Now, tell me, my dear wife, how many times have you asked me these very questions? Wouldn't you rather have these lovely ladies' opinions instead of from one who doesn't know the difference between a pleat and a tuck?"

Katie shook her head. "You have to get used to it—in fact, all of you do. You have to understand that women talk about weighty things just as much as men do. We just choose not to smoke cigars."

"If you're going to talk like this now, what'll it be like when these suffragettes get women the right to vote? We will never have any peace," Yhomas said. "But, speaking of peace, I think you'll get some tomorrow. Christian and I think Clarence should ride up to the Tonto Basin to get the 'lay of the land,' so to speak, before he meets with the committee. Mrs. Woodson, I do hope you have no objections."

"Of course not. That's why we came here."

"Just so you know, we'll be gone at least a week," Yhomas added.

"Oh, would it be all right if I come as well?" Ina Claire asked. "I'd love to camp out for a few days. Especially if we're not dodging cannon shells," she added with a smile.

"I don't think it'd be very convenient, my dear," Yhomas said. "We'll have only one tent, you see."

"You stay here and help your mother get settled," Clarence said. "Until I see how long I'll be needed, we need to find temporary lodging."

"Yes, sir, I understand," Ina Claire said.

"Nonsense," Katie said. "There's no need for you to look anywhere else. We have plenty of room, and Gwen and I love to have other women around."

"I appreciate that," Clarence said, "but it has to be on a temporary basis."

"You're free to stay as long as you like."

"Speaking of which, I'd better get Will back home before he forgets where he lives," Phoebe said.

"Mama, I won't forget. Come on, Wet, let's go home."

Christian knelt down beside the boy. "Will, I can't go with you tonight. Mr. Prinsen told me we have to get up before the sun comes up in the morning. Now, would you want me to wake you up so early?"

Will's eyes grew large. "Who's going to put me in bed tonight?"

Christian pulled the boy to him. "You're a big boy and I need you to take care of your mother while I'm gone. You remember how sick she was? Well, she needs you to be strong. Can you do that?"

Will nodded, but he didn't say anything.

Christian hugged him. "Let's go find your things and then you can help me bring the buggy around."

Phoebe watched Christian interact with Will. Was Christian slipping away from them? Was he just letting Will down easily, and by extension her? It was going to be a long week until he came back. The question was: Would he be coming back to her?

On the drive home, Will kept up a running commentary about everything that had happened during her absence. He recalled Hannah's taking his picture with her new Kodak folding camera, and how he and Adeline had written a story. Then they helped Miss Gwen pick up the pears that had fallen so she could make preserves.

"But, Mama, Hannah and Adeline couldn't play in the daytime. When do I get to go to school?"

"It will be a while," Phoebe said, not being any more specific.

She was glad that Will had been so talkative because it helped keep her mind off the evening. But after she put Will to bed and crawled into her own, her mind began to wander.

How could one of the happiest days of her life have turned so miserable? When she and Christian had left Hot Springs, she was sure her relationship with him was on solid ground.

"Am I your woman?" she'd asked.

"What do you think?" he'd answered. Why couldn't Christian have said, "Yes, I love you, and I want to be by your side forever."

There had never been a suggestion of marriage, but Phoebe had assumed that would be the natural outcome. He was so good with Will, with mutual affection between them.

But tonight, when Mrs. Woodson had suggested that "fate has brought us together again," Phoebe had been jolted back to reality. Christian had had another life before he came to America. In passing, he'd told her bits and pieces of his history, but he'd never shared the things Ina Claire and her mother had talked about this evening.

As Phoebe had sat across the table from them,

she had watched Ina Claire fawn over every word Christian said, as if she were entranced by him. But when her mother said "Fate has brought us together again," Ina Claire's expression could only be described as pure joy.

Phoebe had no doubt that Ina Claire Woodson was in love with Christian De Wet.

And so was Phoebe Sloan.

But the question was: Did she have the will to fight for him?

Out at the Tonto Basin, Christian, Yhomas, and Clarence examined the dam site. Yhomas pointed out what they intended to use as the catchment basin and where the dam should be built. Clarence got out the transit and level, and the tripod, and measured from one side of the gorge to the other, establishing the distance as well as the angle of inclination with the help of the other two men.

That night they cooked bacon and beans over an open fire. As the fire burned, glowing embers drifted up to add pinpoints of red to the myriad stars in the night sky.

"Look at that." Yhomas pointed to the vault of blackness. "I wonder how many stars there are."

"If you're talking only about the stars visible to the naked eye," Clarence said, "it's a total of about nine thousand, but that's in the total sky from both hemispheres. It breaks down to about forty-five hundred depending on the season of the year and where you're located on the face of the earth."

"Don't tell me you've counted all the stars. I know that engineers love numbers, but this . . ." Yhomas said.

"I haven't, but some astronomers have."

Yhomas laughed. "Now, you show me a man who has counted every star in the night sky, and I'll show you a man who has nothing to do."

In the distance, they heard a long, plaintive howl.

"What sort of creature is that?" Christian asked.

"A coyote—nothing to worry about. They're afraid to come around people."

A few minutes later they heard another sound, heavy and long, rising and falling, sort of an *oh wouh uu* sound.

"And that, my friend, is a mountain lion," Yhomas said. "We don't want to run into one of those if we can avoid it."

Christian stretched and yawned. "Well, you two can talk all night if you want. Neither one of you had to move around much today. But Clarence had me running all over the place with that blasted measuring stick of his."

"A surveying rod," Clarence said. "If you're going to be an engineer's assistant, you have to know the terminology."

Throughout the week, Clarence continued his work. Then he announced that he thought he had enough data to make his assessment, and after taking a few bore samples they'd be ready to go home.

Christian had enjoyed the time spent with Yhomas and Clarence. Although he'd teased Clarence about being run around, he was actually enjoying it. During the surveying, he was separated enough from the other two that it was almost as if he were alone. He'd heard no sound made by man, only the sounds of nature: the rattle of ocotillo limbs moving in the wind, the quiet scurrying of a desert mouse, or the occasional coo-coo-cooing call of a roadrunner. He liked the towering and graceful saguaro cactus, extending its arms as if reaching for the sky, and he was particularly impressed by the variegated hues of the mesas that rose from the desert floor.

His stay in the desert had been much more pleasant than he'd anticipated, and he found himself thinking about how he would enjoy camping out here with Will when the boy was old enough. He fantasized that they might shoot some game, and he, Phoebe, and Will could cook it over a fire.

Hmm, how had Phoebe worked her way into his thoughts? He wondered what she was doing this week while he was gone. He'd asked her if he could court her, but she didn't quite understand that he was serious. When he'd asked her if she'd let someone fall in love with her, Phoebe had deflected her answer by saying that Will loved her.

What did she think of Christian?

He wished he knew the answer.

Clarence said he'd be finished with his surveying today, so Christian walked slowly back to the campsite to begin packing up.

He'd brought his Martini rifle and had intended to fire it, but Clarence had kept him so busy, he hadn't found the time. He'd hoped he might see a bighorn sheep while they were here, but that opportunity never presented itself. He was determined to find a target to shoot at, just so he could zero in on the sights; so as Yhomas continued striking their camp, and Clarence made a few final drawings, Christian loaded the rifle, sliding the long, slender .303-caliber round into the chamber, then lifted the lever.

Clarence was squatting under a rock overhang, boring out a rock sample, when a mountain lion appeared on the precipice, about ten feet above him.

"Oh, my God, look!" Yhomas pointed to the lion.

"Maybe I can scare him away." Christian raised the rifle to his shoulder and sighted in on the animal. It was magnificent, and he didn't want to shoot it.

"Woodson, look out!" Yhomas yelled.

Whether activated by the shout or by Clarence's sudden move, the lion leaped. Christian fired, and his bullet struck the cat in midair. It fell to the ground exactly where Clarence had been but a moment before.

"What the . . . ?" Clarence shouted.

"Get back!" Yhomas called. "The cat might just be wounded."

Clarence moved away several feet, keeping a wary eye on the lion. When the lion didn't move, he started back toward it, taking slow and cautious steps, examining the creature closely. Then, boldly, he moved right up to it.

"Beware, Clarence," Yhomas said.

Clarence chuckled. "Beware of what? This cat is as dead as a doornail. Great shot, my friend."

"It's a wonder I made the shot at all," Christian said. "This rifle seems to be a bit out of balance. It's somewhat stock-heavy."

"There's your problem," Yhomas said. "The butt plate looks like brass, but I wouldn't be surprised if it was brass-plated lead."

Christian looked at the butt plate. "You might be right."

"Well," Clarence said, "I'd say that's a fitting conclusion to our exploration."

Clarence's close call was the subject of conversation when the men returned home.

"You should have skinned him," Andy said. "You could've hung the skin on the wall as a trophy."

"I didn't want a trophy," Christian said. "I really wish it hadn't been necessary for me to shoot him: he was a magnificent animal."

"Well, you should've brought him back for me. I'd be glad to hang a pelt like that," Andy said.

"Isn't that July?" Yhomas asked as he saw an approaching buckboard.

"It's him. I hope there's nothing wrong at Phoebe's place." Christian's words and expression showed genuine concern.

"July," Christian said, greeting him as he came in. "Is everything all right?"

"Yes. I wasn't expecting to see you here."

"We rode in pretty late last night and decided to spend the night here."

"Well, you got here at the right time. Phoebe thinks we should pluck the birds today, and she sent me over to get Andy to come help us out— that is, if it's all right with you, Mr. Prinsen."

"Of course Andy can go help," Yhomas said.

"Would it be all right if I went, too?" Ina Claire asked. "I'm not sure there'd be anything I could do, but I don't have anything to do here."

"I'm sure Phoebe would be glad to have you." Yhomas chuckled. "Everybody needs to be around for a plucking at least once in their lifetime."

16

"**W**et, you're back!" Will ran out to meet the buckboard, his arms spread wide.

Christian jumped out of the wagon before July stopped it and scooped Will up into his arms. He whirled him around in the air, causing the child to giggle uncontrollably.

"Did you miss me?" Christian asked.

"I really, really did." Will planted a big kiss on Christian's cheek.

"Now, that's a welcome." Christian turned and saw Phoebe coming out of the house.

Phoebe had wanted to run to Christian and kiss him as well, but when she saw Ina Claire, she held back, saying, "Will speaks for both of us. I missed you, too."

Christian smiled at her. "It's good to be missed."

Turning to Ina Claire, Phoebe said, "Ina Claire, I'm happy to see you again."

"I hope you don't mind I came, too."

"Of course not. We can always use another pair of hands to sort feathers."

"I'm glad she came along," Christian said. "We greenhorns need to stick together."

"A greenhorn? Do you mean to tell me you've never seen an ostrich plucked?" Phoebe asked.

"That is correct, madam," Christian said with an exaggerated nod. "I've seen my share of ostriches running wild on the Karoo and I've eaten ostrich eggs, but this'll be the first time I've ever seen the taking of the feathers."

"It's not a particularly hard job," Andy said, "but it is . . . how should we say it, Phoebe?"

"It's messy." A wide smile crossed her face.

"You're going to miss seeing the hard part," July said, "because Trinidad and I already brought them in from their pens. I'm glad you don't have any more adult birds than you do, Phoebe, because you can't bring in more than two or three at a time."

"That doesn't make sense," Ina Claire said. "Why couldn't you bring them all in at once?"

"The males are very feisty, and I guess the females would be, too, if they thought another female was trying to take their mate." July looked directly at Phoebe when he said these words.

"Well, they're all in the plucking pen now, so we'd better get organized. Andy, why don't we all step onto the porch for a cup of coffee and you can tell our greenhorns what they can expect," Phoebe said.

A short while later, they all gathered at what Phoebe called a pen but July insisted was a kraal. This small enclosure forced the birds to crowd together so that the more disagreeable birds wouldn't have a chance to attack. All one could see was a forest of long necks, huge eyes, and gaping beaks. Since their normal routine had been drastically interrupted, the birds were all emitting short, hollow sounds that sounded like a cross between a grunt and a cough.

"This isn't exactly how I pictured this," Ina Claire said, "but I'm ready to do whatever you say, Phoebe."

"At this stage, it's better that you and I just stand back and watch," Phoebe said. "The men do this part."

"Is Wet going to die?" Will's eyes were large and questioning.

"No, honey, he's not. You see how close the wood is in the plucking box. If a bird started kicking, the sides of the box would stop him from hurting anyone."

"I don't want Wet to die."

"Neither do I." Phoebe put her arm around her son.

Ina Claire was curious about Will's seeming fascination that something might happen to Christian. "Phoebe, I don't understand. Why would Will ask such a thing?"

"Will saw his father killed by an ostrich."

"Oh!" Ina Claire gasped. "Oh, you poor child, what a terrible thing for you to have seen!"

Ina Claire leaned over and wrapped her arms around the child. Phoebe thought Will might resist the embrace and was surprised that he didn't. She was also surprised to see that Ina Claire's eyes had welled with tears. Her concern for Will was genuine.

"I'm not sure that he's ever gotten over it," Phoebe said, remembering his reaction to her own injury.

"I can see how such a thing could be so traumatic—for anyone, especially someone as young as Will. Oh, but, Phoebe, you have done such a wonderful job with him. The Prinsens and the Bucknells think the world of him, and I can see why. He is such a delightful child."

Phoebe could see exactly how Christian could have found comfort in Ina Claire's company when they were in Africa. She was a good woman.

Christian and July cautiously singled out the first bird. They guided him away from the rest of the troop, and July, coming from behind, slipped a black hood over the ostrich's head. Once he was covered, he was easily maneuvered into the narrow plucking box. Trinidad stood on one side and Andy was on the other. July followed the bird into the box and began removing the tail feathers while Andy and Trinidad, with a few rapid snips of their shears, took the wing feathers.

"Now it's your turn, Christian. Try to tie all the

feathers of the same length together and then hand them over to Phoebe. The actual sorting will come later," Andy said. "Open the front gate and let this poor critter out. We've got fifty-one more birds to go."

Phoebe always thought the birds seemed somewhat crestfallen when they ran off, as if they were humiliated by their ordeal. She smiled when she thought of the first plucking she and Edwin had tried to do by themselves. It was nearly a disaster—Edwin thought it was inhumane to take the feathers, but Phoebe convinced him that cutting the feathers didn't hurt the birds, and besides, it was the only way they were going to make any money.

"Ina Claire, you and Will can carry some of these bundles up to the house. Leave them on the porch, because most of them will be quite dirty," Phoebe said.

When the plucking was over, a long, busy day of sorting began. Everything had to give way to the feathers, which had to be washed, starched, and sized before they were tied into bundles. The entire surface of the porch was covered with feathers, with more feathers spilling into the kitchen. The table, the chairs, the floor—every place had an assigned size where the feathers would be grouped.

"I had no idea there were so many kinds of feathers and that you'd have to sort them out," Ina Claire said.

"It's all about money." Phoebe picked up one particularly long, graceful feather. "On the London market, this feather could fetch as much as sixty to eighty dollars."

"For one feather?" Ina Claire asked. "That seems hard to believe. Who would pay that?"

"Don't say that around Mr. Prinsen," Andy said. "He intends to make the Salt River Valley competitive with the biggest ostrich ranches in South Africa."

"But it still comes back to who wants one of these," Ina Claire said.

"They've been around for a long time," Christian said. "Themei, the Egyptian goddess, wears one. It's the symbol of justice because it is perfectly even and equal on both sides."

"I don't know about that," Phoebe said, "but as long as women in high society want feathers, I intend to see that they're available."

"What about the boos, Mama? Who wants these?" Will threw a handful into the air.

"Now, there's a future feather man." Christian moved over to bundle some of the tail feathers, which were indeed called boos. "It looks to me like these would make good feather dusters."

"I think these are Wapi's feathers," Will said. "Can I make a duster out of him?"

"And who is Wapi?" Ina Claire asked.

"He's our pet ostrich," Phoebe said.

"Wapi can talk," Will said.

"Really? Wapi can talk?" Ina Claire had a questioning look.

"July says parrots can talk, and ostriches are bigger than parrots."

Ina Claire laughed. "That's true. Ostriches are certainly a lot bigger than parrots. What does Wapi say to you?"

"He doesn't talk to me. Wapi can only talk Afrikaans, so July and Wet are the only ones who know what he says."

"If he came from Africa, I can understand that," Ina Claire said, smiling, and obviously enjoying her play with Will.

"July's teaching me how to talk Afrikaans. Then Wapi can talk to me. You want to hear me say something?"

"Yes, I would," Ina Claire said.

"My *naam* is Will *en ek vier jaar oud*. Do you know what I said?"

"I do. You said your name is Will and you're four years old."

Will's eyes widened and his mouth opened in surprise. "You can talk Afrikaans?"

"I know a few words, but not enough to talk to Wapi."

Phoebe watched the interaction between Ina Claire and her son. During the evening at the Prinsens', she'd felt disquieted while listening to what the young woman had gone through. That night, she'd definitely been jealous, thinking Ina Claire and Christian might have had a romantic involvement; but if Ina Claire was her rival, she wished she could dislike her. Ina Claire had a friendly way about her; it was easy to see that Will was taken with her, and Phoebe had to admit that she liked her as well.

Just then the hall clock struck nine.

"Oh, dear," Ina Claire said, looking toward Andy. "I didn't know it was that late. I need to get back. Are you going back to the Prinsens'?"

"There's no need for that," Phoebe said. "I have plenty of room for everyone. There are three available bedrooms upstairs, since July moved to the bunkhouse."

"There are two rooms," Christian said. "You can't have mine."

Phoebe tossed and turned far into the night. She was extremely tired; the work that day had been exhausting, but here she was wide-awake. Why couldn't she go to sleep?

Even as she asked herself the question, though, she knew exactly what was causing her to be so restless. She couldn't sleep because Christian was in the room just above her. And even more disturbing was that Ina Claire was in the room next to his. She was reasonably certain that Christian wouldn't go to Ina Claire's room tonight, not while he was staying in Phoebe's house. But what if Ina Claire went to his room? Would he be able to resist her? Would he want to?

Two days later Phoebe, Christian, and Will were in the office of J. L. Stein, an ostrich-feather broker who represented the New York market. On a blackboard he'd written the prices per pound, listing the classes of feathers: whites, primes, firsts, feminas, and spadones, among a dozen other classifications. The prices ranged from a high of $300 per pound all the way down to $5 a pound for drabs and tails. Before leaving home, all Phoebe's feathers had been graded, with Andy and July making the final determination.

The feathers were in sacks, each separated by grade. Will insisted on dragging in one bag himself.

Mr. Stein had asked that the feathers be emptied onto a long table in the back of his office so he could gauge them. The primes were brought out first.

"Oh, yes." He separated the bundle into individual feathers. "These are fine feathers, Mrs. Sloan. I do believe you've outdone yourself."

Phoebe was flattered by Mr. Stein's praise. "Thank you. I appreciate that, coming from you, sir."

"I'm not just saying that. The Arizona feathers seem to be more luxuriant than the African. I believe how you grow the alfalfa makes the difference, and when the irrigation system is improved, I think this valley will surpass the biggest producers abroad."

"That would be wonderful," Phoebe said.

Stein inspected each bundle of feathers, and when he was finished, he went to his cash box and began withdrawing money. He counted out $1,170. "I believe this is my best offer, ma'am. I can pay a little more because these feathers will stay in the New York market, and that will save the transport cost to London. I hope this amount meets your expectation."

"I understand." Phoebe desperately tried to control the trembling of her hand as she accepted the money. "Perhaps when you return for the next plucking, you can do better."

"I would hope so. With the US market continuing to grow as it is, I can see a very profitable partnership developing between us. I believe our company will import at least a half million dollars' worth of feathers this year, and there's no reason why feathers from you and your cohorts here in the valley shouldn't become a big part of our inventory."

"I look forward to that, Mr. Stein."

When Phoebe and Christian and Will had walked a short distance from the brokerage house, Phoebe turned to Christian, a broad smile spreading across her face. "I want you to pinch me. I can't believe this."

Will turned to Phoebe and immediately pinched her arm.

"Ouch!"

Christian laughed. "He just did what you told him to."

"I guess I did ask for that. I know you're used to dealing with millions upon millions of dollars, but this is the most money I've ever seen."

"It means more to you because it's yours—you worked for it, you made it. Now that you're a rich woman, what're you going to do with your money?"

"I hardly think I'm rich, but I know the first thing I'm going to buy."

"And what is that? A new hat, maybe even one with an ostrich feather?"

"I'm going to buy a pound of butter—no, make that a keg of butter!"

Christian laughed as the three of them continued down the street to the Maricopa Loan and Trust.

When they entered, Phoebe stepped up to the teller. "I'd like to make a deposit."

"Yes, ma'am," the teller said. "And your name is . . . ?

"Phoebe Sloan."

The teller checked his register. "Just a moment, ma'am, I need to get Mr. Forbes." He went into a room walled off with glass and soon returned with the president of the Loan and Trust.

Charles Forbes stepped to the window. "Good morning, Mrs. Sloan, Mr. Henshaw says you want to make a deposit."

"Is there something wrong with that?" Christian asked.

"Does this gentleman speak for you?" Mr. Forbes asked.

"I speak for myself, but to repeat his question, is there something wrong with my making a deposit?"

"If you recall, I lowered your interest rate when you made your mortgage payment in June, but your part of the bargain was to pay five percent. I'm afraid there was an error in our calculations. You owe an additional thirty-eight dollars."

"Was the error on the part of Mrs. Sloan, or was it on the part of the bank?" Christian asked.

"It doesn't matter. She didn't live up to her part of the bargain."

Christian withdrew a money clip from his pocket and pulled off two $20 notes and laid them on the counter. "Now she's paid."

"Christian, you don't have to do that. Take your money back." Phoebe opened her reticule and took out the cash she had received from Mr. Stein. "I believe you said thirty-eight dollars." She counted out the exact amount. "Now, I want to know what kind of interest you're paying on savings."

"That felt good," Phoebe said as she, Christian, and Will walked back out to the wagon. "Ever since Edwin died, I've struggled, and now for the first time I have enough money to take care of the next mortgage payment and still have enough to support Will and me."

"Do you know what I think?"

"What?"

"It calls for a celebration. Suppose we go to the Phoenix Restaurant and have something to eat."

"What's a restaurant?" Will asked.

"It's time you found out, my boy," Christian said as they headed for the courthouse plaza.

17

Will looked around the Phoenix Restaurant with an expression of awe. "Mama, look at all the people sitting at the tables. The people who live here sure do have a lot of company."

"They do indeed," Christian said with a little laugh.

They were met by the maître d', who escorted them to a table, then left a menu with Christian and Phoebe.

"Why don't I get one?" Will asked.

"Well, little man, if you want a menu, I shall certainly give you one," the maître d' said.

After Christian explained the purpose of the menu, Will challenged him. "You mean all I have to do is say what I want to eat and they'll bring it?"

"Sure, if they have it."

"Do they have apple pie?"

"Yes, here it is, right here."

"I want apple pie."

"That's for dessert. You'll have to order something else first." Phoebe said.

"Wet said I could have anything I wanted."

"I did say that, Phoebe. And since this is his first experience with a restaurant, shouldn't he get whatever he wants?"

"Ohhh, you are spoiling him rotten," Phoebe said, though her complaint was ameliorated by a broad smile.

A few minutes later, while Christian ate lamb chops and Phoebe had baked chicken, Will was enjoying a slice of apple pie.

"How is your chicken?" Christian asked.

"You know what I like best about it?"

"What's that?"

"I didn't have to cook it."

Christian laughed. "Well, I can see how that might appeal to you."

"This is the first time I've been in here." Phoebe glanced around the room.

"Edwin didn't like this restaurant?"

"No, you don't understand. This is the first time I've been in any restaurant since I came to Arizona. I think"—Phoebe glanced over at Will, who was enjoying his pie—"I think Edwin didn't particularly want to be seen in public with me."

"Edwin must have been a"—Christian started to say that Edwin was a fool, but didn't want to say so in front of Will—"very busy man, not to have time to take his family out on occasion."

"He was." Phoebe knew exactly what Christian was about to say, and why he didn't.

A man stepped up to their table then and said by way of introduction, "Amon Hancock."

"Yes, Captain, I remember you." Christian started to stand, but Hancock held his hand out.

"No, stay seated; you and Mrs. Sloan enjoy your meal. I just wanted to say that I've looked over the report that you, Thomas, and this Woodson fellow prepared. I'm really beginning to believe that we'll get this water project done after all."

"Oh, that would be wonderful!" Phoebe said.

"Yes, ma'am, it truly would." Hancock looked at Will. "Maybe by the time this young fellow is a grown man, the valley will have so much water that it'll truly be a Garden of Eden. Well, I'll leave you; please forgive the intrusion. I just wanted to express my appreciation for what you're doing."

"That was very nice of him," Phoebe said after Hancock walked away.

"I'm a little uncomfortable with all the accolades. The project isn't done yet."

"No, but thanks to you, and Mr. Woodson, it will be."

"If so, it'll be because of Clarence, not me."

"I'm glad Mr. Woodson was able to come out here, not only because of the water project, but because it allowed you to reunite with your friends."

"It was good to see them again."

"Tell me about Ina Claire."

"What do you want to know?"

"I heard the talk about the siege, and how terrible it was. Ina Claire says she doesn't think she could have gotten through it if you hadn't been there to help her."

"That may be true, but she also helped me. Seeing a strong woman having to go through all of that made me stronger."

"But the time you two spent together wasn't all bad, was it? Surely you must have something pleasant to look back on."

"Oh, yes. Before the siege, Saturday afternoons were particularly pleasant. There was always some sort of entertainment, whether it was some Brit or Dutch orchestra, with fine instruments and wonderful music, or a Kaffir band put together from the diamond-mine workers, with such instruments as they could gather. Sometimes there'd even be dances."

"I expect Ina Claire is a very good dancer."

"Much better than I am. What about you? Do you enjoy dancing?"

"It's been a very long time since I've been to a dance."

"Really? Well, then, we'll have to go sometime."

"No, I'm sure I've forgotten how to dance. That's something for you and Ina Claire. She is"— Phoebe paused, trying to come up with the correct word—"a most captivating young woman. One can't help but like her."

"She is an extraordinary woman. She made living through that awful siege bearable."

"Yes, I can see how she would."

"Phoebe, I want you to know that I think a great deal of Ina Claire. As I told you, I've never had a family of any kind, so that means that people like Ina Claire, her mother and father, are very important to me, and they always will be."

"I understand." But did she?

"Mama, you know what I want for dessert?" Will's question was a welcome interruption to the way the conversation was going.

"What do you mean, dessert? You just had dessert."

"No, that was my dinner. We're in a restaurant and I can have anything I want, remember? That's what Wet said. I had apple pie for my dinner, and now, for dessert, I want cherry pie."

"Will . . ." Phoebe said.

"Oh, indulge him just this once," Christian said. "After all, this is his first time ever in a restaurant. We should make it memorable for him."

Phoebe shook her head. "I can tell, right now, that if the two of you gang up on me, I'll never have a chance."

At the same time Christian, Phoebe, and Will were in the restaurant, many of the city's elite were having lunch in the Phoenix Country Club. Here, at the "Bankers' Table," business competition was left behind as the bankers celebrated their affluence and importance to the city. W. F.

and Frank Sloan were both there, as well as the officers of several of the other banks. Daniel Murphy, president of the Prescott National Bank, was in town, and everyone was commiserating with him over his brother's loss in his bid to be Arizona's delegate to Congress.

"There had to be some kind of shenanigans going on," Murphy said. "He shouldn't have lost."

"At least Oakes will keep his job as governor," Frank said as he took out his pocketknife and began to pare his fingernails. "Bryant didn't have a chance against McKinley."

"No, there was no question McKinley was going to win the presidency," Charles Forbes said. "Now we'll just have to wait and see if Marcus Smith can get some traction on our petition for statehood. I'd feel a lot better if we'd elected a Republican."

"I don't think there's a chance we'll get anything done on statehood until we get the water situation settled," Emil Ganz said.

"Yhomas Prinsen brought in this new engineer Ben Fowler hired," Bill Ainsworth said. "Named Woodson. He seemed like a nice enough fellow, but I don't know what he can do."

"The question is what can that other South African do—the one who supposedly worked for Cecil Rhodes? Fowler says he's come up with a plan to get the money without relying on the government," Ganz said.

"You mean Christian De Wet?" Ainsworth asked.

"Christian? That's not a very common name

around here. Is this fellow tall . . . sandy hair, wears tall boots and jodhpurs?" Charles Forbes asked.

"That's him," Frank said. "I think he's pulling a fast one. There's no way he worked for Cecil Rhodes."

"Frank, why do you say that? Have you met this man?" W.F. asked.

"Damned right I've met him. Pop, that's the guy who's moved in with Phoebe."

"Well, now, that explains things," Charles Forbes said. "Your sister-in-law came into the bank this morning. She deposited quite a bundle of cash, but this guy—I seem to recall now, she did call him Christian—offered to pay off her interest and she wouldn't let him."

"A bundle of cash? I wonder where she came up with that?" W.F. asked.

"Well, you can be sure she didn't make it off those damned birds," Frank said. "She probably thinks she's hit the mother lode with this guy. You say he offered to pay her interest?"

"He did," Forbes said. "Had a wad of cash."

W.F. shook his head. "Poor little Will. What's going to become of him?"

"You don't have to worry about him, Pop." Frank opened his hand where his knife lay. "Every morning when I drop my brother's knife into my pocket, I make a vow that I won't allow that woman to ruin his son."

When Christian, Phoebe, and Will returned to the farm, Ina Claire was sitting in the front porch swing with Andy Patterson, and they were laughing.

"I was beginning to think you two ran off with the money," Andy said as he rose from the swing. "It's about time you got here."

"Wet took me to a restaurant," Will said. "Do you know you can eat anything you want there? And nobody has to cook?"

"Someone had to cook the food, but it wasn't your mother," Phoebe said. "Andy, Mr. Stein was amazed at what a good job you'd done grading the feathers. He accepted every one in the grade we delivered."

Andy beamed with Phoebe's compliment. "I'm glad it turned out that way, but it was really July who made the final decisions. The more I'm around that man, the more I admire him."

"He's a good man," Christian said. "You both are."

"Well, I'm going to be in a heap of trouble if I don't get you back over to Mr. Prinsen's. He says the Board of Trade is having a meeting with the Water Storage Committee, and he thinks you should be there."

"Is it at Yhomas's house?" Christian asked.

"No, I think he said it'd be at the Dorris Theater, so we'd better hurry if you're going to make it in time."

"All right, just let me step inside and get a jacket. I need to look like I know something if anybody asks me a question."

"I think I'll go back with you," Ina Claire said.

"I want to tell my mother about all the work it takes just so she can have a feather in her hat."

When Christian stepped out onto the porch, he'd put on a brown cashmere jacket. He had a black strip of cloth in his hand. "Do you think I should put on this butterfly?"

"A butterfly? You can't wear a butterfly," Will said.

"I guess that takes care of it." Christian laughed. "If Will says I can't wear a butterfly, then I won't." He handed the tie to Phoebe. "I don't suppose I'll be back tonight." Then he did something unexpected. He kissed Phoebe in full view of both Ina Claire and Andy.

"Mama, Wet kissed you," Will said with a big-eyed expression.

"Yes, he did," Phoebe said with no embarrassment.

"All right, Will. I'm leaving you in charge. Can you do that for me?" Christian asked as he climbed up into the wagon.

"Yes, sir." Will stepped over in front of Phoebe.

Phoebe watched as the wagon pulled away. She'd never felt happier in her life. Her grand experiment with the ostriches had paid off, and she now had money, but most of all, there was no question she was in love with Christian De Wet.

Christian, Yhomas, and Clarence Woodson went directly to the Dorris Theater, where about fifty men were gathered.

"I didn't think you were going to make it on

time," Captain Hancock said when Yhomas stepped down from the surrey. "Ben is back from Washington and he's brought some gasbags with him."

Yhomas laughed. "I take it they don't agree that we should own the water rights outright."

"That's it," the captain said, "and I'm afraid they've convinced Ben that the government route is the way to go."

"It may be," Christian said. "I know it'd be possible to raise the capital privately, but it would take a lot of cajoling."

"More like horse trading," Captain Hancock said. "Already Alexander Chandler and Dwight Heard are maneuvering to make certain they increase their advantages."

"Do you think the committee still needs my services?" Woodson asked.

"Depends on whether or not they agree with what you've come up with. We'd better go on in now."

Captain Hancock led the way, and the four found seats near the front of the theater. When they were seated, Ben Fowler began to speak.

"I want to thank all of you who came out tonight. It is my privilege to introduce several dignitaries among us. First, there's the secretary of the interior, Ethan Hitchcock—I'll be glad to serve as his interpreter for those of you who can't understand him."

Several of the men cast questioning glances toward one another.

Then the gentleman in question rose from

his chair. "Despite what Ben says, ya'll won't be needin' any interpreter. I'll just slow down a little mo', and when ya'll come on down to Mobile, why, ya'll will fit right in."

The room erupted with laughter.

"His accent takes a little getting used to, but talking to Yhomas Prinsen gave me good practice before I went to Washington," Ben said.

"Hear, hear," several others called.

"That brings me to George Maxwell, and believe me, the people in Washington understand him. What shall I say your position is, George?"

"I prefer to be called an irrigation propagandist," the man seated beside the secretary said.

"He'd rather be called that than a wire-puller," Fowler said, "but he's a lobbyist through and through. If he can do for us what he's done for California, we'll have our water project, and we won't be out a penny of our own money."

Captain Hancock took a deep breath and said, "That's what we're all afraid of," his voice audible only to Christian.

For the next hour both Hitchcock and Maxwell advocated for the government to step in and take over the project, while several others advanced their ideas that the local people should control their own water. When the subject of money was brought up, they turned to Christian, and he methodically laid out his plan again. However, he could tell that the enthusiasm was rapidly turning toward government financing.

When the merits of the project had been discussed ad nauseam, Fowler introduced Frederick Newell, the surveyor from Washington, and finally he called on Yhomas to introduce Clarence.

"Thank you, Yhomas," Clarence said when he got up to speak. "Gentlemen, I wasn't sure what I was getting into when I came here, and I don't know anything about the annual rainfall, or how much water you expect to move, but I can say that, in my opinion, where you've chosen to locate the dam is excellent. The gorge offers a favorable site for a masonry dam, and the sedimentary formation, with the strata inclined about thirty degrees to the horizontal, and dipping toward the reservoir, is a most favorable condition, both for retaining water and the stability of the dam. The foundation and rock abutments are excellent. In short, gentlemen, I see no geological or physical impediments to this project."

"Mr. Newell, do you have anything to add?" Fowler asked.

"Nothing," Newell said, "except that I agree entirely with Mr. Woodson and I congratulate him on the excellence of his report."

"Then, if that's the case, I make a motion that we hire the man. Are there any objections?"

The next morning Phoebe was still in a good mood. Will was sleeping later than usual, and she was out watering the orange trees that Katie Prinsen had given her. Even though the trees were young, they'd bloomed, and she now had several oranges beginning to color. She hoped she could find a piece of fruit that was sufficiently ripe for Will to pick. Then she heard a vehicle approach. Smiling, she was sure it'd be Christian and they could all have breakfast together. But she was immediately on the defensive when she saw that it was Frank.

"Oh, no." A knot formed in her stomach. "I don't need this."

Frank climbed down from the buggy and withdrew a valise from behind the seat. "Get in the house," he said as he advanced toward her. It wasn't a request but an order to which he fully expected compliance.

"Whatever you have to say to me, you can say it right here." Phoebe still clutched the bucket. She felt safer out here. Christian was gone, but July and Trinidad had to be somewhere nearby. She knew all it would take was a scream and one of them would come running.

"Phoebe." Frank's tone of voice changed. He held up the valise. "I have some papers here that are important. They concern Will, and it will be easier for you to examine them if I can spread them out on the table. Please, can we go inside?"

"What do you mean, they concern Will?"

"If you look at them, you'll understand."

Phoebe paused for a moment, then she heard July speaking to Trinidad. If she could hear him that easily when he was just talking, she knew he'd be able to hear her if she screamed.

"All right." She started toward the house.

Once in the kitchen, Frank sat at the table. She was glad to see that he'd chosen the side of the table with his back to the wall and the table between him and the door. If Phoebe needed to run, she'd have a slight advantage.

"My father and I had lunch with Charles Forbes yesterday."

"Oh?"

"He told us you made a rather substantial deposit at the Loan and Trust."

"I did, but I don't see how that's any business of yours."

"Where'd you get the money?"

Phoebe let out a long sigh. "I know you find this hard to believe, but my 'silly little ostrich farm' is making money, in spite of the Sloans."

"May I remind you that you wouldn't have this place without the Sloans—or, more specifically, Aunt Gertrude?"

"I agree, it was Aunt Gertrude's money that allowed Edwin to buy this place, but she didn't leave him enough to pay for it outright. I'm the one who's made this place work, and I'd have a lot more money if you hadn't broken all the eggs in my brooder."

"What makes you think I did that?"

"When you came out here, you knew what'd happened."

"I told you Rojas told me, and Cornello told him."

"That's not possible. Cornello didn't know anything about the eggs, and Trinidad was in jail.

The only way you could have known about my eggs was if you hired someone to break them, or did it yourself."

Frank had no answer. He opened the valise and took out an envelope. "You may say you got that money from all your hard work, but you're not fooling me. I know who you are, and what you are."

"And what's that supposed to mean?"

"Charles Forbes told us about your paramour, how he tried to pay your debt. 'Christian, you don't have to do that. Take your money back,'" Frank said, mimicking a woman's voice.

"Get out! Get out of my house!" Phoebe rose from the table as she pointed toward the door.

"Not so fast. You haven't listened to my offer."

"If it's coming from you, no matter what it is, I'm not interested."

He withdrew a piece of paper from the envelope and slid it across the table. "Take a look at the third paragraph."

Phoebe picked it up and began to read. She furrowed her brow and then turned her eyes toward Frank. "What're you trying to do?"

"Exactly what it says. My father has set up a trust fund for Will."

"But this paper says it's worth twenty-five thousand dollars. That can't be."

"Ha! If you know how much money W. F. Sloan really has, you'd treat us all a lot better."

Phoebe sat down as she continued reading. It stated that Will would have access to the trust when he was eighteen, and that the only stipulation was that he wouldn't leave Arizona.

Frank took out a bottle of ink and a pen. "Will you sign the paper?"

"If the only stipulation is that he stay in Arizona, I have no problem with that. Where do I sign?"

"The last line on the second page. Oh, and make sure you date it." Frank turned the page.

Phoebe took the pen and wrote the date. Then she glanced up at the paragraph above where she would affix her signature.

"Go ahead. Sign it. I need to get back to town."

"Wait. This says that I can't get married. What does that have to do with Will's trust?"

"It's just a precaution. My father wants to ensure that you don't get married and run off with Will or, worse yet, that you let some man come along and adopt his only heir."

"I will not sign this." Phoebe put the pen down and slid the paper across the table. "As I said before, get out of my house." She worked hard to control her anger.

"You oversexed little chippie." Frank's lip curled. "You would throw away Will's inheritance just so you can diddle the South African?"

Phoebe picked up the bucket sitting at her feet. She threw the water at Frank, and it went splattering everywhere.

Wiping his face, Frank turned to her. "Mark my words, you will regret not signing this paper."

18

After Frank left, Phoebe began to clean up the mess she'd made in the kitchen.

"What happened?" Will said. "I heard yelling, and then a loud noise."

"I'm sorry, sweetheart. Come here, I just want to hold you."

"Mama! I'm too big for that."

"I guess you are, but I can still muss up your hair." Phoebe ran her hand through his hair, which showed he'd just climbed out of bed. "What would you like for breakfast?"

A big smile crossed his face. "Can I have anything I want?"

"If we have it, sure. What would you like?"

"I want bread . . . and *butter*." He shouted that last word.

"I think that's a good idea. It's been a long time

since we had butter, but you know what? We're going to have it anytime we want it from now on." Phoebe took out a loaf of bread.

For the rest of the morning, Phoebe entertained Will. She read to him and helped him set up some of his animals. When she spotted a new animal, she wondered where he got it. "What is this and where did it come from?"

"July made it. He says it's a giraffe."

Just then she looked up to see July running from the paddocks. For a big man he was moving quickly.

"Oh, dear, something's happened." She left Will on the floor and went out to meet July.

"Utshani on fire! *Sinazo ukusindisa izintshe!"*

Phoebe didn't understand everything he was saying, but the word *fire* jolted her into action.

"Will, stay right here!" she yelled. "Don't move! Play with your animals, do you understand?"

"What happened?"

"I'm going with July to find out, but promise me you won't leave the porch unless someone comes for you."

When Phoebe found July, he was running out of the shed with an armload of gunnysacks.

"Where is it? Where's the fire?" She tried to match July's stride.

"Out by the south paddocks." He started running down the dirt road that separated the pens for the ostriches.

She looked south and saw a plume of black smoke that was widening at its base as it spread rapidly. She ran, following July until he reached the canal.

"Get these wet for me," July said. "And when Trinidad gets here, send him out with some more."

"Where is he now?"

"I sent him to cut the wires on the paddocks."

"But the ostriches—won't they get out?"

"Yes, Phoebe, but isn't that what you want?"

Phoebe thought of the alternative. Taking the pile of sacks, she waded into the canal and began dipping them as fast as she could and then threw them onto the bank.

As she was working, she watched the smoke. The color was changing from black to brown and then to white as the area on fire was getting wider and wider.

Trinidad came running up.

"Take these"—she threw some sacks toward him—"but I'm coming, too."

All three using the wet gunnysacks began frantically beating at the advancing conflagration. The blaze, feeding on the late-season alfalfa, sent flames leaping into the air.

Phoebe was exhausted, and she could hear the loud, anxious sounds coming from some ostriches—not the bass-octave, thrumming sounds that she was used to hearing, but sounds of panic.

"They're trapped." She dropped her sack and ran toward the sound.

"No, senora!" Trinidad shouted, grabbing her.

"Don't be foolish," July said. "Think of Will."

"But my birds! They're going to die."

"And so will you if you try to go after them."

They continued to beat at the flames, but it was a losing battle because the wind whipped the fire into whirling vortexes that threw out sparks and set even more fires.

"We have to retreat," July said. "Let's try to head it off from the buildings."

"Phoebe!"

She turned around to see Christian and Ina Claire running toward them. "Christian!" Phoebe's voice broke as she ran to meet him. "I'm going to lose everything."

"Not if I have anything to do with it. Ina Claire!" he yelled. "Get back to the Prinsens'. Have Andy bring the spring cart and as many men as he can muster."

"Ina Claire, wait!" Phoebe called. "Take Will with you! He doesn't need to be here if . . ."

"Understood!" Ina Claire called as she started toward the house in a run.

Phoebe gave her wet sacks to Christian and ran back to the canal to get more. As she moved away from the roar and crackle of the flames, she tried to listen for the din of the ostriches, but the sounds were becoming more and more faint.

She couldn't concentrate on that right now. July had said they should try to save the buildings, and she ran to a part of the fire that was racing in that direction. As she ran across the blackened grass, some embers sparked her dress and the cloth began to ignite, Christian ran toward her, knocking her down when he reached her.

"What?" Phoebe called out in alarm.

Christian rolled her over and extinguished most of the flames, but to be certain, he finished it off by applying a wet sack to her.

"Thanks." She grinned sheepishly.

Phoebe didn't know how long they'd been fighting the fire when Andy arrived with a spring cart carrying a water tank, a dozen buckets, and several men. One man pulled a hose out in front of the cart while two others manned a pump as water began to spray toward the fire.

At least a dozen people were running behind the cart, each with sacks to beat the flames. Phoebe saw that Gwen, Katie, Mrs. Woodson, and Ina Claire were among those coming to help.

With more people, there were enough to spread across the path of the approaching fire, but even then, the flames were moving closer to the buildings.

"We need to start a backfire," Buck said. "Phoebe, do you have any kerosene?"

"Yes, it's in the lean-to."

"I'll get it." Trinidad took off in a run.

While most of the men continued to fight the fire, Phoebe and the other women started a bucket brigade, wetting down a strip of ground from the canal all the way to the road.

When the strip was wet, Phoebe ran back to the men who were still battling the blaze. "We've got the water down," she said, her breath coming in gasps.

"Come on, men, let's get the backfire started,"

Buck called, and carrying their sacks with them, the men, their eyes red and their faces blackened with smoke, retreated about a hundred yards from the fire.

"Everyone spread out," Buck said. "In this wind, it's going to be your jobs to keep this thing going in the right direction."

Buck poured out a line of kerosene between the wet ground and the approaching fire. Then Christian lit one end, sending a fire racing down the line as the men started fanning the flames, forcing them to burn back toward the main fire.

All the firefighters lined up to beat any of the flames that started in the wrong direction until finally a blackened strip was about twenty feet wide. The backfire was moving toward the advancing flames, thereby robbing the fire of fuel. The two lines of fire joined and burned even more fiercely for a few minutes—until it died down and at last the flicker of flame was gone and only a few wisps of light gray smoke curled up from what was a great blackened field of at least fifty acres.

Phoebe looked out across the field and saw several blackened lumps. She put her hand to her mouth as tears filled her eyes. "They didn't have a chance."

"I'm sorry, senora," Trinidad said. "I should've seen the fire sooner."

"It's not your fault, Trinidad. We all did what we could."

Gwen came over to put her arm around Phoebe, and Ina Claire came to stand beside her.

"I'm so sorry," Gwen said.

"What about Wapi?" Phoebe asked. "Did you happen to see if he was one of the birds who escaped?"

"I don't know," Trinidad said. "When I cut the wires, I didn't look at the birds."

"Poor Will. If he's lost Wapi . . ." Phoebe shook her head as she looked toward Edwin's gravesite, where the fence was gone.

"Look at the bright side, Phoebe," Buck said. "You've got over a hundred acres that weren't burned, and thanks to Trinidad, some of your birds did escape, and the best thing of all: none of your buildings are gone."

"I know." Phoebe looked down at her burned and blackened dress. "I don't know how to thank you all." Her lower lip began to quiver.

"You don't have to thank us," Yhomas said. "Your fire could've just as easily become our fire. If it had gotten out of control, who knows how many acres would be gone. But we took care of it."

"I wonder how it started," Christian said.

"It's hard to say. Sometimes a discarded bottle will start one of these things. The sun shining through the glass, the dry grass . . ." Buck shook his head.

"Who's that?" Andy looked toward a galloping horse.

"It's Hannah!" Gwen said. "What's she doing over here?"

"Mama! Mama!" Hannah was calling.

She stopped the horse and Buck grabbed the halter, then helped his daughter down. "What is it, Hannah? What happened?"

"It's Will, Daddy." Hannah fell against her father's chest.

"Will? Hannah, is he hurt?" Phoebe asked.

"No, ma'am. He's gone."

"Gone? Where is he?" Phoebe asked, her voice rising.

"Some man came and took him. Will called him Uncle Frank. He cried and cried and said he didn't want to go with that man, but he made him go. I tried to stop him, but he pushed me down and said he was taking his nephew and I couldn't stop him."

"It's all right, sweetheart." Phoebe patted the girl on her shoulder. "Will's uncle is a very persuasive man. I know you did all you could to stop him from taking Will, but don't worry, I'll go get him and bring him home."

"I'm going with you," Christian said.

By the time Phoebe and Christian got cleaned up, it was nearly dark, and Christian drove Phoebe into town. They went to Frank's house.

Ostentatiously, every window in Frank's house was glowing, his house being the only one on the block to be lit with electricity. Christian pushed a button that rang a bell within the house.

When the door opened, a maid met them; she was not anyone Phoebe had seen before. "Are you expected guests?"

"Probably," Phoebe said. "Is Mr. Sloan here?"

"May I tell him who is calling?" The maid moved aside, allowing them to step into the entry hall.

"Tell him it's Mrs. Sloan."

"Yes, ma'am."

When the woman left, Phoebe reached over to squeeze Christian's hand. She felt a degree of confidence because he was with her.

She was prepared to see Frank, but Myra came to meet them. "Phoebe. This is a surprise. What are you doing here?"

"I've come to get Will."

"Will? Why on earth do you think he'd be here?" Myra seemed genuinely surprised at the suggestion.

"Because Frank took him."

"Phoebe, don't be so dramatic. If Will is missing, you know Frank didn't take him—not unless he found him wandering around somewhere."

"That's not true, Myra. Frank took him." Phoebe's voice rose. "We had a fire out at the farm today. I'd sent Will to the Prinsens' to be safe, and Frank came to their house and took him."

"Be reasonable, Phoebe. I know you and Frank have had your differences since Edwin died, but he loves that child."

"Is he here?"

"You mean Will? Of course not."

"She means Frank," Christian said.

"Oh. He's not here either. I expect he's at the bank."

"We'll go look for Will somewhere else," Christian said, raising his voice. "Come on, Mama, let's go."

"Phoebe, if Will is missing, I really am sorry." Myra took Phoebe's hand. "I know how distraught you must be, but I've not seen him or Frank. If Frank has the boy, he's probably taken him back to your house by now. If I were you, I'd go on home."

"All I ask is that if Frank does bring him here, you see to it that he brings him home tonight, no matter the time."

Myra smiled sympathetically. "I promise. If I have to, I'll bring him myself."

"Do you think she was telling the truth?" Christian asked when he and Phoebe reached the buggy.

"I think so. I picked up on your ruse when you raised your voice and called me 'Mama.' Had Will been within hearing distance, he would've come running."

If he wasn't tied up somewhere, Christian thought. "Shall we go by the bank, just to make sure?"

"He won't be there. His father might be, but not Frank."

Christian drove by the bank anyway. A metal accordion gate was pulled across the door and all the lights were out.

"Should we go by Mr. and Mrs. Sloan's house?" Christian asked.

"No. I'm hoping Myra is right and Frank's taken him home."

They rode for some time before Christian broke the silence. "It doesn't make sense. First of all, why would Frank take Will, and secondly, how did he know to go to the Prinsens'?"

"He did it to teach me a lesson."

"Kidnapping is a pretty serious offense just to teach you some kind of lesson. What did you do to deserve this?"

"He wanted something and I wouldn't do it."

"That bastard." Christian's thoughts went immediately to the time Phoebe told him Frank had wanted her in his bed. Christian made up his mind that when Will was safely retuned, he'd settle this with Frank Sloan once and for all. That man would never bother her again.

When the buggy pulled up in front of Phoebe's house, Ina Claire came out on the porch, closely followed by Andy.

"Did you find Will?" Ina Claire asked.

"No," Phoebe said. "Frank didn't bring him here?"

"No." Ina Claire shook her head.

"What do you want to do, Phoebe?" Christian asked. "Should we go back to town and get the sheriff?"

"Not yet. As ornery as Frank is, I don't think he'll hurt Will. At this point Will is the only grandchild W.F. has, and even though he doesn't act like it, I think that's important to the old man."

"You have more faith in Frank than I do," Christian said. "I'd have the sheriff on his doorstep tonight."

"I'm hoping that when Frank gets there, Myra will make him bring Will home tonight."

"It's your call, but you know how I feel," Christian said.

"I do, and I appreciate your being here with me, but I think I know Frank well enough to understand what he's doing."

"Ina Claire made a bite to eat for you two," Andy said. "We thought you'd be hungry."

"Thank you, I guess in all the excitement, I forgot to eat."

"Well, I didn't forget." Christian moved up the steps. "What did you make?"

"She made a pot of soup, and is it ever good!" Andy said.

"Does it have any mangel-wurzels?" Christian asked.

"It does, and they're not dried-up little nubs," Ina Claire said.

"Do you have a clue what they're talking about?" Andy asked.

"Beets," Christian said. "Ina Claire and I had lots of soup with wizened carrots and dried-up beets but very little else." He got two bowls and ladled a healthy serving into each one. "Come, Phoebe, sit down with me."

"Now that you're here, we're going to go on

home," Ina Claire said. "I know everyone's anxious to find out about Will, especially Hannah. She feels so bad about what happened."

"I know she does, but it wasn't her fault," Phoebe said. "I can't thank both of you enough for staying here. By the way, where are July and Trinidad?"

"Trinidad is out making sure there aren't any hot spots that could flare up again, and July is trying to round up any stray ostriches. He thinks they can outrun any predator that might chase them, but if they fall into a ravine or even step into a hole in the ground, a bird can break its leg, and—well, we'll just say he'd want to put it out of its misery."

"My poor birds. They didn't deserve this."

"Neither did you, Phoebe." Ina Claire embraced her warmly.

"Thank you, Ina Claire. You've been a big help today, and I can't tell you how much I appreciate it."

Phoebe could barely eat. Her stomach was churning as she thought about Will. She had to keep telling herself that Frank wouldn't do anything to harm Will, or she'd lose her sanity.

Christian looked up from his meal. "Why don't you go to bed? I know you have to be tired after today. I'll take care of everything here." He took the bowls to the dishpan.

"I am tired." She began to rub her neck.

Christian stepped behind her and began knead-

ing her muscles. "You have to hurt—all the beating and the buckets of water. I'm very proud of
you." He leaned down and encircled her chest and
gave her a hug.

"Why, Christian, why?"

"I don't know, but tomorrow we're going to
find out."

Phoebe went to sleep immediately upon putting
her head on the pillow, but it wasn't a restful
sleep and she awakened after about an hour. She
lay there willing herself to sleep, but it wouldn't
come.

"Frank, why would you do such a thing? Do
you hate me so much that you'd take Will away
from me?" Tears streamed down her cheeks.
She closed her eyes and willed the tears to stop
and the knot in her throat to go away. Thinking
through it all, Phoebe realized Frank's motiva-
tion.

He knew she'd never give in for money, but
he'd hit her in her most vulnerable spot. Will.
And he'd nearly succeeded. She'd almost signed
to secure Will's inheritance, but she couldn't
stand to sign away her possibility of a future with
Christian. Now Frank was pitting Will against
Christian. Whom did she love more?

She loved them both, but if it came down to the
safety of her son or marriage to Christian, she'd
choose her son. And Frank knew that. He'd won.

She couldn't stay in bed any longer. Part of her
wanted to go upstairs and climb into bed with

Christian, but she wouldn't. She couldn't—she had to say good-bye to him.

She put on her robe and stepped out onto the porch. As she stood there, the acrid smell of burned vegetation and feathers assailed her nose.

"Can't sleep, huh?"

Phoebe jumped at Christian's voice. "You startled me. I didn't expect to find you out here."

"I can't sleep either. All I can think about is Will. There's something fishy about this, and I can't figure out why Frank did this."

Phoebe moved to sit beside him and shivered in the night air.

"Are you cold?" Christian put his arm around her shoulder, pulling her closer.

It seemed like the most natural thing in the world, and Phoebe put her head on his shoulder. "Poor Will, I wish he was here with us. I know he has to be so scared right now. Do you think he thinks I've abandoned him?"

Christian's first inclination was to say no, that Will knew Phoebe would come for him, but in that instant Christian saw two men dragging him away from his own mother. He had been just about Will's age at the time, and he never saw his mother again.

"Which one is a balloon?" Phoebe asked, breaking the silence.

"What?"

"Didn't you used to look for balloons in the night sky?"

Christian chuckled. "You've been talking to Ina Claire, haven't you?"

"She said you were the best at finding them."

"Let's find a spot where we can see the open sky. And whoever finds the first balloon gets the first kiss."

"Is that a game you played with Ina Claire?"

"No. It's new. I've never played it with anyone."

Christian entered the house and soon returned with a quilt and a blanket. He spread the quilt and sat down, waiting for her to join him. When she did, he wrapped the blanket around her.

"Did she tell you how to do it?" Christian asked.

"She said you had to stare at one particular star for ten minutes and not blink. If it moved, you could prove it was a balloon."

"There." Christian pointed. "That has to be a balloon."

"Ha, even I know that's Venus."

"That's the first one. The rules say you have to give me a kiss."

"Who found it? You or me?"

"We'll have to kiss and find out." Christian kissed her—not a passionate kiss, but a comfortable kiss. "Tomorrow, Phoebe, I swear we'll bring Will home, no matter what it is that Frank is holding against you. If I have to do bodily damage to that son of a bitch, I will find your son."

"I know you will." Phoebe lay down on the quilt.

Christian joined her and pulled her close. Soon she was sleeping, drawing long, even breaths.

But sleep wouldn't come for Christian. He was a child kicking and screaming as he was torn from a young woman, a scene that he'd kept at bay for many years. He closed his eyes, and once again he was a scrawny little boy, cowering under the table as he hid from the master. He was coming after him with a strap because Christian had dared to suck his fingers in hopes of getting the last of his gruel.

To this day he couldn't stand oatmeal.

He pulled Phoebe closer to him and finally fell into a fitful sleep, his waking thoughts becoming more vivid as he relived them in his troubled dreams.

The orphanage was a large stone hall with high, inescapable windows where the vermin had free range, and in his nightmare a large rat was coming toward him in his hiding place.

"No!" He sat up quickly and kicked at something that had come near his foot. In the moonlight he saw a rather small animal with a long black-and-white-striped tail. His heart was beating wildly until he realized it was probably a ringtail.

Phoebe had shifted when Christian sat up. "Go back to your own bed, honey. I love you," she said in her sleep, then turned over and snuggled closer to Christian.

19

The next morning Phoebe was aghast that Christian had allowed her to sleep out under the stars with him. "What if Trinidad or July saw us?"

Christian smiled. "I expect Trinidad did. I saw him early this morning. He and July are trying to track down any of the birds that may be somewhere close."

"Do you think I'll get any of them back?"

"Some, but probably not many. We'll have to wait and see, but right now we can't worry about them. How fast can you get ready to go to town?"

"By the time you get the buggy hitched up, I'll be ready." Phoebe hurried into the house.

When they got to town, they rode by the bank and found the accordion gate was pulled back.

"Do you want to stop here first?" Christian asked.

"No, I want to go to the house first. If Myra was telling the truth last night and she knows something this morning, I think she'll tell me."

They got to Frank's house a little after nine o'clock. Christian rang the bell, but no one answered.

"That's strange," Phoebe said. "Even if Frank and Myra aren't here, you'd think their maid would come to the door."

"Maybe she was told not to."

"Let's go around back. When I was the maid, I had to do a lot more than answer the door."

When they reached the back of the house, the maid was beating some carpets that were hung over a clothesline.

"Pardon me," Phoebe called, trying to sound as friendly as she could. "I came to get my little boy. I know he probably caused a lot of trouble last night."

The woman's face showed contempt. "Look . . . Mrs. Sloan." The maid set the words apart. "Miss Myra told you last night there was no child here, and no child came with Mr. Frank." She immediately went back to beating the carpet, dismissing them without further comment.

Christian shook his head when Phoebe started to speak again. He took her arm and guided her back to the buggy.

"Christian, I don't believe her. Will may not be here now, but I know he was here last night."

"Why do you say that?"

"I just feel it. What do we do now?"

"I think it's time to go see your in-laws. Do you think they know anything about where Will is?"

"What makes you think I know where Will is?" Juliet Sloan asked. "When was the last time you brought him to see his grandparents?"

"I'm sorry," Phoebe said, for the first time having some empathy for the Sloans. "Are you sure you haven't seen him, Mrs. Sloan? Frank didn't tell you where he was taking Will?"

"You've always been a delusional young woman. Frank adored Edwin, no matter what hateful nonsense you planted in his heart. If Will is missing, whatever would make you think Frank had anything to do with it?"

"Ma'am, there was a young woman who was caring for Will while everyone was fighting a fire at Phoebe's place. We know that it was Frank who came for him because she told us," Christian said.

"And who are you? Oh, yes, I've heard about you. What respectable man goes into a women's establishment and buys underwear for her? It's scandalous! I'm ashamed that this woman carries the name of Sloan," Juliet said before slamming the door in their faces.

Phoebe was devastated when they climbed into the buggy. "I don't know what to do. I don't know who to go to. I never thought that I might be part of the problem. Mrs. Sloan's right, I never brought Will to see them. I thought they hated me so much that they wouldn't want to see Will either, but maybe I was wrong."

"We should get the sheriff, Phoebe."

"Not yet. If there is a chance I can find Will without going to the sheriff, I want to try it."

"If that's what you want to do, all right. But if we don't know where he is by tomorrow, promise me you'll go to the sheriff. Or if you're not ready to do that, I'll personally find Frank and beat him to within an inch of his life."

"No, Christian, please." Phoebe reached out to put her hand on his arm. "If you did something to Frank, you'd certainly wind up in jail. You don't know how much power these people have in this town."

Phoebe was quiet on the drive home, but her mind was full of thoughts. Where was Will? She had to trust that he was still in Phoenix and that Frank wouldn't do anything to harm him. Last night she had decided that if it took her signature to get Will back, she would sign anything.

"I'll go see if July is back," Christian said when they got back to the house.

Phoebe nodded, but she didn't speak. He watched her head for Edwin's burned gravesite. He wanted to go with her and take her in his arms to comfort her, but he felt she was pushing him away.

Christian headed for the paddocks to see if he could find either July or Trinidad, but neither man was around. He walked out to the burned acreage, only to find many carcasses.

So much carnage. What could possibly have started this fire? Then he remembered Buck's saying it might have been started by a discarded bottle, but that didn't make a lot of sense. This was November. Wouldn't that scenario have had more credence if it was the middle of the summer?

There had to be a starting point for a fire. Christian decided he'd walk over the area to look for some physical indication of where and how the fire had started. The logical place to start was the back of the field where the unburned alfalfa was still standing.

It took a while to get to that point, but when he arrived, something caught his attention. The back of the fire had a relatively straight line that stretched for a couple hundred feet. Beyond that point, the line of demarcation appeared to be meandering—much as you would expect a fire to move. Christian knelt beside the line, picking up some of the pieces of alfalfa. The bottoms of the plant were burned in two, but the tops were lying flat, pointing away from the fire line. The tops weren't burned, suggesting the flames ignited rapidly.

"Damn, this fire was set!"

He hurried along the line looking for something to prove his speculation—a discarded kerosene can, a cigar butt, anything he could take back as proof.

If someone had set the fire, he had to come from somewhere. Christian saw a break in the vegetation that was visible on both sides of the canal. He went to that point and, looking down, he saw boot prints. He broke off a limb of a scrub willow that was growing beside the canal, intending to mark the spot for the sheriff, should Phoebe agree to get him involved.

Then he saw a piece of polished metal hidden in the grass. He smiled as he picked it up. This has to belong to somebody, and I have a good idea who, he thought.

Christian started across the blackened field, heading for the gravesite, where he could see Phoebe still standing. But then he saw her start running toward the house, and Christian was encouraged. Frank must be bringing Will home.

He, too, started running. As he got closer, he heard the unmistakable brooming call of ostriches—two low staccato calls and then a third prolonged sound.

When he reached the house, Trinidad was leading the birds by dropping a trail of grain while July came up behind.

One bird ran to meet Phoebe.

"Wapi!" she yelled. "You're alive."

The denuded bird followed along behind Phoebe as obediently as a puppy would follow its master.

"I'm glad that one survived," Christian said when he reached the men. "How many did you find?"

"It's not good." Trinidad opened the first paddock on the unburned side of the road. "Sixteen."

"That's all?" Christian asked.

"There were about twenty on this side of the road," July said, "but they are all feather birds. We only found one pair of adults."

Christian shook his head. "There won't be many plumes at the next plucking."

"Did she find Will?" July asked.

"She knows where he has to be, but he's not home yet."

"The brother-in-law?"

"You know it is," Christian said, "and now I think he's the one who set the fire."

"How do you know that?" July asked.

But Christian didn't have a chance to answer, because just at that moment a buggy turned into the lane.

"Christian, where's Phoebe?" Ina Claire asked as she jumped down. "We know where Will is."

When Phoebe came outside, Gwen was taking a carpetbag out of the buggy. "Do you know this lady? We picked her up about a mile back. She was walking along the road and she's got some news to tell you."

A rather large, gray-haired black woman stepped out of the buggy.

"Crecy!" Phoebe cried as the two women embraced. "It's been a long time since I've seen you."

"I came as soon as I could. They've got your baby."

"W.F. and Juliet?"

"No, ma'am. I don't work for them no more. I work for the Evanses—Miss Myra's mama and daddy. This morning when Mr. Frank brought that child bright and early, and he a-cryin' for his mama, I knew something was wrong. When I was fixin' his breakfast, Miss Myrtle left me with him and I asked him who he was. He told me he was your little one and I had to come and tell you. He said Mr. Frank stole him. Now, that ain't right."

"Oh, Crecy, you don't know how grateful I am that you were there," Phoebe said. "They forgot that you and I worked together at the Sloans and that you'd know me."

"Yes'm, that they did."

"I'm going to go right now. I should have known Frank would take Will to his in-laws."

"Wait a minute," Christian said. "Why don't you let me go get him?"

"And I'll go, too," July said. "Christian and I will do whatever it takes to bring that little guy home to you, Phoebe."

"I can't let you do that. I need to be the one to go get him."

"Think about it for a minute. These people won't know us, but if they see you—if Frank's told them to keep him from you—they may do what they can to stash Will away."

Phoebe took a deep breath. "All right, but, Christian, don't . . . no, do whatever it takes to get him back."

"We will," Christian said. "Gwen, may we take your buggy?"

"Of course."

"Where are we going?" July asked.

"Do you remember where the feather brokerage was, on Washington?" Phoebe asked.

"Yes."

"They live one block behind, on the corner of Seventeenth and Adams. It's a big yellow house."

"They keep two red chairs on the front porch," Crecy added.

"Oh, Crecy, I hadn't thought. They will have to know that you're the one who told us. You'll be in trouble."

"I won't be in trouble, because I won't go back. I threw my things out the back window and gathered them up before they saw me. I can't work for such people no more."

"The longer July and I stay here, the longer it'll be before we bring Will back to you." Christian laid his fingers gently on Phoebe's cheek, then bent down and kissed her lightly on the lips. "Don't worry, we'll bring him back. Maybe you should bake some cookies. I've never known anyone who liked cookies as much as Will. Well, maybe Wapi."

Phoebe smiled through her tears. "I'll do that."

"I do believe that one is the biggest man I ever did see," Crecy said as Christian and July drove away. "Why does he talk like that?"

"He's from Africa." Phoebe turned toward the house.

"My grandma came from Africa. She always wanted to go home."

"Actually, July is a Zulu."

"A Zulu? My grandma was a Hottentot. and my grandpa was a Zulu, so that makes us kinfolk."

"I guess that's right, but according to Christian, July is Shaka's grandson," Phoebe said. "Shaka was the greatest Zulu monarch in Bulawayo."

"Shaka? Everybody in South Africa has heard of him," Ina Claire said. "I didn't know that about July."

"So this July is a prince?" Crecy asked.

Phoebe chuckled. "I never thought about it like that, but, yes, I suppose he is."

"This is the house," Christian said, stopping the buggy at the corner of Adams and Seventeenth.

Christian tied the horse to the hitching post, then he and July knocked on the door.

A man appearing to be in his early sixties opened the door. He looked irritated. "What do you want? We don't engage with solicitors of any kind."

"We're here to take Will Sloan back to his mother," Christian said.

"There's nobody here by that name."

"Wet!" Will shouted as he came barreling through the house.

"Come back here, you little brat!" a woman called as she chased after him.

"Myrtle, you were supposed to keep that kid out of sight!" Chauncey Evans said.

Will darted around Evans's legs and Christian picked him up.

"Wet, you've come to get me! I knew you would!" Will wrapped his arms around him. "I want to go to my house."

"Then that's where we'll go," Christian said.

"I don't think so," Evans said. "I was entrusted to care for this child, and I'm afraid I can't let him go with strangers."

"It's obvious we're not strangers to Will. Let's go home." Christian turned and started down the steps of the porch.

"Mister, I don't know who you are, but I wouldn't do that if I were you."

Christian heard the distinct double clicking sound of a hammer pulled back on a revolver. He turned around to see Evans pointing a gun at him.

"Put that kid down now or I'll shoot you where you stand," Evans said with an angry growl.

In a lightning-quick move, July wrapped his big hand around Evans's gun hand, squeezing down so hard that the man cried out in pain. When July eased his grip, Evans dropped the pistol.

"You son of a bitch! You broke my fingers!" he shouted, grabbing his wounded hand with his other. "Just you wait, you'll pay for this."

Christian set Will down, then picked up the revolver, which was now lying on the sidewalk. Opening the cylinder, he removed all the shells and dropped them in his pocket before he handed the empty pistol back to Evans.

"Good day, Mr. Evans," Christian said.

"Take me home, Wet. Please take me home." Will reached up to grab Christian's hand, and the three of them walked back to the buggy with Evans screaming invectives at their backs.

"Will!" Phoebe shouted happily, running out to the buggy when Christian returned. She had her arms open and was laughing, Will stood up in the buggy, then fell into them.

"I'm so happy to have you back home!" Phoebe smothered him with kisses.

"I didn't like that man, Mama."

"I don't blame you, honey, I don't like him either."

"That man was going to shoot Wet, but July made him drop his gun."

"What? Christian, is that right? Did Chauncey actually try to shoot you?"

"Let's just say that he attempted to prevent us from taking Will, but July found a way to dissuade him."

"Oh! I never dreamed he'd take it to that extreme."

"No harm was done," Christian said, "except Mr. Evans may not be using his hand for a few days."

"Oh!" Despite herself, Phoebe laughed. "Then he got just what he deserves. I only wish it'd been Frank. But it's over now and Will is home."

"And do you know what I think he needs? Cookies and milk," Christian said.

"Then he shall have them," Gwen said. "We made the kind you like best."

"Are they oatmeal?"

"Yes, with currents," Ina Claire said as she and Will ran toward the house.

As they sat around the table, Will recounted how Frank had come to Prinsen House to get him. "I told Uncle Frank that you wouldn't like it if you came to get me and I wasn't there. Hannah tried to stop him, but he pushed her down." Will motioned to show how Frank had done it.

"When Mr. Frank brought Will to the Evanses, all that boy could say was 'I want to go home,'" Crecy said. "When I found out who he belonged to, I told Miss Myrtle I'd bring him back to you, but Mr. Chauncey told me to mind my own business. I knew that wasn't right. That's why I came here, even if I had to walk."

"And I can't tell you how much I appreciate that, Crecy."

Crecy flashed a broad smile. "I remember when we both worked for Miss Juliet, how when she fussed at me you'd take up for me. We were friends then."

Phoebe walked over to embrace her. "What do you mean *then*? We're still friends."

"Crecy, you said you didn't want to go back to the Evanses," Gwen said. "Do you want a job?"

"Yes, ma'am, I expect I need to work."

"How would you like to work out here in the country? Just the other day, Katie said we needed a full-time cook over at the ostrich farm, and it seems to me like you would be a good candidate for the job."

"That's a wonderful idea," Phoebe said. "I can vouch for her cooking—except I seem to recall she has a little trouble with rarebit."

"You would remember that."

Both women laughed together.

At that moment there was a loud knock, and Phoebe went to the door. Three armed men were standing on the porch, and each was wearing a badge.

"Mrs. Sloan, we're looking for a big black man who we think works for you. Do you know if he's here?"

"Why do you want to know?"

"May we look around?"

"I . . ."

"We don't need your permission: we have a warrant to search the premises."

"There's no need for that." July stepped up behind Phoebe.

"Man oh man, this is a big one, all right, Enoch," one of the other deputies said. "I'd say he fits the description, wouldn't you?"

"Were you at the home of Chauncey Evans today?" the deputy asked.

"We both were." Christian joined Phoebe and July. "Can you tell me what this is about?"

"It's about assault and battery, and about kid-napping."

"Nobody kidnapped anybody," Phoebe said, "unless it was Frank Sloan, who took Will with-out my permission. He's the one who took him to the Evanses', and I sent these two gentlemen to get Will back."

"Ma'am, we have a warrant to arrest this man," the deputy said. "It's not our duty to decide whether he's guilty or not. But it is our duty to bring him back to Sheriff Sturgeon."

"How dare you accuse July of kidnapping? I told you, I asked him to go get my son."

"It's all right. I'll go with them." July looked at the three deputies. "But I'll not let you tie me to a whipping post."

"A whipping post? What are you talking about? I don't even know what that is," the dep-uty said. "All we're going to do is take you to jail. What happens to you after that will be up to the judge."

"Don't worry, July, we'll get a lawyer," Phoebe said. "We'll get this all straightened out."

"Put your hands behind your back," a deputy said.

"Do you have to handcuff him?" Phoebe asked.

"Ma'am, you can see what a big man he is." The deputy shook his head. "If he was to try anything, why, all three of us couldn't bring him down. We'd have to shoot him."

"No!" Will yelled. "No, no, no. July is my friend.

Don't take him away." Will wrapped his arms around July's legs.

July bent down to Will. "I won't be gone for long, but while I'm gone, I'm leaving you in charge of Wapi. Make sure he has water and he gets alfalfa. Can you do that for me?"

Will nodded.

July stood and then put his hands behind his back. One of the deputies slipped on the handcuffs.

Christian patted his friend on his back as the three deputies led him out to an enclosed and barred wagon.

Christian had a sinking feeling as he watched the wagon roll away. His thoughts went back to their arrival in New York, where July was treated as second-class. He was a foreigner and a black man. Phoebe had said, "We'll get this all straightened out." Christian hoped she was right.

20

"**J**uly? His name is July?" Clifford Frazier asked. Frazier was the ex–attorney general of the Arizona Territory, and he'd represented Yhomas when he established his ostrich farm.

"July is the only name I've ever heard him called," Yhomas Prinsen said.

"He's got to have a last name. Can you come up with something?"

Christian smiled. "He does have another name. When we were coming through Ellis Island, he registered as Julius Van Koopmans."

"Van Koopmans," Yhomas chuckled. "Of course, that makes sense."

Frazier looked at Yhomas with a questioning expression. "Is there something significant about the name Van Koopmans that I should be aware of?"

"Just that she's a wonderful lady and a friend to us both," Yhomas said.

"A friend to all three of us," Christian said. "July worked for her for close to twenty years."

"All right." Frazier wrote the name on a piece of paper. "As of now, I am officially the counselor of record for Mr. Julius Van Koopmans."

Christian, Phoebe, and Will, the Bucknells and the Prinsens, were all in the courtroom, sitting on the left side of the gallery. Chauncey Evans and his wife, along with both sets of Sloans, were there as well, and they sat on the right side. July was before the bar, sitting at the defense table with Clifford Frazier.

Judge Johnstone looked at the charge sheet that was before him. "Is counsel for the defense present?"

Frazier stood. "I am, Your Honor."

"Prosecution?"

The district attorney stood. "T. W. Flannigan, Your Honor."

"Mr. Frazier, I've been informed that your client has waived trial by jury and wishes his case to be heard by the bench."

"That is correct, Your Honor."

"Mr. Van Koopmans, are you aware that in forfeiting a trial by jury you are agreeing to abide by my decision?"

"Yes, sir, Your Honor."

"I object!" Frank shouted. "I think a case this important should be heard by a jury."

Judge Johnstone hammered his gavel loudly on the sound block and pointed to Frank. "Mr. Sloan. You have no standing in this case. You are forbidden, sir, from speaking at all, except from the witness stand, and then only in response to questions from counsel. One more outburst from you, and I'll have you removed from this courtroom until such time as your presence is required as a witness. Do I make myself perfectly clear?"

"Yes, Your Honor," a chastened Frank replied.

"Mr. Prosecutor, make your case."

Flannigan stood. "Your Honor, this case consists of two charges against the accused—one for assault and battery, and one for kidnapping. I ask that the charges be severed as to verdicts."

"Do you have any objection, Mr. Frazier?" Judge Johnstone asked.

"No objection, Your Honor."

"Very well, you may proceed, Mr. Flannigan."

"Prosecution calls Frank Sloan to the witness stand."

Frank glared at Phoebe as he went to the witness stand and was sworn in.

"Mr. Sloan, did you remove Will Sloan, a boy of four years and your nephew by blood, from the Prinsen House?"

"I did."

"Why did you take him?"

"I found him to be totally unsupervised, running loose on an ostrich farm. And because my own brother was killed by an ostrich, I was naturally worried about him. My late brother's wife has, by her scandalous behavior, shown herself to be an unfit mother, and I was preparing to sue for guardianship of Will on that alone. . . . But when I found Will to be abandoned by his mother, I felt that, for my nephew's safety, I had no choice but to move him."

"Where did you take him?"

"I took him to the home of Chauncey Evans, my father-in-law, and a gentleman of impeccable reputation."

"Thank you. I have no further questions."

"Mr. Frazier?"

Frazier stood, but he didn't approach Frank. "Mr. Sloan, where was Will when you took him?"

"I've already answered that question. He was at the Prinsen farm."

"Was he outside, among the ostriches?"

"Well, no."

"Isn't it true that he was in the house, being looked after by Hannah Bucknell?"

"She's nothing but a child herself."

"She is fourteen years old, and it's standard and acceptable procedure for young ladies, even younger than fourteen, to look after children. In addition, it was broad daylight and they were in the house. Do you know why he was there?"

"Yes. There was a fire at Phoebe's farm."

"Thank you. No further questions. But, Your Honor, I reserve the right to recall this witness."

The next witness called was Chauncey Evans, who, under questioning and at the prosecutor's urging, showed his bandaged hand to the judge.

"How many fingers were broken?"

"Three," Evans said angrily. "That black son of a bitch grabbed my hand and squeezed so hard I thought I was going to pass out from the pain."

The judge rapped his gavel on the sound block again. "Watch your language, sir."

"I'm sorry, Your Honor."

"Did you turn Will over to them?"

"No, why should I? I'd never seen either one of them before. I know that Will was my son-in-law's blood nephew, and he left him with me for safekeeping. I felt obligated to do just what he asked me to do."

"Did you point a gun at Mr. De Wet?"

"I certainly did. As I said, I didn't know who he was. Why should I have turned the child over to them?"

"Thank you. No further questions."

Again Frazier stood, but did not approach the witness.

"Mr. Evans, did Mr. De Wet tell you that Mrs. Sloan had sent him for her son?"

"So what? Any stranger could have said that."

"What was Will's reaction to Mr. De Wet's appearance at your door?"

"I don't know, I didn't pay any attention to his reaction. I was more concerned with my obligation to keep him safe."

"Thank you. You may stand down."

"I have no more witnesses, Your Honor," the prosecutor said.

Phoebe was the first witness whom Frazier

called, and unlike in his cross of the witnesses for the prosecution, he approached her.

"Did you leave Will in Hannah's keeping?"

"I did."

"Have you ever left her with Hannah before?"

"Yes, Hannah and her sister, Adeline, are very responsible young ladies who think the world of Will, and he thinks the world of them. I felt no apprehension at all in leaving him with them."

"Did you ask Mr. De Wet and Mr. Van Koopmans to go to the Evanses' house to pick up Will?"

"Yes."

"So as far as you're concerned, there was no kidnapping involved."

"Will is my child; they were picking him up for me. And I hasten to add, Will wasn't there by my authority in the first place. Frank Sloan had no business taking my son there."

"Your witness, Counselor."

The prosecutor stood. "Mrs. Sloan, is it true that you are living with two men: Christian De Wet and this black man, who I understand goes by the name July?"

"No, that isn't true."

"May I remind you that you are under oath? I ask you again, are you living with two men?"

"No, I live with three. Mr. De Wet, July, and Trinidad Arriola."

"Four men, Mama! I live with you, too!"

Those on the left side of the gallery laughed, as did Judge Johnstone. The prosecutor, realizing that the question may have backfired, stepped away.

Frazier's next witness was Hannah Bucknell. "Hannah, when Mr. Sloan came for Will, what did he say?"

"He said he was taking Will."

"What did you say?"

"I asked if Miss Phoebe sent him. He didn't answer me. He just came in and grabbed Will."

"And did Will agree to go with him?"

"No, sir, Will cried and told me not to let his uncle Frank take him. I asked him again if Miss Phoebe had sent him, and he told me it was none of my business. When I tried to take Will back, Mr. Sloan pushed me down. Will yelled at me to go get his mama and ask her to come get him, so that's what I did."

"Thank you, Hannah."

"I have no questions of this child," the prosecutor said.

Christian was the next witness and he said that, yes, he and July had gone to retrieve Will for Will's mother. And, yes, July had grabbed Evans's hand, but only after Evans had pointed his pistol and threatened to shoot Christian.

"As far as I'm concerned, July . . . that is, Mr. Van Koopmans, saved my life."

"Are you sure he intended to shoot you?"

"I know that his gun was loaded."

Frazier walked back over to the defense table, picked up an envelope, then brought it to the bench, where he dumped out six bullets. "Your Honor, I submit these bullets as defense exhibit one."

The prosecutor did not cross-examine Christian.

Defense's last witness was Will.

"Will, when Mr. De Wet and July came to Mr. Evans's house, what did you think?"

"I was happy. I yelled at Wet to take me home."

"And did you see Mr. Evans point a gun at Mr. De Wet?"

"It scared me. I thought he was going to shoot Wet."

"Your witness."

"No questions."

"Your Honor, I have no more witnesses to call but I would like to—"

"Put that black giant on the stand! Make him tell how he broke my fingers!" Evans shouted.

Again Judge Johnstone pounded his gavel. "This is the second time my court has been interrupted, and I will not have it happen again!"

The judge looked back toward Frazier. "Please continue, Counselor."

"I would like to call Mr. Frank Sloan back to the stand."

"The court reminds the witness that he has been previously sworn in," the judge said as Frank took his seat.

"You testified that you went to pick up Will because you knew there was a fire at Phoebe Sloan's place."

"That's right."

"How did you know there was fire?"

"I saw the fire."

"You saw the fire? Or you started the fire?"

"I don't know what anyone has told you, but I didn't start that fire!" Frank yelled.

Frazier returned to the defense table, then removed something from a second envelope—the object Christian had found in the brush near the canal.

"Mr. Sloan, do you recognize this?"

"Yes, that's my brother's knife."

"Your brother's knife, you say?"

"Yes. As you can see, it has his initials." Frank told Frazier to turn the knife over. "JES."

"Isn't it true, Mr. Sloan, that you've been carrying this knife since his death? And I remind you that you're under oath."

"Yes, I've been carrying it. But I lost it, and I thank whoever found it." He reached for the knife, but Frazier pulled it back.

"Suppose I told you that this knife was found near the uninvolved part of the alfalfa field that was burned? And suppose I told you that evidence shows use of an accelerant to start the fire? The location of this knife, and the way the fire was started, might suggest that whoever was carrying this knife started the fire, don't you agree?"

"Objection, Your Honor. Calls for a conclusion," Flannigan said.

"Sustained."

"Mr. Sloan, do you have any idea how your

brother's knife, the knife that you admit you've been carrying, might've turned up near the point where the fire originated?"

"I suggest you ask that Mexican who works for Phoebe. I lost this knife months ago. I thought I'd misplaced it and that it would show up. But now that I think about it, I'm sure Trinidad or Cornello stole it. If you want to know how the knife got there, ask one of them."

"No further questions, Your Honor," Frazier said. "Defense rests."

"Your Honor, I—"

"You may stand down, Mr. Sloan," the judge interrupted.

Judge Johnstone looked out over the courtroom. "I've heard the witnesses, and I see no need to retire before I pronounce the verdicts.

"For the charge of assault and battery, I find that the action of the defendant, Julius Van Koopmans, also known as July, was entirely justified, as he had reasonable cause to believe that Chauncey Evans had every intention of shooting Christian De Wet. Therefore to the charge of assault and battery, I find the defendant innocent.

"As to the charge of kidnapping, it is obvious that the only person guilty of kidnapping is Frank Sloan, who took the boy without consent of the boy's mother. As Sloan was not charged, I cannot find against him. However, as to the kidnapping charge against the defendant, I find him to be innocent, and I hereby release him from custody. Court is adjourned."

Those sitting on the left side of the court hurried forward to congratulate a smiling July. Will seemed happiest of all, and he tackled July's leg before July picked him up and set him on his shoulders.

"Mama! Look how tall I am!" Will said excitedly.

Christian stood in the back of the courtroom, watching. He was approached by Frank and W. F. Sloan.

"Well, I suppose you're pleased with the outcome," W.F. said.

"Yes, sir, I am. July was an innocent man, and I'm glad the judge saw it that way."

"Is Phoebe going to pursue arson charges against my son?"

"Arson?" Frank said in surprise. "Pop, what are you talking about?"

"I'm talking about the fact that you set fire to Phoebe's farm. A fire that, during this drought, could have gotten out of hand and destroyed thousands of acres."

"That's not true, Pop! They are lying!"

"Mr. De Wet, where did you find that knife?"

"Not thirty feet from the fire line."

"I explained that. I lost that knife more than a month ago."

"You're lying, Frank," W.F. said. "I saw that knife in your hands just a few days ago. And so did several other witnesses."

"I . . . I . . ." Frank mumbled, unable to go any further.

"I guess breaking all her eggs just wasn't enough for you," Christian said to Frank.

"Eggs? What eggs? I haven't heard about this," W.F. said.

"It was back in September when Trinidad and Cornello were celebrating at the fiesta. Phoebe was at a meeting for the water project, and when she got home, all her eggs were smashed."

"How do you know it was Frank?"

"Frank knew about it the next day. He told Phoebe that one of her men had told him, but that was impossible. One of her men was in jail, and the other was at the fiesta."

W.F. glared at Frank.

"Pop, I did all of this for her own good. You know she can't make a living there for herself and Will. I thought if I forced her off the farm, she would come to her senses. I even offered to put her up in . . ." Frank, seeing the expression on his father's face, stopped in midsentence. "I was looking out for Will. He is your grandson; I just wanted what was best for him."

"How is Will?" W.F. asked Christian.

"He's happy to be back with his mother. Will is a fine young man."

"I'm afraid I haven't seen much of him, but if Phoebe will let me, I intend to remedy that."

"I obviously don't speak for Phoebe, but I feel like she'd be most amenable to that. I know she grieves for your son."

"And so do I. Frank says she was responsible for Edwin's death, but the more I think about it, I don't know how she could've been. As I see it, if Edwin was out among the ostriches, it had to be an accident." Then W.F. smiled. "You can't force one of those ornery birds to do anything."

"I have to agree," Christian said.

"Do you think she can make a good living raising those damn things?"

"She made more than a thousand dollars on just this last plucking, and according to Prinsen you can pluck every eight months. Yes, I'd say two thousand dollars a year is a pretty good living, but it'll take her a while to get back there. She only has two adult birds left after the fire, and that's where the prized plumes come from."

"I'd like to make her an offer," W.F. said, "and you seem to have some sway with her."

"I wouldn't say that. Phoebe is a very capable businesswoman who doesn't need me to tell her what to do."

"Well, perhaps you will be my arbitrator. If Prinsen will sell them to me, do you think she'll accept ten pairs of adult birds?"

Christian smiled. "That sounds like a very reasonable offer."

"There's one more thing Frank has done that I need to untangle." W.F. withdrew a folded piece of paper. "This was a lie, too. It says that I established a trust for Will that he'll access when he's eighteen. That's not true. My will gives the boy Edwin's half of my estate, and I have to say, with some humility, it's much more than the twenty-five thousand dollars Frank was willing to give him."

"Pop, why would you give half of all your money to that boy? We don't even know for sure that Edwin was the father. I mean, you've seen how eager she's been to give herself to a perfect stranger. She—"

"Frank Sloan, if you say one more word about Phoebe, I am going to knock your teeth out, right here in front of your father."

"Then it would be you in jail instead of that black cretin," Frank replied.

"I would testify that you just tripped and fell," W.F. said.

"What? Pop, I'm your son!"

"Unfortunately, that is true."

"But I—"

"Shut up, Frank. Just shut up. I've heard about all that I care to hear from you." W.F. turned to Christian. "About this agreement. The second part is inexcusable." W.F. handed the paper to Christian. "I suspect it has a lot to do with you."

Christian read the document. "This explains a few things."

"To be honest, my respect for Phoebe has grown tremendously. I think I've misjudged her all along."

Christian sat in the back of the courtroom watching as everyone congregated around July.

He couldn't take his eyes off Phoebe. She was so animated and effervescent, did he dare hope that she had refused to sign Frank's paper because of him? He had told W.F. that she was a capable businesswoman who didn't need him, and that was true. For a moment, he was concerned that, with the new birds, she didn't really need him.

But then he smiled. There was one thing all the money in the world couldn't satisfy for his Phoebe.

Phoebe noticed that Christian wasn't among the celebrants. She looked around and found him sitting at the back of the courtroom, a huge grin across his face.

She walked back to join him. "You look like the Cheshire cat." She took a seat beside him. "Why didn't you tell me you found Edwin's knife?"

"I planned to, but then we got so excited when Wapi came home, I forgot."

"I'm glad he was one of the survivors." She lowered her eyes and they began to cloud. "I guess I was too prideful. I thought my money troubles were over and I thought you would be working for the water project, but now I know both of those things are not to be."

"Maybe I could take Cornello's place. You know he's never coming back."

"With only two birds producing prime feathers, I'm afraid I couldn't pay you very much."

"Maybe you can."

"How?"

"Your father-in-law just offered to buy you twenty adult ostriches."

"He did not!"

"No, he really did. He said he's misjudged you and wants to make it up to you. And he gave me this."

Christian handed her the paper W.F. had given him.

She took one look at it and ripped it in two. "No. If he expects me to sign that thing, he can keep his ostriches."

"He said he admired you because you didn't sign it. He doesn't have a trust for Will."

"Then I didn't lose anything, because—"

"Because you wouldn't sign a paper saying you wouldn't get married."

Phoebe nodded her head.

Christian chuckled. "He isn't going to hold you to that either. He says that his grandson is definitely in his will."

"Hey, you two," Gwen called. "We need to get going. Crecy and Ina Claire are cooking up a big celebration dinner for July."

"For me?" July asked. "How did they know the judge would rule in my favor?"

"Crecy said that she divined you would be found innocent."

"She divined it?"

"Never question Crecy," Phoebe said. "If she tells you she's divined something, you'd better listen to her."

When the Prinsens' surrey pulled up, closely followed by Phoebe's buggy, Will was the first to jump down. He went running into the house, calling out at the top of his lungs, "July's here! He's out of jail!"

By the time Christian, Phoebe, and July reached the house, everyone was in the foyer to greet them.

When the congratulations were over, Ina Claire led them all into the dining room. "Crecy made a rib roast and I've been smelling it all afternoon. I can't wait to try it."

During the meal, talk was of the trial, of how it was obvious Frank had set the fire, and the new revelation that W.F. wanted to partially replenish Phoebe's troop of birds.

"He wants to buy twenty birds from you, Yhomas—that is, if you're willing to sell them," Christian said.

"I'm in the business of buying birds, not selling them. If it was for anyone else but Phoebe, I'd say no."

"I appreciate that, because I may be taking on two new hands." Phoebe looked toward Christian and smiled. "I know July can do the work, and I think he can teach a greenhorn what to do."

"A greenhorn? You couldn't have found a better ostrich wrestler than me," Christian said, continuing the banter.

"What makes you think you're the one I'm going to hire?" Phoebe cocked her head to one side.

Christian's eyes opened wide. "It'd better be me!"

"Well, I think the first thing we ought to do is

go round up some birds. I assume you want them as soon as possible," Yhomas said.

"I'll go," Buck said.

"All right," Yhomas said. "I think the birds pastured on the north forty will be the easiest to move."

"You'll need help," July said. "I'll go, too, if Crecy will hold back another piece of that apple pie."

"Don't you worry about that," Crecy said. "I've got a whole pie that has your name on it."

July smiled. "That's what I like to hear."

When July and Buck were gone, Crecy and Ina Claire began clearing the table.

"Ladies and gentlemen, this has been a very rewarding day," Clarence Woodson said as he rose from the table. "Our friend July has been exonerated, W. F. Sloan has been rehabilitated, and Phoebe gets her livelihood back, but there is something else I'd like to say.

"I am an engineer, and by definition I like to tinker; if something doesn't work right, I want to know why. You've all heard the story of how Christian saved my life by shooting a mountain lion. What you don't know is that Christian was complaining about the balance of his rifle.

"I took it upon myself to inspect that rifle, expecting to find that the butt plate was a mixture of lead and brass, instead of the standard copper-and-zinc alloy. But I was wrong. It was just as it should be.

"Christian was right. The rifle was out of balance, but everything seemed to be standard-issue for a Martini. I took it upon myself to remove the butt plate, and I'd like to show you what I found."

Clarence stood and left the dining room. When he returned, he had the rifle and a screwdriver. He handed both to Christian. "If you'll remove the butt plate, I think you'll find the cause of the imbalance."

When Christian took off the plate, several small items fell from the hollowed-out section of the stock. Christian's mouth fell open when he saw what looked like octahedron-shaped alum crystals. "Raw diamonds. Where did these come from?"

Clarence laughed. "Well, they certainly didn't come from Arizona. Where did you get this rifle?"

"Mrs. Van Koopmans gave it to me before I left Cape Town. It's funny when I think back on it. It caused such a problem getting through customs that I almost got rid of it, but because it had been a gift from Mrs. Van Koopmans, I kept it."

"Do you think she knew about the diamonds?" Yhomas asked.

"We're talking about Marie Van Koopmans. Was there anything going on that she didn't know? More than likely some IDB runner came through and needed money and he sold her this rifle."

"An IDB runner? What's that?" Phoebe asked.

"An illicit diamond buyer. Until Cecil Rhodes consolidated De Beers, there were almost as many diamonds stolen as sold."

"What do you think these are worth?" Yhomas picked up a couple of the stones.

"It's hard to say"—Christian looked at Phoebe—"but I'd guess it might be pretty close to twenty-five thousand dollars."

Phoebe smiled broadly. "A pretty good inheritance."

A single candle burned on the bedside table, its light casting shadows on the wall of a man and a woman making love, not hurriedly or furtively, but with slow, sensuous kisses and strokes, a giving and taking of shared possessiveness.

Then, after mutual, satisfying climaxes, they lay together, naked skin against naked skin.

"Oh, what a wonderful day this has been!" Phoebe said. "Will is upstairs in his own bed, July was found innocent, W.F. is replacing the birds"—she snuggled closer to Christian—"and I'm in bed with the man I love. This day could not possibly be better."

"Oh, I wouldn't say that. There is something that would make it better."

"What's that?"

"If you tell me you'll marry me."

Phoebe sat up and looked at Christian, his face gleaming gold in the candlelight. "Is that a proposal?"

"Yes. I'm asking you to marry me."

"Let me think about it," Phoebe teased.

"All right, think about it, but I have to warn you, there is a time limit on the offer."

"How long would that be?"

"Oh, I'd say about seventy years or so. If you haven't agreed to marry me by then, I'm going to take the offer back."

"Well, if you're going to be that way about it, I guess I'd better say yes now."

"I guess you had better." Christian put his arms around Phoebe's neck and pulled her down to him.

"Oh, my," she said after a long, deep kiss. "Again?"

"I want to keep trying until I get it right."

Don't miss these other titles by SARA LUCK!

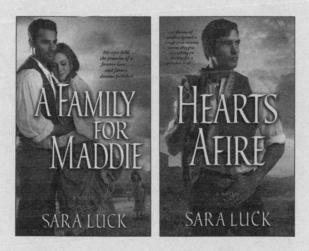

Pick up or download
your copies today!